PUFFIN BOOKS

DOT.
ROBOT
CYBER GOLD

Jason Bradbury likes gadgets – a lot! He has scoured the globe to find them and rarely stops talking and writing about them. He also likes computer games – perhaps even loves them. The first computer game he ever played consisted of nothing more than two dots and a straight line, but it was enough to ignite a lifelong passion for the (pixellated) pastime – and despite having real *human* children and a robot called Vernon to look after, Jason still finds time for more game playing than is wise.

He is best known as host of UK TV show *The Gadget Show*, on which he swims with sharks, rides rocket-powered skateboards and breaks tech world records – but before his TV career took off he was also a comedian, a scriptwriter and a breakdancer.

Jason lives in London, where he travels the streets on various electric vehicles and newfangled devices.

The science and technology in the Dot.Robot series is real and Jason has witnessed much of it first-hand, including a trip in a self-driving car in Las Vegas, a flying robot test flight and a look at an invisible jacket – if you can look at something that's *invisible*!

To find out what Jason is up to go to his website *www.jasonbradbury.com* or find him on Twitter (@jasonbradbury)

JASON BRADBURY

DOT.
ROBOT

CYBER GOLD

PUFFIN

PUFFIN BOOKS

Published by the Penguin Group
Penguin Books Ltd, 80 Strand, London WC2R ORL, England
Penguin Group (USA) Inc., 375 Hudson Street, New York, New York 10014, USA
Penguin Group (Canada), 90 Eglinton Avenue East, Suite 700, Toronto, Ontario, Canada M4P 2Y3
(a division of Pearson Penguin Canada Inc.)
Penguin Ireland, 25 St Stephen's Green, Dublin 2, Ireland (a division of Penguin Books Ltd)
Penguin Group (Australia), 250 Camberwell Road, Camberwell, Victoria 3124, Australia
(a division of Pearson Australia Group Pty Ltd)
Penguin Books India Pvt Ltd, 11 Community Centre, Panchsheel Park, New Delhi – 110 017, India
Penguin Group (NZ), 67 Apollo Drive, Rosedale, Auckland 0632, New Zealand
(a division of Pearson New Zealand Ltd)
Penguin Books (South Africa) (Pty) Ltd, 24 Sturdee Avenue, Rosebank,
Johannesburg 2196, South Africa

Penguin Books Ltd, Registered Offices: 80 Strand, London WC2R ORL, England

puffinbooks.com

First published 2011
001 – 10 9 8 7 6 5 4 3 2 1

Set in AbsaraOT Light 11.25/17 pt
Printed in Great Britain by Clays Ltd, St Ives plc

British Library Cataloguing in Publication Data
A CIP catalogue record for this book is available from the British Library

ISBN: 978-0-141-32397-8

www.greenpenguin.co.uk

MIX
Paper from
responsible sources
FSC
www.fsc.org   FSC™ C018179

Penguin Books is committed to a sustainable
future for our business, our readers and our
planet. This book is made from paper certified
by the Forest Stewardship Council.

For my heart and soul – Claire, Marnie,
Jackson and Harrison

● PROLOGUE

Master Kojima was a boy of few words. He let his actions do the talking in the biggest professional gaming tournaments in the world. The only problem was that right now he needed to find the power of speech – quickly.

Standing in a prison tunnel, the boy who held three of Master Kojima's fingers in an excruciating finger lock was running out of patience.

Master Kojima hadn't heard a sound since his sister had slipped into the darkness twenty minutes ago. Her escape plan had been hastily made. But a half-baked plan was better than facing a beating from one of the other boys. Despite his own predicament, Master Kojima kindled the faint glimmer of hope that his twin sister might just have made it out.

Hope was a rare commodity in this place, something most of the other kids in here had let die. Without hope, some of Master Kojima's fellow inmates had lost the ability to cope at all. The younger ones were especially vulnerable, crying so much they couldn't even do the work they'd been brought here for, and then being marched away by the guards. Some of them had turned up in the kitchen, making the slop that passed for food here. Some of them never turned up at all.

The boy tightened his grip on Master Kojima's hand. 'This is your last chance, *baka*,' he said, using a Japanese swear word in a dialect Master Kojima recognized as from the south of Japan, probably Takamatsu. 'Unless you tell me where your sister is, I'll snap these scrawny little fingers of yours.'

The boy's breath smelled as though he hadn't brushed his teeth in over a month and his bony features made him seem demonic in the flickering light of the candles. Candles were the only source of light in the cells and tunnels of the prison complex. Master Kojima thought that was funny, in a perverse kind of way – high-tech computers and high-speed broadband routers in the gaming hall where they worked but buckets of water to drink from and candles in the cells.

The finger lock was so painful the ten-year-old could have let tears well up in his eyes, but he had to be strong, for the sake of his sister. The longer he said nothing, the longer she had to escape. By now, he expected his twin sister, Miss Kojima, to have reached the main wall of the compound. Neither twin could ever be mistaken for being athletic, although somewhat ironically they were often referred to in newspaper and magazine interviews as 'cyber athletes'. But of the two of them, Miss Kojima was definitely the most likely to make it over the wall. Her instant game plan involved shimmying up a part of the wall that was connected to the canteen. It was the only place where tall, vertical wooden logs had been used instead of the high slippery concrete wall. Her theory was that the knots in the newly cultivated wood could offer footholds for her small feet and the overhanging section of the canteen's tarpaulin and thatch roof might just be strong enough to support her weight. Once on the roof, she would drop down into what the inmates referred to as the moat. It was a word that summoned up images of medieval castles, but was in reality just a big ditch dug out of the forest floor, then filled with upright sharpened wooden stakes intended to slow any escapees so the guards could catch them. So far, it had proved an effective set up as no one had managed to escape, a fact the guards were keen on reminding the inmates at every opportunity.

In Master Kojima's opinion, the boy who had him trapped was worse than the adult guards. A few weeks ago he had been like the other inmates, snatched from his home and brought here in a blindfold. Along with about twenty others he'd exchanged any humanity he might have arrived with for a few concessions from the guards and whatever sick, sadistic pleasure he got from picking on weaker kids. Miss Kojima had stood up to the boy and he'd decided to teach her a lesson.

The guards allowed this second tier of tyranny because it made the majority of the child inmates feel that bit more hopeless – and the more hopeless they felt, the less distracted they were and the harder they worked.

Master Kojima wished he was big enough to fight back, but it was pointless – not just because of the boy's size, or even the two other boys at his shoulder, but because of the martial arts skills that he and his fellow gang members shared.

'I'll make this easy for you. If you don't tell me where your sister was heading when you made the stupid decision to stand and fight me, I'll not only break your fingers, I'll snap your wrist too!'

The boy's grip tightened and three of Master Kojima's fingers gave way. Intense pain radiated from his hand and shot up his arm. It felt like his tendons had been replaced with live electric cables.

'Well?' asked the boy, switching his grip to Master Kojima's other hand. 'Anything you want to tell me?'

'You can go to hell!' Master Kojima spat the words at the boy. The sound of three more fingers cracking recoiled off the walls in the corridor, followed by Master Kojima's shriek. And his ordeal still wasn't over. With a twisted smile, the boy let his grip slide to Master Kojima's wrist.

Master Kojima's only hope now was that, beyond all reason, his sister's foolhardy plan had got her into the forest – because he could no longer resist.

'OK! Enough. Stop!' he squealed. 'My sister is –'

Master Kojima's words were snatched away by the sound of locks sliding open on a door at the end of the tunnel. The door opened and the figure of a guard with an automatic rifle hanging from his shoulders appeared in the doorway, motioning to the boy holding Master Kojima to come forward.

'Bring him!' the boy commanded two gang members who had watched the interrogation from the shadows. Then he dropped his grip on Master Kojima and walked towards the open doorway, while the two boys took an arm each and dragged Master Kojima after him.

It was dark outside, but as Master Kojima was brought out to an open area surrounded by the concrete perimeter wall, he was blinded by the harsh white light from two powerful headlamps. He instantly knew the source of the intense light and he was terrified.

The fingers of his damaged hand throbbed as he raised an elbow to block the light. What he saw was the outline of a Mech, a five-metre high bi-pedal robotic suit that approximated the shape of a human but was at least twice as high as the tallest person he'd ever seen. The machine had two huge metal arms with large metal pincers for hands, both of which were raised high in front of the steel alloy cage, which served as the cockpit in which the scary-looking robot's guard operator sat. Master Kojima had seen the Mechs at work in the forest in the first few days at the camp. They were used as human-assisted lumberjack robots, which carried and stacked logs and helped with the construction of the wooden parts of the fortress where the children were held.

From what Master Kojima could see in the dazzling light, the Mech towering above him was holding something between its hydraulic pincers – and it wasn't a log.

The earth beneath Master Kojima trembled as the Mech took two steps forward. Then its huge pincers opened, and the object it was holding fell to the ground.

Master Kojima looked in horror. Lying in front of him was the motionless body of his sister.

From: xxxxxxxxxxxx
To: Farley.Jackson@MITedu.com
Subject: Your only warning!

Forget about the Kojima Twins. They are gone.
Stop your meddling or you'll be gone too.

CHAPTER 1

WizardZombie sensed the heat radiating up from the lava fields as the Dragon Hawk swooped down and snarled at a group of spider crabs, before pulling up and soaring towards the city of Venomor.

Venomor was ringed by a sea of flaming lava and patrolled by poisonous crustaceans. The city was only accessible by a flying mount, the most exotic of which was the blue Dragon Hawk. WizardZombie had been awarded this rare flying beast by Dwarf King Claw for helping to repel a group of raiders. It had taken almost five days of near-solid fighting to quell the attacks.

Five days, thought Jackson Farley as he looked up from his tablet computer and stretched his arms out over the dining table where he was seated. Five days of continuous play on his favourite game, *Whisper*, was excessive, even by his extreme gaming standards. But when you were stuck on a slow boat to Tokyo – what else was there to do?

Jackson stood up and opened the fridge in the ship's

kitchen – or *galley* as the ship's captain continually reminded him to call it. There was plenty of food in there, but not all of it was available to Jackson. He'd already witnessed a couple of the crew members being pulled apart when a fight over ownership of a yogurt broke out. It seemed sailors were territorial about their snacks. He grabbed a chocolate bar he knew was *safe*. The crew members weren't the only people on board the massive container ship with cabin fever. It seemed that the best part of a week was enough to send Brooke over the edge. His thirteen-year-old fellow roboteer had walked off in a huff several hours ago – slamming the metal door so hard that flakes of paint had fallen from the door frame, revealing the rusted metal beneath.

Redheads! thought Jackson, even though Brooke kept her hair dyed permanently pink.

Since Jackson had returned from the snowy wastes of Canada a couple of weeks ago – where he'd stared death in the face and seen his father take a fatal fall – he hadn't been much in the mood for conversation. Brooke had been patient with him for the first few days, but since they'd had news of the disappearance of their Japanese friends, the Kojima twins, she'd been like a kitten in a bag, restless with worry about the kidnapped ten-year-olds. Within forty-eight hours, Brooke had packed her robots and hitched a ride on the *Nostromo*, a cargo ship bound for Japan's capital city.

The massive vessel guaranteed anonymous passage for Jackson and Brooke. It would have been quicker to take a plane, but a Japanese police investigator, Detective Yoshida, who had interviewed Brooke and Jackson over a conference call as part of his investigation into the Kojimas' disappearance, had made it quite clear that coming to Japan to look for their friends was a bad idea. Besides, hiding cutting-edge robots in your excess baggage was a great way to get thrown out of an airport. A cash payment of several hundred dollars to a wily old seadog and ten days at sea would get them where they needed to be. What they would do when they reached Japan was the cause of much conversation – at least, it would have been conversation if Jackson had contributed more than a sentence or two since stepping aboard the boat. And therein lay the problem between Brooke and Jackson. Brooke wanted to talk through every aspect of their Japanese rescue mission – how they planned to find the famous professional gaming duo when the Tokyo police had so far failed to turn up any leads. And how she planned to bring to justice the gang boss who they suspected was behind both the kidnapping and many other evil deeds, all of which had affected Jackson in ways he didn't want to think about.

She also wanted to talk to Jackson about her problems with her father, who kept telling Brooke that the robotics laboratory they ran needed to stop producing her 'machines of chaos' and start doing more *commercial* work. This had incensed Brooke every bit as much as the plight of the twins. Her solution was that she and Jackson would form a breakaway organization that she believed could be a real-world version of International Rescue from *Thunderbirds*. The problem was how to pay for it?

When Jackson's only comment was that Brooke wasn't posh enough to be a real-life Lady Penelope, she had blown her top and stormed off.

Jackson didn't want to deal with any of it. For the first time since his life had been irrevocably changed by an Instant Message inviting him to join a secret robot defence force, Jackson didn't want to fight back. He didn't want to be chased or do the chasing. He didn't want to track any more international criminals only to find out that in fact they were closer to him than expected, like the father he'd never known he had or to find out the people he loved were living a lie. Jackson wanted nothing more to do with a world of maniacal billionaires and bad guys, explosions and kidnapping. All he wanted was to be left alone to get his character, WizardZombie, to level 80 in his favourite game, *Whisper*.

So why was he on this rust bucket of a boat? Because, even though Brooke and he weren't on speaking terms, she was his friend – and so were the Kojima twins. Hopefully, they'd get to Japan, Brooke would scare the Tokyo police into working a bit harder and the twins would be found, leaving Jackson to melt quietly into the background. *How is it*, thought Jackson, *that you can think one thing, really believe it, while at the same time know it's never going to happen? The Kojimas are gone. And it's all my fault.*

He turned back to the wafer-thin tablet device in his hands and stroked the screen. The Dragon Hawk banked against the moon and then, tucking its large feathered wings back, began a steep dive towards the stone walls of the town. Just when it looked as if the creature would smash straight through the two-metre-thick ramparts, its wings swept open again and its giant talons brushed the top of the ancient barricade before cushioning a landing in the town square.

WizardZombie stepped down, the heavy armour that covered him from head to toe clinking a tinny rhythm as he walked.

'Buying or selling?' The gruff question came from a stocky dwarf who was holding a two-handed axe, at least twice as long as he was tall.

'Selling,' Jackson typed.

'Auction's in the Drunken Duck Ale House in five mins,' read the speech bubble beside the short bearded warrior.

The clang of a gong signalled the start of trading and lists of goods for sale appeared, floating beside the heads of all the player-characters.

WizardZombie was approached by a blood-elf. There had been a time when no self-respecting Wizard of the Guild would ever consider trading with a member of the opposing Rabble. But these were strange times and, if WizardZombie was going to sell the iron ore he'd toiled so hard to make, there was no room for being too choosy.

'I'll take the lot for 200 gold.' The blood-elf's offer hovered in text form.

'400 gold coins or no deal.' WizardZombie had a reputation for bargaining hard.

'350,' replied the blood-elf.

'We have a deal.'

As an AGREE SALE? window materialized between the two characters, a massive explosion ripped through the ale house. Lined up in the square outside was a group of fifty or so fighters, a raiding party.

A towering human warrior stepped forward and smashed a huge wooden mallet on the ground, cracking the cobbles for several metres around him.

'Each of you must immediately surrender everything you are carrying or we will destroy you!' read the text beside the warrior.

To make sure their message was clear, two stout and heavily armoured gnome gunners fired a shot from each of the cannons they stood behind, the volleys flying over the flaming roof of the Drunken Duck.

*

Jackson sat back and released a long, slow breath. Now even his precious *Whisper* was challenging him to act and make the right decision. All he wanted to do was trade. He'd been doing it for years – gold mining – directing WizardZombie to dig up iron ore and make weapons and potions, all of which could be traded for gold coins, which in turn could be swapped for real-world money on various websites. He was so good at it that with a few hours' play per week he could make enough money to supplement his scholarship at the university where he was studying robotic engineering alongside Brooke, supervised by her professor father. It was strange, but there was something more than the money that Jackson got from gold mining: a sense of achievement that came from making something and finding a buyer.

Jackson reluctantly brought up the inventory of spells.

Two freezing ice streams shot from his hands, instantly immobilizing the cannons and their two stunted operators.

But the raiding party's response was quick, the ground at the wizard's feet crumbling as a wave of energy swept towards him, the combined sorcery of the party's Shaman and Death Knights ripping up the cobblestones, tables and trees in the courtyard and rolling them up inside a thundering tsunami that crashed down on all the Traders. For those still alive, a cloud of Blood Plague Flies blinded them so they could no longer see to run.

The unrelenting attack continued as ten or so Undeads,

the unholy foot soldiers of the party, ran on to the piles of rubble and stripped their victims of anything valuable. Coins, weapons, clothes, pelts, food, spells and potions, all were ripped from the dead and dying. But as one of the vile creatures kneeled to dig by the place where they'd last seen WizardZombie, the rubble started to move. Stone slabs, bricks and splintered beams rose up and started revolving around the scavengers. Within seconds, the Undeads were swept up inside the whirlwind, their skeletal limbs and skulls pulverized by the spinning debris of WizardZombie's Cyclone Strike.

As the dust cleared, WizardZombie was standing before the diminished raiding party. Still, on his own, he was no match for the remaining attackers and he wasted no time in summoning his Dragon Hawk. The elegant creature swooped down, and before its feet had even touched the ground WizardZombie jumped on its back and shot towards the raiders.

A hail of arrows, Death Chill and Boiling Metal spells hit the rider and mount as they crashed through the party, and for a moment the Dragon Hawk faltered. But Wizard-Zombie held on and soon the feathered creature pulled up and flew out over the lava fields, the heat radiating up from the liquid rock floor helping it to rise quickly towards the mountains that ringed the city of Venomor.

But just as Jackson felt it was safe to release his index finger from its continuous contact with the screen of his tablet computer, the view of the rocky horizon on the screen instantly changed. In the space of a single heart-beat, the Dragon Hawk and its rider had been scooped up and dashed against a jagged rock face at least 300 metres in front of them.

He was astonished. WizardZombie was lying on a ridge, under the cold blue corpse of his prized Dragon Hawk – just metres from a sheer drop into the searing lava ocean.

Jackson could only guess that WizardZombie had been struck by a very powerful spell. He'd never seen anything in a game that could throw a mount and its rider with that much force, killing the powerful Dragon Hawk in one strike.

WizardZombie lay paralysed, struck by the combined incantations of four jet-black Death Knights, now hover-ing just metres above him on various species of ferocious flying mounts. Jackson instinctively pressed the key combinations that in any other attack situation would fire off a range of extremely effective anti-magic shields and counter-attacks. But to his amazement nothing happened.

Unable to move, there was nothing WizardZombie could do as three Undeads crawled vertically down the cliff face towards him. On reaching the ledge where he lay helpless, the three scavengers picked away at the Wizard's frigid body.

Jackson watched in shock as first his weapons inventory

was cleared out, then the valuable list of spells and potions he'd played for years to build up.

'This is theft!' he typed feverishly. But there was no reply as the four ghoulish Knights and their detachment of scavengers withdrew into the darkness.

'Damn it!' shouted Jackson, slapping the tablet computer down on the hard wooden surface and pushing the table away from him.

'I need help with some boxes.' It was Brooke. She was standing in the galley doorway. Jackson could see that she had witnessed his outburst by the slightly superior smile she had stuck to her face, as if she was saying, 'I'm actually quite glad you're having a bad time in that goddamn game you never stop playing.' The fact she didn't mention it said a great deal about how badly the two were getting on.

There was a tense silence in which the two of them just stared at each other. He knew it was childish, but Jackson didn't want to answer. Brooke waited a couple of seconds before spinning round and disappearing up the corridor. 'Be on deck in the next minute or I'll rewire that precious slab of yours to electrocute you next time you touch it!' she shouted back.

The light was fading, but as Jackson reached the deck of the ship he could clearly see the outline of a city, its skyscrapers silhouetted like broken teeth, jagged against an angry grey sky.

'Tokyo. Thirty minutes,' said Brooke, using as few words as she could. She was surrounded by flight cases and all kinds of cutting-edge gadgetry – a rugged version of the tablet computer that Jackson had, a scattering of large Li-Po batteries hooked up to their super-quick flash-chargers, and *Tread* – basically a robot inside a low-profile car wheel – who was hooked up to a server in a metal flight case like a patient on life support.

Jackson knew the kit inside out. As far as he was concerned, if you were depending on a machine to save your life, as Brooke's robots had done on several occasions, it was important to have read the manual. He slipped the batteries into foam slots inside a small protective case and disconnected *Tread*, rolling the heavy wheel into an aluminium frame and then into the base of the case inside which the robot was kept for transporting. Brooke had been tinkering with several of her robots on the trip over. *Tread*, originally designed as an alternative to police cruisers in high-speed pursuit situations, had been given a new, proto-type electric super charger which theoretically would give him an improved top speed of 280 kilometres per hour.

Jackson secured *Tread* in the frame, then lifted the four rectangular metal side panels into position. With the panels locked in place there was no sign that the flight case held a robot possessing the same stopping power as a squad of highway police.

'There's tea if you want it,' said Brooke. 'And before

you ask, Jackson, no, it doesn't come with milk and two sugars!' Brooke picked up a tiny bowl from a delicate Japanese tea set she had placed on the wooden deck. She'd taken to drinking the stuff as part of what she called 'acclimatization', her way of preparing for their visit to Japan. And Jackson had noticed she'd also tucked her long bright-pink hair back in a bun, which was skewered with two chopsticks.

'No thanks,' said Jackson, trying not to react to Brooke's attempt to get a rise out of him.

'You see, you Brits think you know tea,' Brooke continued. 'But you stole it off the Japanese.'

Jackson decided it was best to just let Brooke speak, as any attempt to butt in or correct her would probably lead to an argument.

'The Japanese tea ceremony, also called Way of Tea, is a transformative event, a quiet and serious experience in which the drinker meditates on the mellow nature of time and their own existence.' Brooke held up a box featuring the words JAPANESE TEA CEREMONY KIT and a picture of a traditional-looking Japanese lady, bowing with her hands clasped. 'At least, that's what it says on the back of the box!'

'How come you had time to order that before we left Boston?' asked Jackson.

'I came across it in the ship's hold. There's a container with three thousand more of them inside.'

Jackson just nodded.

Brooke was poking the screen of a small, wafer-thin tablet computer as she continued to speak. 'If I'm honest, though, while drinking my tea, I've been less bothered about contemplating the meaning of life and more interested in shape-shifting polymer compounds.' She held up the tablet and presented a picture of a scientist in a laboratory holding up test tubes. Below the picture it read: 'Engineering the compounds of the future in the Department of Applied Chemistry, University of Tokyo'.

Now Brooke and Jackson were on safer ground – science and maths were two subjects that they could talk about.

'Do you have the numbers?' asked Jackson. It was a familiar exchange: whenever Brooke found a new material she thought might inspire another tech creation, Jackson would check it out with a quick mathematical analysis of its properties.

Brooke poked at her skinny computer again before handing it to Jackson. The screen featured a few equations and lists of various compounds alongside their numerical values. To any other thirteen-year-old, it would have been gobbledygook, but for maths genius Jackson the digits built an instant mental image, the molecules and compounds interacting in his head.

'Very interesting. A plastic you can manipulate with light?' said Jackson.

'You got it! It's plastic with shape memory. It's triggered when a particular frequency of light is shone on it. It means that I can build a wing that, theoretically, transforms into the hull of a boat. Or a plastic robot muscle that tightens when a beam of light hits it.' Jackson could see the brilliant engineer's brain imagining all the possible inventions that could come from this new, cutting-edge material. It was how many of Brooke's inventions started, from the announcement of a breakthrough in battery power to flexible bulletproof material or a new, faster electric motor. She'd designed and made all of the robots they'd brought with them to Tokyo with the help of her robotics engineer father, Professor J.P. English, and his high-tech underground laboratory and workshop back in Boston. That didn't mean her father knew anything about their impromptu Japanese expedition. On the contrary, Brooke had only managed to prevent her father calling the FBI to search for her by sending him doctored photographs that showed her apparently camping with Jackson in a forest outside Boston. She'd used her portable satellite broadband link to grab images of a New England campsite from the Internet, then photoshopped herself with Jackson into the picture. She'd even sent the doctored longitude and latitude GPS data to prove that they were close by, but just 'needed some space'.

'And you think you can make use of this stuff?' Jackson ventured, his attention back on the tablet screen.

'If I could get my hands on an electron-beam lithography system and a wafer fusion furnace – sure.'

The two finished packing the equipment into a pile of around ten flight cases and metal boxes. They'd be a little conspicuous wandering around Tokyo with that lot. Hopefully, they'd quickly find a base where they could store the robots. *On the other hand*, mused Jackson, his gaze drifting up the bow of the boat to the shimmery cityscape that loomed ahead, *I wouldn't want to enter the dragon's den without them.*

'We'd better get these below deck,' said Brooke, dragging a case past him, 'if we want to avoid any awkward questions from the port authority.'

Jackson was still gazing at the neon horizon when a shiver ran down his spine. Was it dread or cold? He wasn't sure.

CHAPTER 2

They had docked in the port of Tokyo. Brooke had held back from giving the captain of the *Nostromo* his cash bonus until he'd got them and their boxes through customs without any questions asked, then into the smallest van Jackson had ever seen.

The taxi driver spoke no English, but with a combination of sign language and a Japanese translation application on her phone Brooke had managed to explain their destination – the Capsule Inn, Akihabara district.

'You have got to be kidding!' said Jackson, trying to catch his breath. He'd struggled up and down three flights of steps, dragging the heavy boxes with him. He was standing in a corridor lined with what looked like washing machines. They were the capsules that gave the hotel its name – lozenge-shaped cubby holes, two by one and a half metres in size, stacked two high, five rows on either side of him.

'Oh my God! Are they cute or what!' Brooke exclaimed, swinging open the transparent plastic door to one of the rooms and diving inside. 'Awesome! It's got a TV,' she shouted, her voice echoing around the tiny fibre-glass chamber.

It took Jackson a further fifteen exhausting minutes to heave their gear into three more of the pods, while Brooke bounced up and down on her knees behind the perspex pod door, tinny Japanese pop music blasting from her miniature TV.

Jackson was shattered when he eventually turned his pod's light out, but he didn't go to sleep immediately. Everything about his first night in Tokyo was strange. How bright the streets had seemed, even though it was evening. He'd gazed out of the taxi window at the rainbow canopy of vivid neon that blocked out the sky. The heat and the smell of the city was also new. Even in the plastic coffin where he lay, the toxic scent of antiseptic, which had grabbed him by the nose when he'd first climbed in, was now softened by the faint whiff of fried food. When he eventually fell asleep he was taken on yet another unwilling journey around the places and faces that haunted him every night. In tonight's nightmare Jackson was flying, circling a featureless white landscape, covered in snow and ice. The ice below started to crack as a black hole opened up. Everything near the hole began to revolve round it, like objects in a bathtub when the plug is pulled out, huge chunks of ice and even the dead grey rock beneath them. Jackson was sucked down into the whirling vortex. And as he circled the rim of the jet-black hole in what had become a whirlpool in a torrid black sea, he saw a boat ahead of him. It was the *Nostromo*, the boat that had brought him and Brooke to Japan.

Two figures were on the deck, fighting. As Jackson strained to make them out through the inky-black spray, he recognized the raw-boned face and round blue spectacles of Yakimoto – the creator not just of Jackson's nightmares but of all the misery in his life. Thick strands of the gangster boss's long black hair were blown out around his head like the snakes of Medusa. Jackson watched as Yakimoto shoved the figure in front of him and, as it tumbled overboard, Jackson saw the terrified face of his biological father, the maniacal billionaire Devlin Lear. Jackson fought to swim towards him, but his father kept swirling faster, Yakimoto laughing as Lear called out Jackson's name.

'Jackson!' he cried.

'Jackson! Wake up already!' It was Brooke. She was silhouetted in front of a yellow fluorescent glow that illuminated his transparent pod door. Brooke tapped on the door and poked a finger at a multicoloured matrix of streets and Japanese symbols that crowded her phone's active surface display.

'We're going to the Invader,' she continued. 'It's a

gamer's cafe. Hopefully, something useful can come from all that gaming you've been doing!'

The cafe was in the same district as the hotel, Akihabara, otherwise known as Electric Town, the neon heart that pulsed at the centre of the world's most high-tech city. The two walked in silence, not the awkward silence from the boat but a speechless reaction to this glimmering and glittering jewel of the city. Street after street was lined with walls of TVs for sale, some extending five storeys high. Computer monitors and laptops of every size and colour shone behind glass that was garlanded with fluorescent tubes, and giant mobile phones, cameras and games consoles as big as houses shone down from billboards that blocked out the sky and bathed the midnight streets in light.

'It's not far now. End of this alley,' said Brooke, glancing at her phone and turning into a passageway choked with market stalls. Even at this late hour every stall was manned by an excitable stallholder, shouting words neither Brooke nor Jackson understood, from behind mounds of multicoloured rope lights, connectors and electrical components, all of which flowed on to the pavement like roots in an electric swamp.

The Invader wasn't hard to spot. The front of the cafe looked like a giant Space Invader. The forty-six squares, from which one of the oldest characters in video games was constructed, were each represented as metre-high, red-glowing panels in the tall glass-fronted building. Entrance to the famous gamer's haunt was via the blocky character's mouth.

Inside, rows of computer terminals were arranged over four floors, each the size of several tennis courts side by side. Joining each floor were wide glass stairs, the steps glowing in different colours when anyone stepped on them.

Brooke had mentioned the place on the boat, but if Jackson was honest he hadn't really paid any attention. He should have because it was just like the flashy gaming venues the Kojima twins had described.

During their missions for MeX, the top-secret robot defence force that had brought Brooke, Jackson and the Kojima twins together, Jackson had extracted every ounce of information he could from the twins about their amazing life as professional tournament players of video games. It was incredible to think that, by the age of eight, the famous gaming duo had won their first million-dollar prize. They'd won a great deal more since then in sponsored televised competitions that took place in impressive surroundings like these, watched live on television by millions of gamers across south-east Asia.

It was a long shot, but Brooke hoped to find some gamers who might have some information about the twins.

'We should split up,' said Brooke. 'I'll take the top floors, you take the bottom two.'

'Be careful,' replied Jackson, prompting Brooke to roll her eyes.

'Just get me some info about the twins and I'll be fine,' she replied sharply, before walking towards the stairs.

Directly in front of him, a group of young men were gathered round a single terminal. At the centre of the group was a tall, stick-like figure of a boy seated before a keyboard, mouse and monitor. His fingers were hastily working the keys, but the rest of his body was rigid as he stared intently at the action on screen.

Jackson instantly recognized the figures on screen as from *Starcraft* – a real-time strategy game he knew was popular in this part of the world. The boy was obviously doing well because the group behind him was glued to his every action, whooping encouragement every thirty seconds or so.

Jackson watched at a distance for around five minutes until the boy stood up, putting his hands in the air to the cheers of his friends, like a boxer who had just KO'd his opponent.

One of Brooke's favourite topics of conversation on the boat had been the Japanese language. Once every three or four minutes, Jackson had grunted a monosyllabic response, but they were only stick-and-hoop replies, tiny flicks of a stick intended to keep Brooke rolling along. She'd got the message eventually and stopped talking to him unless it was absolutely necessary. He felt bad about that, but the events of the last eighteen months had left him in such a zombified state he'd been unable to do anything else. What he could do now was to try to extract something useful from the boys in front of him. That might go some way to relieving the guilt he felt about the rift in his friendship with Brooke.

'*Konnichiwa!*' said Jackson. He couldn't have made it sound less Japanese if he'd tried.

The boys looked round at him, paused for a moment, and then erupted into laughter before turning their backs to him.

Jackson sucked in the embarrassment and walked towards the group. 'Good score,' he said, peering round them for a closer glimpse of the boy's computer screen. 'But you're about to lose big time!'

The boys looked at one another before the skinny one spoke. 'Hey, *gaijin*!' he began. Whatever the word meant, Jackson assumed by the way he spat it at him that it wasn't a compliment. 'You no talk to us. We no talk to you. You go away!'

'It's probably easier if I show you,' Jackson persisted. 'May I?'

He moved in front of the boy and seated himself at the terminal. Jackson's fingers danced quickly and expertly over the keyboard and mouse. It took him around a second to bring up the inventory screen where the size and numbers of the boy's army and fighting resources were listed.

'As I thought, your unit deployment strategy is weak. The only reason you weren't seriously pwned in that last engagement is because your opponent was either a complete noob or he'd fallen asleep.'

The boys, who had looked annoyed when Jackson seated himself, now stood frozen in amazement. Except the skinny boy. He had obviously understood the international gamers' speak used by Jackson – *pwned* meaning 'owned' or 'beaten' and *noob*, or *n00b*, meaning 'new player' or 'inexperienced player' – and he didn't look happy. Now Jackson could see him more clearly, he was skinny but a lot taller than Jackson and, he guessed, around four years his senior. The skinny boy stepped forward, but before the situation could escalate Jackson jumped up and pulled out his tablet computer, holding it up so the skinny boy could see the scrawled symbols on its screen.

'What you need is something called a fragmentation formula,' Jackson said, as he moved between swipes on his tablet screen and key presses on the boy's terminal keyboard.

'Good game play is about maintaining a balance of the right choices. Get that balance wrong and you might score some quick showy victories, like you have tonight, but you'll only be setting yourself up for bigger losses in the future.'

Jackson cleared the inventory to reveal the main game screen, which offered an overview of the battlefield where several of the boy's fighting units had surrounded and destroyed his opponent's soldiers and vehicles.

'Look, you've got a swarm of small units instead of one big one. It's the classic mistake of an impatient player.' Two members of the group, who could obviously speak English, drew in sharp intakes of breath. Jackson moved his attention from the screen for a moment and glanced sideways at the boys. 'Oh, come on, be honest,' said Jackson. 'You opted to build small units because you were impatient to get into the action. But look . . .'

Jackson pointed to the thin slab in his hand. On it, drawn in his own rushed handwriting, was an equation.

$$1 + 2(n_1 \, n_2)$$

'The fragmentation formula proves that swarms of small units with a sum effectiveness equal to a couple of larger units are not actually the same in effectiveness.' Aware of the skinny boy's eyes boring straight through him, Jackson was now gabbling his words. 'The swarm of small units is always less effective. This is because a swarm gradually loses power over time as individual units die, while a large unit lasts much longer, and hence doesn't suffer from incremental loss of effectiveness.'

The skinny boy closed the few remaining centimetres

inside Jackson's personal space. This close up, Jackson wasn't so sure the boy was that skinny; he was more sinewy and strong-looking.

'This formula,' the boy whispered. 'Your creation?'

'Not exactly,' replied Jackson. 'But depending on what game I'm playing, I might modify some of the variables.'

The boy broke into a smile and ruffled Jackson's hair. 'English?' he asked.

'I am.' Jackson tried to smile back.

Skinny Boy turned to the others. 'Crazy English *gaijin*!' They all laughed. 'Show more,' he said to Jackson, motioning the other boys to join as he focused his attention on the terminal screen.

'What are you doing?' It was Brooke and she didn't sound happy. The boys parted to reveal Jackson at the terminal. It was a few moments before he turned and his eyes met Brooke's. She stood and glared at him, shaking her head, before turning and walking towards the exit.

'I'm doing what you asked,' said Jackson, jumping up. 'Talking to the locals.' The boys jeered and laughed as Jackson ran after Brooke.

'What's the problem?' he asked, catching up to her on the street.

'You're the problem. You're playing a game, Jackson! The twins are missing and all you can do is play games.' They were back in the alley, Brooke walking in quick strides towards the hotel.

'Those guys might know something. I was trying to break the ice so I could –'

Brooke stopped abruptly. It looked as if she was about to shout, but instead she took a deep breath, then talked almost in a whisper.

'God only knows what Yakimoto has done with our friends or if they're even alive. I came here to find them. I'm just not sure why *you* came, Jackson.'

Jackson was going to correct her, but decided not to. It was the first time he had seen Brooke looking so defeated. The fire in her eyes had gone, washed away by the faintest hint of a tear.

Brooke disappeared inside the entrance to the Capsule Inn. A few minutes later, walking at a more sober pace, Jackson climbed the hotel steps and went inside.

Across the street, a man on a bright-yellow Suzuki sports motorbike pressed a speed-dial button on his smartphone. As the call went live, the phone connected to the wireless-encrypted mic and headphone built into his helmet. He spoke softly in Japanese. 'It's definitely them. They're staying in Akihabara. What do you want me to do?'

'I'll let you know,' said a monotone voice on the other end of the phone. 'For now, stay on them. If they leave, follow them. If they meet anyone, let me know. If you lose them . . . I need not tell you what will happen to you.'

Then the phone went dead.

CHAPTER 3

Jackson woke to find a message on his phone.

> I'm following up on a lead from last night. As you don't
> have any leads, you can stay and watch the kit. I'll be
> back at lunchtime. Brooke

The absence of a smiley-face emoticon was Brooke's way of ensuring Jackson knew she was still furious. He lay back on his thin mattress, looking up at the TV that was moulded into the pod ceiling at an angle enabling you to just about watch it sitting up, assuming you were under six feet tall as most Japanese people were, or lying down. Jackson had left the TV on all night, finding the blend of a language he didn't understand and nonsensical game shows mind-numbing enough to stop him going over everything in his head.

A Japanese man dressed as a salt-shaker was chasing a bunch of his countrymen – who were dressed as various items of food, including a man in an egg costume and one wearing a large tomato outfit – around a giant plate. Jackson mused that the salt-shaker man had anger issues, because rather than simply flipping polystyrene salt crystals at his targets, which seemed to rack up the points, he was grabbing handfuls of costume and virtually headbutting his opponents.

How long would Brooke be? Two, three hours? Jackson was beginning to feel that if he lay in this tube for much longer, there was a real possibility he might go insane. He reached up to switch off the TV, just as an argument broke out between the tomato and the salt-shaker, which Jackson assumed was about the shaker's overly vigorous tactics.

As he stepped outside, the street was busy, mopeds and cyclists buzzing past at high speed in between a slow crawl of buses, cars and delivery vans. Jackson wasn't sure if he was imagining it, but the vehicles all seemed smaller than he was used to in London and Boston. He wondered if perhaps the skyscrapers that had dominated every view of the city since his arrival weren't as big as they seemed, but rather everything else was just really small. Even the bakery that was located in the corner of the hotel had extra-small cakes in the window.

Jackson leaned against the glass and looked more closely at a tray holding six of what he considered to be the most normal-looking cakes from the tens of different varieties displayed. Each of the six cakes looked like a tiny cube-shaped bun, about five centimetres high. The sign attached to the tray was written in Japanese characters, but below these was a description written in English: BIRD MESS BUN.

I'll give that one a miss! thought Jackson. Then he spotted a tray of what looked to be bread buns, labelled MELON PAN. *Can't go wrong with melon*, he thought, and walked in, taking a seat at the bar by the front window where he had a good view of the hotel entrance.

An old lady behind the counter motioned to him in a way that Jackson took to mean 'What would you like?'

Jackson mouthed the word 'Tea' and mimed the tipping of a cup. He then leaned sideways and pointed to the tray of 'melon pan' in the window display.

He glanced to his left. He could see the pavement outside the hotel and through the internal glass panels of the bakery he could also see the foyer. The receptionist was on the phone, performing an improvised manicure on one of her fingernails with her teeth, while listening to someone on the other end of the phone.

Pulling his tablet computer from his bag, he searched for a Wi-Fi hotspot. Like many cities in this tech-savvy part of the globe, Japan, Tokyo had free citywide Internet coverage. But Jackson soon realized that not knowing the Japanese for 'free' was a distinct disadvantage as every one of the sixty or so hotspots that materialized on his screen were named in Japanese characters. After a process of trial and error that lasted around ten minutes, Jackson eventually found a connection that let him out and on to the Net.

He typed 'Kojima Twins' into the search window of the computer's touchscreen.

89,100 results.

Jackson scanned down the page, ignoring references to the twins that he'd either read earlier or that were clearly written before their kidnapping.

Jackson surmised that the first entries covering the twins' disappearance were probably from big newspapers with enough clout for a high search listing. A headline from something called the *Yomiuri Shimbun* caught his eye. Again, he encountered a screen full of Japanese writing, but at the top right of the page was a button marked ENGLISH. The content of the newspaper's home page was instantly translated. Jackson scanned the page, past 'space industry funding' and Japan–China relations, until he found a small article in the 'Culture' section about the Kojimas.

SECOND WEEK OF KOJIMA MYSTERY

Authorities are searching for two of Japan's best-known professional video gamers. The ten-year-old brother and sister were last seen outside the

Metropolitan Hotel in Akihabara, Tokyo,
where several witnesses saw them driven
away in a limousine at high speed.

The twins, who had just won the
coveted Tokyo Smash video-gaming
competition, were reportedly due to
attend a celebratory dinner with their
family when their car was hijacked.

Akira Kojima, the twins' father and
coach, has been openly critical of
police investigators. 'It's been over
two weeks and the police have offered
us nothing. No evidence. No leads. No
hope of finding my children.'

Commentators believe Mr Kojima's
criticism is in reaction to sugges-
tions from the police that the twins
might have organized their own abduction in order to escape the pressures
of their father's famously punishing
coaching practices.

Mr Kojima rejects the police theory,
favouring instead a connection with
the Tokyo underworld, based on one
eyewitness's description of the kidnap
car's driver. The witness, who has
since gone missing, described tattoo

designs consistent with Yakuza gang symbols on the wrist and neck of a man in the car's passenger seat.

The twins' father has gone further in suggesting that he suspects collusion between the police and any gangsters involved. 'It wouldn't be the first time our noble police force was found to have links to the Tokyo underground.'

While the war of words continues between Kojima family members and those investigating the mysterious disappearance, no ransom has been demanded and the kidnappers have not made contact.

The last anyone heard from the Kojima twins was Miss Kojima's Twitter posting an hour after their Tokyo Smash victory.

#TokyoSmash Tonight's victory means a lot to my brother and me - but not as much as your support! x

Jackson had been so absorbed by the information on screen, he hadn't noticed the arrival of his tea and cake. The tea wouldn't have been his first choice. What he'd wanted was the sweet, milky brew he and his stepdad drank by the litre at home in England. What he got was a milkless hot infusion of something that tasted like stewed roses. And the cake wasn't the one he'd ordered; it was a doughnut, which was fine by him, shaped like a Cornish pasty.

Jackson glanced out of the window as he bit into the doughnut. Suddenly a strong taste of curry assaulted his tastebuds. He couldn't help but cough, spitting out a gooey lump of doughy yellow doughnut on to his plate. He checked the counter behind him, embarrassed by his involuntary ejection, but the old lady simply smiled back at him, putting two wrinkly thumbs in the air. Still spluttering, Jackson held up a thumb in response before turning back round to gulp down two mouthfuls of tea.

With the effects of the curry flavouring still tinkling on the roof of his mouth, Jackson checked the pavement outside the hotel. A tramp had brought a shopping cart filled with cardboard and a small stained mattress alongside a green flip-top bin on the road outside the hotel. He opened the lid of the bin and started to root around inside. Jackson shared one thing with the tramp, he thought. *A desire to drop out of society. No work pressures, no fixed abode, no run-ins with evil gangsters. Hotel receptionists, however, they could still ruin your day.* He watched as the woman from the hotel reception came out to shoo him off.

Jackson leaned forward to examine the picture that accompanied the article on his tablet's screen. It featured a man who looked like the classic gumshoe detective: silvery-grey mackintosh raincoat, even greyer tie, bedhead of relatively short but messy grey hair, misty round spectacles on the end of his nose and a limp cigarette hanging perilously from his bottom lip. The description below the picture read: 'Twins behind their own disappearance, say Tokyo detectives.'

It must be Detective Yoshida, mused Jackson, the Tokyo Police investigator who had interviewed him and Brooke over the phone a few days after the twins' disappearance. Brooke had been suspicious about him from the start and it looked from the article as if she might be right. Jackson had clearly explained the sequence of events to the detective. Yakimoto was a career gangster who Jackson's own mother had tracked as part of a British intelligence team. Jackson had asked for information on him from the Kojimas who in turn had engaged the services of their bodyguard. The bodyguard was now dead. Jackson had omitted some other details about Yakimoto, like the fact he'd been in a fight to the death with him in which one of his and Brooke's robots had torn a huge scar in the scumbag's face, and the involvement of Jackson's biological father, disgraced dot.com billionaire Devlin Lear. But he had shared with Detective Yoshida the contents of an email, warning him to forget about the Kojimas, which he was sure came from Yakimoto.

And yet there the detective was, in the newspaper,

talking about the twins staging their own disappearance. *No question about it*, thought Jackson. *He's a dirty cop, a Yakuza puppet.*

Jackson knew the detective wasn't telling the truth. He knew it because he had asked the twins to investigate Yakimoto. Their information had enabled him to track the Yakuza boss to his diamond mine in Canada, where the gangster leader had killed Devlin Lear and almost killed Jackson before fleeing with a stash of diamonds.

Jackson had played the events of those days over and over in his head. If anger and revenge hadn't driven him to the diamond mine, or if he'd been just too scared to face the man who – through the most horrible quirks of fate – had murdered both his mother and father, then the charade of the last eighteen months would now be over. The Kojima twins would never have been taken. He wouldn't be in this bakery waiting for a huffy Brooke. He'd be an ordinary thirteen-year-old studying robotics at MIT in Boston. *Strike that last one*, he thought. *There's nothing ordinary about a boy who can figure out cube roots in his head, quicker than a calculator.*

He glanced out of the window again. A white van had parked outside the hotel. One of its two rear doors was open. The closed door had big red Japanese characters on it that Jackson guessed might mean 'Removals' or something like that, as three men were loading several metal cases into the back of it. They were being directed by a fourth man, who in turn was arguing with the receptionist from the hotel.

Jackson would have looked back down and carried on surfing if it wasn't for the fact that he found something familiar about the removals guy. Silvery-grey mackintosh, messy hair, stub of a cigarette. Jackson shot a glance at his tablet computer and then the scene unfolding on the roadside before him suddenly came crashing into focus. The face on the man just ten metres away from him was the exact one pictured in the article in his hand. It was Detective Yoshida. And now Jackson looked more closely, those were his and Brooke's metal cases – the cases that contained their robots.

Jackson jumped up and ran out of the bakery towards the van. He had no idea what he would do, but he couldn't just stand by and watch all their gear being taken. Then he stopped in his tracks. He'd spotted the English version of the Japanese text on the back of the van: POLICE.

What was he thinking? How was his arrest, and by a dirty cop at that, going to help their quest to find the twins? Jackson turned and pretended to look in the bakery window. He watched the reflection of the van, helpless, as the detective closed the doors, climbed into the front cabin with his men and drove away.

CHAPTER 4

'Let me get this straight!'

Brooke's face was as pink as her hair. Jackson wasn't sure if that was from running to the bakery after he'd called to tell her about the police visit, or just because she was boiling with anger. Behind Brooke was a Japanese boy in a baseball cap, who she'd been too consumed with anger to introduce. The boy simply stood quietly while Brooke raged.

'You sat here drinking tea, while Detective Yoshida removed everything from our capsules? Everything we need if we are to stand even the slimmest chance of rescuing the twins. Now we have no gear and nowhere to stay!' Brooke jabbed a finger towards the bakery window, in the direction of a man who was leaning against the outside of the hotel, smoking a cigarette. Jackson had seen him talking to Detective Yoshida before taking up his position by the hotel wall when the detective and his men drove away. He'd told Brooke to avoid the hotel and come straight to the bakery. The plain-clothes officer was completely unaware that the subjects he'd been posted to watch for were just metres away, watching him.

Brooke was right, thought Jackson. He had completely messed up. Everything, the whole trip, was now in jeopardy because of his stupidity. All she'd asked him to do was watch over the robots and he had failed – spectacularly. He waited for a response to form in his head, but as had been the case over the last two weeks, there was nothing, except perhaps a desire to vanish on the spot.

Things had gone from bad to worse – and once again, it was all Jackson's fault.

'Well, Jackson?' Brooke said reproachfully. 'What are we going to do now?'

'*Anjiru yori umu ga yasushi.*' The Japanese voice came from behind Brooke. The boy in the cap stepped forward and snapped a quick bow to Jackson.

'It's a Japanese proverb,' the boy said in perfect English, with a slight American twang to his accent. 'In translation it's something like *It is easier to make it, than thinking about it.*'

The boy was obviously Japanese, with a characteristically round Japanese face and features, jet-black prongs of gelled hair sprouting from below the cap, suggesting a tamed version of the spiky hairstyle that Jackson had noticed so many young guys sporting. But his accent and clothes were all American. Levi jeans, Nike Hightop boots, rusty-coloured Puffa bodywarmer over a plaid shirt. And Jackson recognized the symbol on his cap – the white interlocked L and A on a blue background of the LA Dodgers baseball team.

'But don't think that all Japanese go around spouting proverbs the whole time. It just seemed like a cool way to snap you two out of your samurai stand-off!'

'This is Marty, by the way,' said Brooke in a flat tone, looking through the bakery window in the direction of the police officer, in order to avoid eye contact with Jackson. 'He's a computer-games blogger. A girl I met last night put me on to him. I would have told you, but you were too busy showing off your gaming skills.'

'Marty McFly,' said the boy, slicing his hand through the awkward space between Jackson and Brooke. Jackson shook it. It was an unusual name for a Japanese boy, even one dressed so convincingly as an American teenager, and there was something familiar about it – Jackson was sure he'd heard the name before; he just couldn't put his finger on it.

'*Back to the Future!*' said Marty, reading the recognition in Jackson's face. 'It's my absolute favourite movie of all time. I started wearing Marty's clothes from the film and the name just stuck. Have you seen it?'

'Yeah, I've seen all three of the films,' said Jackson.

'So have I.' Brooke broke the uncomfortable silence she'd maintained during Marty's colourful introduction.

'Me and my dad tried to make the Hoverboard from the second film once.'

'No way! Did it work?' Marty asked excitedly.

'We managed to make it hover using two inverted pulse-jet turbines, but one of them malfunctioned during testing and incinerated the board and most of my father's garage.'

'*Majide!*' exclaimed Marty. 'Sorry, I must remember to speak English. That's awesome!'

'So, you know the Kojimas?' said Jackson.

'Of course. Every gamer in Japan knows the Kojimas,' said Marty. 'My posts feature them at least every couple of weeks. My readers want to know about them. They win every tournament they enter. At least, they did before they went missing.' He glanced at Brooke when he said this. It was clear to Jackson that Marty considered she cared more about the Kojimas' fate than Jackson did.

'According to Marty, the Kojimas are not the only gamers who've gone missing.' This time Brooke glared straight at Jackson, her eyes still cold.

Marty dug into a tatty brown leather satchel slung over his shoulder and pulled out an equally tatty netbook. He opened the miniature laptop, placed it on the bar in the window where they were sitting, and opened a folder containing several saved websites. The Japanese writing on the web page he'd loaded was indecipherable to Jackson and Brooke, but it also contained a couple of pictures, one of a boy about their age and a second featuring a pretty girl.

'I first noticed it a few months ago. Several of the regulars at tournaments around Japan had stopped attending. I followed up on a few.' Marty pointed to the picture of the boy. 'Kenji Takahashi, from Nagoya. He was the first Japanese player ever to win the South Asian Cyber League Cup. I even travelled to his house and talked to his parents. They told me that one night they went to bed, leaving him playing in his room. Next morning he was gone. And Cho Kobayashi. Known as "Baby Face".'

'She's beautiful,' said Brooke, looking at the JPEG of a girl of around thirteen. She had huge green eyes and her pale, perfectly oval face was framed by a tousled bob haircut of shiny black hair, the tips of which were electric blue.

'Most Japanese don't know her, but within the gaming community she is a kind of pin-up. She vanished about three months ago on the way home from college. Her gaming friends launched an online search for her, using Twitter and Facebook and banner adverts on the most popular tournament forums and blogs. The WHERE IS BABY FACE? banner was everywhere online for weeks.'

'And did anything come of the search?' asked Brooke.

'Nothing. And you can add to those two at least five other regular competition players and three members of a team visiting Tokyo from South Korea for a big annual LAN party we hold in the capital each year.'

'So you think these disappearances are connected?' asked Jackson.

'It's hard to say. I guess other kids go missing too. But, yes, if I was going to put my money on it, I'd guess that amount of high-profile gamers going missing in a short space of time is more than just a coincidence.'

Jackson looked over to Brooke. *What was Yakimoto up to?* Jackson wondered. *What possible reason would he have for rounding up gamers? Surely it wasn't just coincidence?* He had to admit to an instant and illogical sense of hope, a sensation that had been in short supply since he'd learned of the Kojimas' disappearance. If the Kojimas weren't the only ones abducted, did this mean there was a better chance they might still be alive? What was the mathematical rationale of safety in numbers? Jackson suppressed his thoughts. He'd come back to this mystery later. For the time being he wanted to concentrate on what else Marty had to say.

'What about the police?' asked Brooke, motioning to the man outside. The officer was continuing to chain-smoke. It had begun to rain so he had to shield his cigarette inside his jacket. 'What have the police said about the missing children?'

'I read one interview with a Tokyo Met detective who said he was investigating the possibility of a kidnapping, but all the others told a similar story about the Kojima disappearance.'

'They said they think the twins ran away?' suggested Brooke.

'Yes, as far as I can tell, the police and the newspapers haven't spotted the gaming connection. Each case, the Kojimas' included, has been treated as discrete and unrelated. Just kids who up and ran away,' said Marty.

'I knew it!' said Brooke, shaking her head fiercely. 'Do they think we're idiots? The twins were abducted in front of a crowd of their own fans and still the official police line is that they staged the whole thing to run away from their father. It's Yakimoto – the police are in cahoots with the Yakuza, I just know it!'

'Yakimoto?' asked Marty.

'He's the head of the Yamaguchi-gumi. I believe it's the biggest Yakuza gangster family in Japan,' said Jackson.

'Wow. You guys have really done your research,' said Marty.

'There's a lot we don't know,' replied Jackson. 'We're keen to learn as much as we can about Yakimoto and his organization.'

'Well, you are correct, Yamaguchi-gumi are the biggest Yakuza group in Japan. They virtually own whole districts like Roppongi here in Tokyo, where they run protection rackets and gambling operations. How do you know this boss man, Yakimoto, is involved with the Kojima kidnapping?'

'We just know,' said Jackson firmly. The last thing he wanted to do was repeat the details of the call to Miss Kojima in which he'd first asked for information about Yakimoto and, in so doing, had put the Kojima twins on the Yakuza radar. He could feel the regret threatening to overwhelm him. He'd learned that the only way to deal with it was to avoid thinking about it. And there was something else bothering him: Brooke's new friend. Jackson didn't want to appear rude, but should he and Brooke be sharing what they knew about one of Tokyo's most dangerous men – with a complete stranger?

'Brooke, I need to ask you something,' he said, smiling at Marty before turning away from him. 'Who is this guy?' he whispered, motioning over his shoulder. 'And how do you know we can trust him?'

'I don't know if you've noticed, Jackson,' said Brooke sternly. 'We don't have an awful lot to go on here! Marty was a chance encounter. Before I told him anything I checked up on him online and took a look at his blog. It all checks out. He's given us the best lead so far, and after you so efficiently disposed of our robots we need all the help we can get.'

Brooke's words stung, but Jackson had to admit Marty's missing gamers theory did offer a new dimension to their search for the twins. That was it then, what choice was there but to trust the boy in the Puffa?

'Do you think Yakuza could be behind the other kidnappings too?' Brooke asked Marty.

'There's one sure way to find out,' added Jackson. 'Do you think you could help us get to Yakimoto?'

'Wait a minute, Jackson-*san*,' said Marty, adding the traditional Japanese sign of respect to his name. 'You don't just walk up to Yamaguchi-gumi. They are a powerful force here in Japan. Asking the wrong kind of questions can land you in a lot of trouble.'

'Yeah, we kinda found that out already,' replied Jackson, glancing at Brooke. The words from the threatening email he'd received, just before they set off for Tokyo, lined up in his mind: *Forget about the Kojima Twins. They are gone. Stop your meddling or you'll be gone too.* 'Let's just assume we tread carefully – can you find us some Yakuza hang-outs in Tokyo?'

'Just a minute, Sherlock,' said Brooke. 'Before we go announcing our intention to take on Japan's criminal underground – it might be an idea to get back the kit you lost for us. Where do you think they'll have taken it, Marty?'

'Let me see.' Marty opened a browser on his netbook and entered some more Japanese characters. A few seconds later an image flashed up on the computer screen. It showed an imposing wedge-shaped multi-storey building with a cylindrical tower on the top.

'My God,' said Brooke, looking at the small screen. 'They've taken my robots to Tokyo's version of Alcatraz.'

'Yes!' said Marty. 'The headquarters of the Keishicho – the Tokyo Metropolitan Police – does look a little like your famous prison in San Francisco. Except it's not surrounded by shark-infested waters.'

'Great, so it's not all bad news!' said Brooke.

'Well, Brooke-*san*,' said Marty, 'I'm guessing they make up for the lack of man-eating predators in the Kasumi-gaseki district of Tokyo with state-of-the-art security measures.'

The small pink car was parked in the centre of a massive interchange, where eight pedestrian crossings and thousands of pedestrians converged. Traffic was already backed up and the pavements had begun choking up too, with people taking pictures of the dangerously parked car.

Taped to the windscreen was a handwritten note in Japanese:

Dear Officer,
Gone shoe shopping.
Back in an hour xxxx

The shocking-red sky didn't make the snaggletoothed silhouette of the massive Tokyo Metropolitan Police building look any less monstrous.

Jackson and Marty stood in an alleyway opposite the building, waiting for a call from Brooke. Her plan was typical Brooke: audacious and highly technical, with a good chance of complete and utter failure, but Jackson had to admire its ingenuity.

They'd been waiting for around an hour when Jackson's phone pulsed.

'Cute, ain't she?' said Brooke.

'I'm sorry, what's cute?' said Jackson, before he noticed a police truck towing the small shocking-pink car towards two large metal doors at the front of the building.

'She's a Nissan Figaro. One litre, turbocharged and water-cooled. I've always wanted to pimp one of them. I reckon I could squeeze a V8 under that hood. Can you imagine me burning off some dumbwad in a Camaro in that precious little pink lady?'

'Brooke, can we get back on topic? Did you plant the transceiver?'

'You bet I did, sugar. You should be able to pick it up now.'

Jackson glanced at the phone in his hand. A pale-blue message icon was blinking on the phone's glossy white surface.

'*Kawaii!*' exclaimed Marty. 'What kind of phone is that?'

'It's one Brooke designed and prototyped in her lab back in Boston. It uses an active surface display. Unlike most phones it has no screen. Instead, its whole surface is capable of displaying imagery which all reacts to touch.'

Jackson expanded the message icon by pinching it

between two fingers and then moving them apart. The icon opened into a full-colour map of Tokyo's Kasumi-gaseki district, with the phone in Jackson's hand and the one in the Nissan's boot represented as glowing dots. Jackson glanced up as the car disappeared inside the police building, the large metal doors closing behind it.

Brooke's idea had been to find a vehicle, break into it and hide her smartphone inside. Then, somehow, get it towed away by the Tokyo police. Working on the assumption that her robots had most likely been taken to a vehicle pound somewhere deep inside the police building, she hoped that by tracking her phone until it stopped, she'd stand a good chance of locating the storage facility where *Punk, Fist, Tread* and the rest of their gear were being kept. If any normal thirteen-year-old girl had attempted such a plan, she would have fallen at the first hurdle – hot-wiring the car. But Brooke spent every hour of every day, building, rewiring and modifying any and all vehicles she got her hands on, from the robots she designed and built to her self-driving Hummer, and even her father's Jet Ranger helicopter, which was maintained by Brooke and, in her words, 'hot-rodded' by her. And as she'd created both her own and Jackson's smartphone herself, she also had the requisite electronics skills to set up the handset's iner-tial navigation sensor to transmit from the boot of the car as it was taken inside the police building.

*

'You can have that back,' said Brooke, joining the boys in the alleyway and dropping Marty's grubby mobile phone into his hands, the way you'd put a snotty tissue in the bin.

'Don't suppose you'd consider a swap?' asked Marty.

Brooke just smiled. 'How we doing?'

'The tow truck just went inside.' Jackson presented the handset to Brooke who inspected the glowing full-colour map on its surface. Beside the pulsating dot that was now inside the outline of the wedge-shaped police headquarters was a series of figures.

'It's going down. It just descended around sixty-four metres.'

Jackson looked at the building across the road. He estimated the height of each floor.

'I'm guessing that's six floors underground.'

'This is incredible. What are you guys, like secret agents or something?'

'Us, secret agents?' Brooke smiled, keeping her eyes fixed on the graphical display on Jackson's phone. 'You gotta be kidding me. The toys we get to play with are way better than a secret agent's!' She paused, frowning. 'As I suspected, their Wi-Fi is encrypted. The only way we'll connect to *Fist* is via my phone in the boot of the Nissan.'

'Wi-Fi? What, your robots use Wi-Fi?' said Marty.

'Dot.robots use the Internet as their communication

medium, same as a remote-control car uses radio waves. They are too deep in the building to get a signal from the street, and while I could probably brute-force the password on the internal police network it might take all night to crack it. Instead, we can configure our phones as Wi-Fi hotspots. It's really no big deal. If you jailbreak your phone, you could probably get it to do the same.' Jackson looked at the ancient flip phone in Marty's hand. 'OK, maybe not. The robots connect to Brooke's phone and then out on to the Web, so we can control them from here.'

'Wow, you guys are something else,' gushed Marty.

'Sending out a hailing signal now,' said Brooke. She waved her handset in the air, moving it to and fro, as if beckoning to someone across the street.

'Now that's just weird,' said Marty.

'Brooke's phones have a gestural interface.'

Marty looked confused.

'Many of the features on Brooke's handsets can be controlled using gestures or movements of the hand, like a wave or a shape drawn in the air which initiates a program or application. And our robots have a Mirror Mode in which they can follow the movements of the phone holder.'

'And I'm working on adding mind control to this baby,' said Brooke, her head down as she typed on the surface of her phone.

'Very funny!' said Marty.

'She's being serious,' said Jackson. 'Brooke's modified a Bluetooth earpiece to read her mind.'

Brooke fished in the back of her jeans and momentarily flashed an earpiece before slipping it back in her pocket. 'I can still make calls on it and stuff,' she said, 'but it's also a high-fidelity BCI!'

'Brain–Computer Interface,' said Jackson. Brooke's fondness for acronyms left most people clueless. 'It touches the skin behind her ear and picks up her alpha and theta brain waves.' The project had been Brooke's obsession before news of the twins' disappearance. Now she was obsessed with finding them.

'I can already trigger the ringtone, just by relaxing. I call it my chill-tone! It's just in the first stages right now, pretty pointless really, but you know what they say – it's the thought that counts!'

'You guys are truly amazing, but I'm not sure how all your tech is going to help you get your robots out of there.' Marty pointed across the road. 'You do realize, that's one of the most secure buildings in all of Japan?'

Jackson looked at the building. The sun had dipped below the concrete horizon and he could see that most of the windows in the massive structure were lit. They would be taking back the robots from right under the noses of several hundred police officers.

'It's nothing we can't handle,' said Jackson confidently.

*

The invisible pulse of electrical energy that was radiating from the boot of the small pink car in Pound 12, Area B, was imperceptible to the guard on duty. Not that 'guard' was a particularly useful moniker for Sergeant Kinshobi as he wasn't really guarding anything. The vehicle and goods lock-up was six floors below ground level. It was accessed via bombproof steel doors at the street entrance and a spiral concrete tunnel with ceiling-mounted CCTV cameras every fifteen metres. There were twenty evidence pounds in total, each large enough to hold fifteen standard-sized vehicles. Each pound was secured behind high-tensile steel sliding doors and biometric locks, which required an authorized fingerprint to access. As far as Sergeant Kinshobi was concerned, his job was more like that of a museum curator than a guard. Sure he got to wear the gear, the shiny badge and even a sidearm, but his days of running down handbag snatchers or chasing carjackers in a high-speed highway pursuit were far behind him. Now he simply checked in and out an increasingly exotic collection of recovered vehicles and large-scale possessions. Most weird object in his inventory? Pound 17, Cage C: a whole stuffed moose. Vehicle in the lock-up he'd most like to take home? Pound 11, Area E: Lamborghini Gallardo LP560-4 Polizia. The exotic vehicle was in the squad car-parking area and was a special model of the supercar donated by the Polizia Stradale, the Italian Traffic Police Force, and decked out in Tokyo Metropolitan Police colours for use in special ceremonial occasions. The sports car was meant to be part of the general motor pool, but there was an unspoken rule that Sergeant Kinshobi's ultimate boss, Police Chief Shozu, was the only officer permitted to drive it.

Kinshobi had just started the fifth nine-by-nine square sudoku grid of his shift when he heard a creaking sound, followed by quite a loud metallic clang. He put it down to a piece of evidence falling over against the pound gates. He might stand it back upright when he did his final walk around, before clocking off, but he'd probably leave it for the idiot officer who didn't stand it up properly in the first place.

Three sub-grids complete, six more to go.

Next there was a clattering sound that seemed to pass quickly from left to right, below his office window. This time the sergeant glanced up from his puzzle book but he saw nothing.

Six three-by-three square sub-grids complete. The sergeant checked his wristwatch. He'd only taken two and a half minutes so far. He was flying tonight. A soft whirring sound caught his attention. This time he actually got up and stuck his head out of his tiny office doorway, but the sound had stopped.

Just one region of nine little squares left, thought the sergeant as he returned to his chair, *and even with all these distractions, a time under four minutes!*

Sergeant Kinshobi's focus was shattered by the shrill yowl of a car alarm. Throwing his pencil down in disgust and leaving his puzzle unfinished, he got up and walked over to a line of filing cabinets. He opened one of the drawers, fished around inside and pulled out a metal coat hanger. He then walked towards the source of the alarm.

It was a trick he'd been taught by one of his regular informants when he'd worked the streets. Depending on the car's make and model, a wire coat hanger could be bent into one of several shapes and used to open the bonnet and disconnect the battery, thus disrupting the alarm's power source.

Following the sound, Sergeant Kinshobi strode across the main squad-car pool area, checking each pound as he went. His eye was drawn to what looked, in the low light of Pound 5, like a large elliptical hole in the steel bars of the pound's electric gate. He walked towards it slowly, wishing he'd brought his torch so he could have a better look. As he neared the gate to the pound, he could see it was still firmly locked in place, but the four bars that made up its centre section had been bent to form a hole about as wide as his shoulders. Kinshobi was still trying to make sense of what he was seeing when the noise from the alarm ceased. He turned round and began to walk briskly towards where he thought the alarm had been coming from. As he turned a corner, he could see the lights flashing on an old-fashioned pink Nissan. Its open bonnet was facing him as he slowed his pace towards it. He was sure this hadn't been the case when it had been delivered a few hours ago. The police officer instinctively dropped his right hand to the holster on his hip and rested it on the butt of his gun.

'Hello!' he shouted. 'Guys, if this is some kind of prank, I'm too old for it. You're spooking the hell out of me.'

When he reached the car he noticed that the bonnet had been twisted and ripped from its hinges, and rather than being upright on its stabilizing arm the bonnet had been left against the windscreen. The sergeant drew his pistol and crabbed around the car. The boot lid was equally mangled and, when Kinshobi summoned up the courage to glance inside, he could see it was empty.

Just then the sergeant caught the sound of creaking again. This time he knew exactly what it was. What he'd heard before, and was listening to now, was the sound of high-tensile steel bars bending. And it was coming from the main entrance.

'Oh my God!' Marty was shaking his head in disbelief. 'He's bending those bars like they're made out of liquorice!'

'Yeah, *Fist* is stacked, ain't he?' Brooke replied.

Marty and Jackson were standing either side of Brooke, all three of them huddled in the shadow of a fire escape in an alleyway from which they could clearly see the police building. Jackson's tablet computer was serving up a live video feed from *Fist* as the robot ripped its way effortlessly through the main gates to the lock-up level. They'd watched as Brooke's HAIL command had woken the remote robotic grappling machine while he sat curled up inside the metal flight case in which he'd been shipped. It had taken *Fist* just a couple of seconds to boot up and a further few seconds to rip free from the case. Waving her mobile in front of her, with the skill and precision of a conductor, Brooke had directed *Fist* to apply around fifteen per cent of the total pressure his four arms were capable of producing on the locking mechanism of the gate that secured the cage where he'd been stored, more than enough power to rip the gate clean off its hinges.

The robot had then prised open the cages that contained the rest of Brooke's belongings and, clasping their handles between his rugged plastic hands, dragged the three metal containers towards the last obstacle on the lock-up level, the high-strength carbon-steel entry gates. Brooke had then remembered that she needed to retrieve her phone and sent *Fist* over to the Nissan, where he'd ripped the boot open to retrieve the phone, and then the bonnet to disconnect the alarm. With *Fist* back at the gate, she had focused him on the metal channel that guided the sliding wheels on the top and bottom of the gate, the engineer in her instinctively seeking out the weakest part of the gate assembly. Fifteen hundred pounds per square inch – around fifty per cent of the total pressure *Fist* could apply as leverage – was directed at the bars and bottom section of the gate. The force contorted them upwards until the line of wheels that enabled the gate to slide open was dislocated from the runners bolted to the concrete floor, allowing the whole half-tonne structure to be swung upwards like a huge cat flap.

The shape and size of the three cases *Fist* was carrying made moving quite awkward, and he limped up the spiral exit ramp towards ground level using two arms to walk and two to carry the cases above his body, like a baboon with a ball.

'What happens when he makes it out on to the street?' asked Marty, transfixed by the feed from *Fist* on the tablet's screen, which showed a tunnel bathed in fluorescent yellow light, curving gently towards the entrance gate at street level.

'I figured I'd wear *Fist* and you'd hail us a cab.'

Marty began to laugh, waiting for the other two to join in. But instead Jackson and Brooke looked at Marty with straight faces. Brooke was referring to what she and Jackson called *Fist*'s 'Backpack Mode'. The robot was extremely strong but he was also relatively light, about the same weight as a small child of around six years old, and he could be directed to climb up and cuddle his wearer from behind, his arms stretching round the shoulders and waist like a backpack.

'Seriously, how are you planning to get your gear out of here?' Marty persisted.

'I am being serious,' said Brooke. 'Despite what you might think, I ain't in the habit of jacking folks' cars without good reason. You got the number of a cab firm in that quaint little cell of yours?'

'Er . . . yes, I think I have,' said Marty, pressing the keys on his handset and cupping the microphone with his hand as he began to speak in Japanese.

'Coast is clear!' shouted Jackson. He was standing where the alleyway met the road, looking up and down the street. At that moment, two of *Fist*'s yellow plastic hands appeared from behind the bars of the entrance gate to the police HQ building, ready to wrench the two sliding sections apart.

'Wait!' shouted Jackson. A couple of streets up, two police squad cars had pulled out and were approaching the HQ building. When the two cars were in line with the mouth of the alleyway they paused for oncoming traffic in the centre of the road, before turning towards the entrance gate. Moments later the large gates began to slide open.

Brooke had to act quickly, sending a series of mimetic commands to *Fist* who responded by instantly darting sideways like a crab, his strong, agile hands finding holds around a fuse-box, then a metal electricity cable that traced the curvature of the ceiling, and finally the casing of one of the yellow strip lights, until he was flattened against the roof of the tunnel, Brooke's cases held tightly against the concrete surface in a way that made them look like air-conditioning vents when the squad cars' headlamps momentarily picked them out. To everyone's relief, the two cars glided smoothly under *Fist* and down into the depths of the building.

Jackson signalled the all-clear, and a few motions from Brooke's handset later *Fist* was scampering between the closing gates and across the road towards the alleyway, dragging the cases behind him.

'Marty, how's that cab doing?' said Brooke, still directing *Fist*. 'We need to get us out of here as soon as possible.'

''Bout five minutes,' said Marty, looking in amazement as *Fist* walked past him. Brooke brought the robot to rest in the shadow of a scaffolding tower that stretched several storeys up the side of what appeared to be an apartment block. He looked like a huge, bright-yellow spider, with black-and-yellow hazard warning stripes on sections of his arms and oval-shaped body. Even in the dimly lit alleyway, it was impossible not to spot him.

'I'm thinking we might look a little conspicuous bundling into a cab with a bright-yellow robot,' said Marty.

'Don't worry yourself, cowboy. *Fist* has his own unique way of travelling,' said Brooke, retrieving her phone from him. She dropped a shoulder and let her rucksack slide to the ground, then dipped a hand inside and brought out a tightly scrunched red plastic poncho. She cut some more shapes with her phone, each of which resulted in a burst of movement from *Fist* that made Marty take a few steps backwards. Within seconds, *Fist* had walked towards his operator and climbed on to her back, wrapping his arms round her waist and shoulders. Brooke opened out the thin plastic poncho before pulling it over her head, replacing the yellow robot on her back with the outline of Mickey Mouse and the words WELCOME TO DISNEYLAND.

'The cab, Jackson! Anything?' Brooke shouted, impatiently this time.

But Jackson did not react to Brooke's insistent question. His head was turned slightly, his ear pointed directly at the gates across the street as they opened again.

A wave of sound from inside the entrance tunnel confirmed Jackson's suspicions as the last of the two squad cars came up the ramp backwards, siren blaring.

Jackson, Brooke and Marty instinctively threw themselves against the walls of the alleyway as the two cars flew out of the opening, rear bumpers first, before swinging their front ends in opposite directions. Then the throaty growl of a sports-car engine reverberated through the tunnel, growing in intensity, until its source, a Lamborghini decorated in police blue, leaped into the space between the other two squad cars.

The alleyway, along with Brooke, Marty and Jackson, was instantly illuminated by the car's headlamps.

'Wow!' shouted Brooke, ducking her head to get a better view. 'Your cops drive Gallardos! I love this town!'

A loud Japanese voice echoed from the car's loud-speaker.

'What's he saying, Marty?' asked Brooke.

'Like your American cops say in the movies – *come out with your hands up!*'

'They'll never take us alive!' shouted Brooke.

'They'll never *what*?' Jackson yelped.

'Don't sweat it, partner!' replied Brooke. 'Just get you and our luggage down that alley!'

Jackson had worked alongside Brooke for long enough to know when she had a plan and he dutifully turned and ran. At the same moment *Fist* leaped up to meet the scaffolding above him, grasping the horizontal steel bar that supported the first level, swinging vertically round its axis with the agility of an orang-utan. The robot continued its climb with a series of interconnected swings, ascending the temporary steel structure until he was on its third level. Jackson caught a flash of white out of the corner of his eye as Brooke swished her phone like a knife blade, then *Fist* suddenly jumped from the scaffold platform towards the opposite side of the alley, one hand still firmly clenched around the framework. The force of his jump made the entire structure buckle in the middle.

Within seconds, ten-metre lengths of tubular steel were falling to the ground along with planks of timber, bricks and even a small cement mixer. And in front of the cascade of building materials, sprinting towards Jackson and Marty through a cloud of dust, was Brooke.

'Go, go, go!' she shouted, grasping the handle of the case which Marty was having trouble dragging behind him.

Jackson was doing his best to run too, with a flight case in each hand so heavy that every time their metal edges snagged on a drain cover or the edge of a rubbish skip it felt like his arms were being pulled out of their sockets. As he glanced over his shoulder, he could see the blue flashing lights of the three squad cars disappearing in different directions through a barricade of broken scaffolding. This chase wasn't over yet.

The Gallardo was a monster, every bit the snarling, road-eating animal Sergeant Kinshobi hoped it would be. He'd clearly seen the three kids and that weird mechanical spider-like thing of theirs before the scaffolding had blocked his way. Kinshobi had almost cheered when the route to them had been blocked because he wanted to chase them. He wanted to see what this Italian dream machine could do. The other two cops were behind him in their Mitsubishis, quite a long way behind him, as the combination of the 5.2 litre V10 power plant under the

Italian car's bonnet and his blue flashing lights meant that Kinshobi had a straight run up to the interchange. He'd actually shouted out a short section of the rule book under which he and his lock-up colleagues worked, as he drifted the car's back-end round the first corner at nearly 180 kilometres an hour. 'Section Fourteen! Clause 3! An officer may commandeer any official police vehicle for the pursuit of persons in the act of a crime.'

Stuff the Police Chief, thought Kinshobi. *The little* manuke *could never drive this beast like I can, anyway!*

'Aren't they just going to be waiting for us?' Marty couldn't see any flashing lights at the end of the alleyway towards which the three of them were shambling, dragging the cases awkwardly behind them.

'No problem,' said Brooke between desperate breaths. 'Look, the alley branches off ahead. Hopefully, there's an exit down there.'

The unmistakable stench of fish was the first thing that hit them as the three renegades turned left down a narrow offshoot of the alleyway. The passage was only just wide enough to get the cases through; polystyrene crates that had once held fish were stacked twenty or thirty high on either side. The noxious smell and puddles of congealed gloop that oozed from the towers of crates suggested not all of them had been cleaned out before stacking.

The passageway terminated at a set of open double doors, in front of which four men wearing white plastic pinafores sat on crates playing some kind of card game. Brooke was the first to arrive at the door, but as she attempted to go through it one of the men stood up, blocking the doorway.

'You no go in here!' said the man, his thick folded arms resting on top of a large belly. To Brooke's horror, he was holding a curved blade in one of his hands and both the blade and his white plastic apron glistened with what looked like blood. As Brooke took a shocked step backwards she could see that the men weren't playing cards but filleting fish, removing the heads, tails and scales of big silver fish with long curved blades, throwing the fillets into crates of ice.

As Marty and Jackson arrived the whoop of a police siren found them. They turned to see flashes of blue light licking at the brickwork of the alley behind and a police car's search beam probing every hiding place. When they turned back the man guarding the door squinted at them curiously. It was obvious what he concluded because he smiled and held up a finger and thumb, rubbing them together to suggest that if they wanted to use his door to escape from the police, they'd need to pay him.

Another whoop from the police car's siren told them the squad car was getting closer.

'OK, I'll pay the man,' said Brooke. It was obvious to Jackson from her voice that she was furious, but what choice did they have – the police car could block off the passageway at any time. She dipped her shoulder to reach into her backpack, but Marty placed a hand on her arm and stopped her.

'No need,' he said. 'Leave this to me.'

Marty stepped forward and immediately the hulking fish butcher unfolded his arms and held up two hands in mock defence. Jackson had to admit, Marty was about half the height of the man in front of him. The other men, who had continued to gut fish unabated, burst out laughing.

Oh no, thought Jackson. *It's never nice to see someone get a beating. Even worse when it's a fellow geek.*

Marty whispered something in Japanese. It was so low that Jackson could hardly hear him speaking and the fishy doorman had to lean forward and turn his ear in the boy's direction. To Jackson's amazement, Marty's words had an instant effect on the man. The smile vanished from his face and he straightened, then moved immediately to one side before subtly bowing to Marty. Marty reciprocated with his own gentle nod before walking back to Brooke, grasping the handle of one of the flight cases and marching through the door.

Jackson and Brooke followed behind, Brooke pausing for a moment by the man in the bloody apron and waving her hand in front of her nose. 'You know, you really could use some new cologne.'

The door led to a large warehouse filled with lines of tables around which traders haggled over boxes of fish, racks of meat and piles of vegetables.

'What did you say to that guy?' Jackson asked as he towed his cases past a stall containing what looked like squid in big fish tanks.

'It helps if you can talk the language,' said Marty. He then pointed to a large opening across the hall that looked as if it might lead to the street outside.

Brooke was looking around, frantically waiting for a solution to form, when her eyes rested on a big glass motorbike showroom across the street.

'I've got an idea,' she said. She dropped to her knees and tipped flat the smallest of the three metal flight cases that were lined up at their feet. She entered four numbers into a combination lock near the case's handle and opened its lid. Inside the square case, set in a snug lining of compact foam, was a dull metal sphere about the size of a beach ball.

'What is that?' said Marty.

'I prefer *who*,' replied Brooke. 'It's *Punk*.'

The police squad cars had gathered round the branch of the Tokyo City Bank like vultures encircling their next meal. Every time there was a bang or a smash from inside, the officers, who were stooping behind the open doors of their cars, guns at the ready, would duck and shout to each other nervously in Japanese. Little did they know that the real action was taking place further up the road – in a motorcycle showroom.

For Brooke, her choice of vehicle had been love at first sight. Despite the rather desperate nature of their situation, the excitement at seeing an actual Cherban Urban Jet was hard to suppress. It was an electric tricycle – but its two rear wheels almost merged into one big, fat dragster-style tyre, giving it the appearance of a low-slung, sparkling, aquamarine motorcycle from the future with a two-seater cockpit. Brooke didn't hesitate in ordering *Fist* to smash a four-metre-squared section of the showroom's glass front. *Punk*'s role as bank robber was intended merely as a temporary distraction. After all, what cop would choose to investigate an alarm at a motorcycle dealer's over the excitement of an active bank robbery? This particular diversionary tactic was made possible by a test mode built into *Punk*'s root-level programming that enabled him to recognize and seek out any given object. Brooke simply showed him an object he couldn't possibly find in a branch of a Tokyo bank – a picture of a seagull she'd snapped using her phone on the boat coming over. *Punk* had been turning the place upside-down, looking for the seabird, ever since.

It took Brooke around four minutes to hack the complex electronics of the electric street racer – a process that started with the delicate examination of the vehicle's starter solenoid and ignition chip-set and ended with a letter opener, borrowed from a salesman's desk, which she'd rammed in the key slot and brutally twisted.

An array of turquoise system indicators glowing on the Urban Jet's dashboard told Brooke the pure-bred racing machine was ready to go. Brooke cut a few shapes in the air with her handset and *Fist* responded by grabbing *Punk*'s empty case and climbing into the back seat of the vehicle, behind its driver. Brooke then lay almost fully back in the contoured leather driving seat and placed both hands on the handlebars, which were so low they almost touched her thighs. As she squeezed gently on the leather throttle grip in her right hand, the slimline tricycle rolled forward, over the threshold of the broken window and on to the pavement. Before she joined the road, Brooke turned a sharp left, riding down part of the pavement until she stopped next to a section of the building's glass frontage that was still intact. She dropped her shoulder and unclipped her backpack, swinging it round to her front so she could fish inside. Her fingers felt the shapes of several tools, all instantly familiar to the young engineer: her treasured ratchet given to her by her father on her fifth birthday, a tiny palm-sized electric screwdriver that packed a targeting laser, and the distinctive cold chrome of a spirit-level hand gauge that Brooke used for balancing her robots' servos. Then she felt something less familiar, a small, square-edged tube. Brooke retrieved the tube of lipstick from her bag. Its chrome plastic case was dulled by scratches, but the black lipstick itself was in almost pristine condition as Brooke had only used it once when she'd attended a Blink 182 gig at MIT, during fresher's week. She wasn't big on make-up and had only kept it in her tool stash because she figured that one day it might come in handy for something.

Brooke leaned sideways, stretching an arm out of the Urban Jet's cockpit. She used the lipstick to scrawl something on the glass before zipping up her bag and speeding away, head down.

> Dear Sir,
> Sorry for all the mess.
> Lovin' the Urban Jet!
> I'll send you a cheque in the mail.
> B xxxx

Jackson and Marty had witnessed the scene unfold. They weren't sure at first what Brooke was up to as she'd walked from the bank carrying her rucksack and *Punk*'s case, with *Fist* in backpack mode, his arms wrapped round her shoulders and waist. Then they'd heard the sounds of *Punk* trashing the bank's interior and the alarm going off. They'd watched as two Mitsubishi squad cars and the police Lamborghini had arrived outside the bank, having completely ignored the motorbike showroom.

The police were busy observing what they thought was a bank robbery in process when Brooke arrived at the shop entrance where she'd left Jackson and Marty. She performed a U-turn in the road before them and shouted to Jackson: 'Wait until the coast is clear, then hail a cab. We'll meet at the Invader in an hour.'

'Where are you going?' Marty shouted back.

'Taking this baby for a test drive, of course!'

Then she shot off in the direction she'd come from, passing the showroom with its alarm still flashing, up to the bank where there were now five squad cars. Jackson and Marty continued to watch as Brooke stopped in the middle of the road and performed a series of doughnuts, the wheels of the strange, low-slung racing machine smoking as Brooke spun it round on the spot several times. With all the smoke, it was hard for the boys to see exactly what was going on, but Jackson noticed *Punk* flying out of the front of the bank and dropping into the back seat of Brooke's machine. Brooke then accelerated into the distance, leaving the squad cars to do a series of K-turns in the road before they too shot off in hot pursuit.

Marty cocked his head to one side and folded his arms. 'Wow!' he said. 'You guys are exciting to hang out with!'

'Oh yeah, we're a blast,' replied Jackson. But his reply possessed no conviction whatever. Not that Marty noticed. Jackson hadn't found the events of the last hour even remotely exciting, unlike the young blogger, who'd had a broad grin on his face the whole time. Far from it. Stealing a car so they could break the robots out of the police headquarters, and seeing Brooke pursued by a group of squad cars, had simply added a layer of worry on top of the guilt Jackson already felt for the plight of his friends. What if she crashed? She could kill herself or even someone else. Or she could be locked up. Where would their search for the twins be then?

Jackson told himself he needed to wake up, draw a line under the stupid mistake he'd made at the hotel and get on with finding the twins.

He looked at Marty who was pacing around a few metres down the pavement, talking in animated terms on his mobile phone. Jackson wasn't sure how he felt about sharing so much with the Japanese boy. After all, he was a blogger, a journalist, and weren't you meant never to trust a journalist? Jackson had seen it in countless films, the half-drunk, chain-smoking, greasy-haired hack who would shop his own grandma for a scoop. That wasn't Marty, at least he didn't fit that picture. But he had seen much of the technology Jackson and Brooke usually kept under wraps. Lord only knew what Brooke's father would think.

The robotics professor had a strict policy regarding the public seeing any of the stuff he and his daughter were working on. Not that Brooke hadn't flouted her father's rules on several occasions. The robots' most memorable public appearances replayed in Jackson's mind, like movie clips. There was the time when Brooke was so incensed by her father's reluctance to support her design for a portable self-driving car unit that she fitted her prototype invention to a forklift and remotely directed the driverless lifter to pick up a porta-toilet, drive it down the main hall of MIT university and place it in the middle of J.P.'s lecture theatre. The only thing was, the technology was untested and, when the digital link to Brooke's handheld controller failed, the forklift – with the toilet full of chemicals and excrement on the front of it – went haywire, eventually tipping over on some stairs and flooding the canteen with its evil-smelling liquid cargo. And only a few weeks ago he and Brooke had deployed *Fist* to rescue a pensioner trapped in his truck. It would have been a quick job and the old man would have put the strange yellow machine that peeled back his crumpled bonnet down to some new-fangled fire-brigade gadget. But the fact that Brooke insisted on using *Fist* to rip the wheels off the sports car of the ignorant jerk who'd caused the accident in the first place wasn't so easy to hide. Her father's influence – not to mention a chunk of his bank balance – had silenced the man. But nothing could prevent the YouTube footage of *Fist* that was uploaded by a passer-by.

Jackson smiled to himself. Three million hits. Not that he and Brooke were counting.

Brooke was convinced that the sports-car incident was the catalyst for her father's recent change of heart. He'd decided they should move away from the space, military and law enforcement contracts that had been their bread and butter in recent years, and instead focus on the lucrative industrial robots market. Brooke was horrified by the idea of building, in her words, 'Automated Supermarket Shelf Stackers' for which she'd developed the acronym 'A.S.S.S machines'. Jackson suspected that the loss of J.P.'s Chinese investors and the fact that the government had dropped two of his projects, citing the global economic downturn, were the real reasons J.P. now favoured taking a different direction for their robot designs.

Marty signalled to Jackson by raising a finger to indicate he was almost finished. It took a lot of words to order a taxi in Tokyo, Jackson thought. He reflected on Marty's look. It was an odd one. The Puffa bodywarmer had the effect of softening him. It made him seem kind of fat and harmless. But imagining Marty without it, in just the blue plaid shirt he had rolled up to his elbows, Jackson thought he looked quite toned, his forearms not big, but muscular. Was that why Brooke was so keen to accept his help? Jackson stopped himself. *What was that all about?*

he thought. *Jealousy?* Jackson physically shook the thought from his head. Allowing himself to be rational for a moment, he knew it was hardly surprising that Brooke had turned to someone other than Jackson to help rescue them from the mess he'd created. And it wasn't as if he'd been there for Brooke on the boat over. Events in Tokyo were already threatening to spiral out of control. If he and Brooke were to get back on target, he needed to sort his head out, resist the temptation to lose himself in long sessions on *Whisper* and give Brooke the support she needed.

Jackson smiled at Marty as the boy put his phone away and walked back towards him.

When they met up with Brooke, he'd apologize to her for acting like an idiot and let her know he was ready to do whatever was required to find the twins. And he'd give the guy in the Puffa a little more respect. So what if he'd seen the robots and the phones – it wasn't as if he and Brooke had an alternative. Without Marty's help, they would probably still be sitting in the cafe wondering what to do next. With his advice they'd located the robots, and he'd helped Brooke decide how to break them out.

'How long's it going to be, Marty?' Jackson asked.

'Taxis are all booked up. I persuaded a friend of mine to pick us up. Be here in five minutes!' Marty said.

'Cool,' replied Jackson.

*

Pivoting axle! Interesting! thought Brooke. *That's where this vehicle's rapid yaw response comes from!*

Just because Brooke was being pursued by one of the fastest supercars on the planet didn't mean the engineering side of her brain was switched off. A fountain of sparks sprayed from the metal stand underneath the Urban Jet as Brooke leaned as low as her vehicle would let her into the corner.

She'd worked out that despite the engine in the electrically powered racing tricycle being several orders of magnitude less powerful than the police supercar's, like the other high-performance electric engines she'd worked with – the ones found inside her robots, for example – this one had bags of torque. This meant that so far she'd managed to stay ahead of the officer on her tail, despite his skilful execution of some quite spectacularly controlled drifts round very tight corners. But she knew that its higher flat-out speed meant the Gallardo would eventually catch up with her. So Brooke's plan was to keep the Jet light and fast, putting it at speed through the tightest winding streets she could find.

The sparkling aquamarine-blue Urban Jet shot past a small alley, barely wide enough for a car. Doubling back, Brooke spotted the impossibly low blue-and-white police car heading straight towards her, just before she turned into the alley. *Let's see how he likes squeezing his precious little race car down here*, she thought, as she weaved in between doorsteps that jutted out every few metres and ducked beneath low-slung washing lines decorated with all kinds of clothing, which made the narrow cobbled street even narrower. But halfway down the alley and having removed several damp pieces of underwear from her face – *note to self: disadvantage of an open cockpit design* – Brooke could hear her pursuer's siren bouncing off the alley walls. Risking a glance in the side mirror, she could see the crazy man was still on her six o'clock, caring nothing for what the concrete doorsteps and occasional scrapes against the brick wall were doing to his two thousand dollar low-profile rims and custom-paint job. *Tight and fast. Tight and fast!* she repeated to herself, as she shot glances left and right in search of ever more constrictive passageways.

Jackson went instantly from impatience to dread when the police motorcycle cruised past. He'd been examining every car and driver as he waited for Marty's friend to arrive and so he'd been unable to avert his eyes in time to avoid contact with the police officer's. The motorbike continued on its path past them, but it was clear to both Jackson and Marty that its rider was talking into his microphone.

'The market!' shouted Jackson as the officer turned round and headed back towards them.

The bruised skin on Jackson's palms and the meat of his fingers from their last retreat was doubly painful when the heavy flight case clanged against the doors as he and Marty ran back into the market hall. He knew the officer wouldn't be far behind; all he had to do was park his bike and run after them. So Jackson threw his metal case under the first row of stalls he came across before diving down behind it, and Marty followed suit with his case, until both of them were scrabbling through an intricate network of rectangular tunnels constructed from metal table legs and plastic sheeting. If they'd thought the hall was whiffy before, down here, among the rotting fish heads and putrefied vegetables, the smell was positively noxious. Jackson carefully raised the bottom of a white plastic tablecloth that hung down a few centimetres from one of the stalls, as much to get a few mouthfuls of fresher air as to check on the situation. He could see the polished leather motorbike boots of the cop about ten stalls down and the flip-flopped feet of two stallholders standing beside him.

'Exit strategy?' Jackson whispered to Marty.

'Just keep going!' Marty replied.

A few random turns later, and what felt like several hundred painful kilometres on hands and knees now covered in decomposed foodstuffs, Jackson spotted a potential exit route. Between the bowed legs of a stallholder, he could see two stained transparent plastic curtains that looked as if they led outside.

Within seconds, Jackson and Marty were strolling

towards the plastic flaps, walking nonchalantly with their cases in a way that didn't betray how incredibly heavy they were. Nevertheless, as they reached the exit they heard a blast from a police whistle across the hall and the officer shouting. Jackson needed no translation. Yet again, it was time to run. Leaving the hall, the two found themselves at the edge of a large courtyard, with an ancient-looking gold-and-red shrine-like building in the middle. Running wasn't an activity Jackson was practised in. The only muscle group he regularly exercised was the one that enabled him to frown at a particularly testing maths problem, or perhaps whatever muscle enabled his gamer's fingers to move swiftly over the crucial keys during a battle in *Whisper*. Consequently, as Marty led him at speed across the cobbled courtyard, Jackson's thighs felt like they were made of dried-up rubber bands that could snap at any moment, and his throat felt like he was breathing fire. They ran under a long wooden gazebo that led to a busy street. But, just as Jackson was beginning to calculate the amount of steps he had left in him was in the low tens, he spotted a line of rickshaws on the road.

'Hold it,' he spluttered, between desperate attempts to breathe. 'I've got an idea!'

'Whatever it is,' Marty replied, also breathing deeply, just not as deeply as Jackson, 'it had better be quick. That cop will have zeroed his buddies in on us. We need to get out of this area.'

'And that's how we're going to do it!' replied Jackson. He was bent double, his back heaving up and down as he attempted to catch his breath, but he managed to flick a hand in the direction of the line of two-wheeled, cart-like passenger vehicles parked in the road.

'A rickshaw? Those things are strictly for tourists. Even with the fittest dude pulling us, we'll never get out of here before the cops have this place locked down.'

'I wasn't thinking of using a *dude*.' Jackson pushed his case over, so it was lying flat on the pavement. He then kneeled down, entered a five-number code into a tiny digital keypad near its handle and popped its locks open. Marty peered inside. Packed in a tight-fitting, foam-rubber lining was what looked like a single car wheel, with a sparkling chrome rim and a shiny plastic casing sticking out where the hub would usually be.

'And what – sorry, *who* is that?' asked Marty in amazement.

'His name is *Tread*!' said Jackson.

Jackson was working feverishly with an adjustable spanner from *Tread*'s flight case to remove the handlebar of the rickshaw. The bar was connected between a couple of two-metre-long wooden arms that curved up from inside two large spoked wheels, which in turn supported a cushioned bench. The piece Jackson was removing was what the rickshaw's driver pushed against in order to make the ancient Japanese taxi move forward. Marty was alternately focused on Jackson who was working on his knees in the gutter, the road where he thought the police officer might ride up at any minute, and a grimy-looking cafe where the rickshaw owners were gathered. He knew the vehicles belonged to them because all Tokyo rickshaw runners had the same kind of physical appearance. Years of pounding the streets for overweight Westerners had burnt off any trace of flab or fat from their arms and legs, while an outdoor life made their skin leathery and several tones darker than the average Tokyo native.

'You done yet?' Marty enquired.

'Just about,' said Jackson. Finally, it was clear what Jackson was planning. After removing the horizontal handlebar, then sliding it through a section of *Tread*'s body, *Tread* was effectively skewered by the handlebar. The whole operation had taken about a minute and a half. Now all he had to do was fasten it back on to the two horns that rose from the seat and wheels. Jackson was clearly pleased with himself as he looked up to smile at Marty. But Marty was no longer there.

'Stay down!' It was Marty's voice, from somewhere among the line of rickshaws. Jackson shot a glance down the road and instantly spotted the problem. It was the motorcycle cop, cruising slowly towards them, one hand on his accelerator twist grip and the other holding a big Maglite, which he was shining into every nook and alley he passed. To make matters worse, from the noise of plastic chairs scraping the pavement across the street, it was clear that the rickshaw runners were preparing to return.

Jackson calculated that the cop would reach them first. The only course of action was to roll under the rickshaw and hope the officer didn't notice the extra wide, forty-three-centimetre low-profile racing tyre with the shiny, bright red robot centre section that was secured to the front of one of them.

A harsh white torch beam probed the line of rickshaws, picking out the chrome detailing on their wheels and licking at their shiny red leather upholstery, but, thankfully, not *Tread*, who by sheer fluke remained in the shadows. Jackson was about to crawl out of his temporary hiding place when to his surprise two pairs of legs appeared in front of him and he was pulled roughly to his feet.

Jackson stood between two irate-looking young men. He estimated they were in their early twenties and, based on how angry they looked, one of them owned the modified rickshaw. Nearby a man was on his phone, talking very quickly into it and gesturing with his free hand to Jackson.

'He's calling the police!' It was Marty, appearing behind him. 'I'll handle this. When they let go of you, can you get that thing started?' He was pointing at *Tread*.

'Er ... yeah, of course!' said Jackson, surprised by

Marty's carefree attitude to a situation that, judging by the bone-crushing grip one of the men had on his forearm, could result in both of them getting seriously hurt.

Jackson watched as Marty began to speak. He may have seemed strong before, but next to these three young men – the guy on the phone had big round muscular shoulders and bare biceps as wide as Jackson's thighs – Marty was clearly outmatched. Marty had only spoken what Jackson figured equated to around two short sentences but the man on the phone looked up, terminated the call and performed a very subtle bow. Even better, the one holding Jackson released his grip and stepped aside. Marty, who throughout the very brief exchange had kept a polite smile on his face, brought his hands together at chest level, as if he was praying, and dipped gently at the hips in a respectful bow. The rickshaw owners then turned round and walked back to the cafe.

'That was amazing!' said Jackson as he retrieved his handset from his pocket and started tracing shapes on its surface. 'What did you say?'

'I know one of their fathers,' Marty replied, checking up and down the street. 'Don't worry about it. Just get us out of here. I didn't get to them quickly enough. The call to the cops still went through.'

I know one of their fathers. The phrase echoed in Jackson's head as he switched the control of *Tread*'s throttle and steering to his handset's accelerometers and digital gyro. *How lucky is that?* he thought. He was tempted to answer his own question with *Too lucky!* before he pulled himself up. He'd done this many times before, seen something sinister when it wasn't really there – cars whose occupants were staring at him because they were agents sent to kidnap him and, in his early days with MeX, the secret organization run by Devlin Lear that had changed his life forever, teachers and even fellow pupils he'd feared were paid observers. When you'd lived like he had for the past few years, touched by genuine evil, it was hardly surprising he saw intrigue in the smallest detail.

It's a tight community, he told himself. *Everyone knows everyone. Maybe that's the way things go here.* And then his thoughts were drowned out by Marty's cries.

'Go, go, go!' he shouted as he and Jackson clambered into the rickshaw's seat, wedging their cases between them.

Jackson instinctively twisted his handset just enough to enable *Tread*'s tyre to bite the tarmac without losing traction. The rickshaw lurched forward and then, as Jackson turned the phone in his hand just a few degrees, the vehicle swung to the right, forcing the officer who had just arrived on a police motorcycle to slam on his brakes and skid awkwardly, before getting his machine back under control. Jackson touched the edge of his phone. The time appeared in blue numbers on the handset's active surface. He had ten minutes to lose the cop and meet with Brooke at the Invader.

'Hold on!' he said to Marty, as his fingers closed round the phone in his right hand and his wrist twisted it backwards.

The girl was good. And that machine she was riding was unstoppable, finding a fluid route through the traffic with the persistence of water down a hillside. But Sergeant Kinshobi had something she didn't – a siren. The thing that made police work worthwhile, the essence of the job that made the excessive paperwork and the fussy rules and annoying superior officers just about bearable, the soul of every officer on the beat, was present in the sound of a siren.

Like Moses parting the sea, Kinshobi shot past line after line of cars that had pulled over at the side of the road. As he approached a corner, a dab on the brakes shifted the weight of the supercar forward, compressing the front shock absorbers and lightening the back wheels. *Textbook!* thought Kinshobi as he teased the steering wheel left into the corner, then right away from its apex. The back wheels were suddenly sliding, gliding gracefully to the right. *Perfect oversteer!* Kinshobi told himself. Using just the foot pedal now to keep the power on, the sergeant kept the wheels sliding in a geometrically perfect arc, finally flicking the wheel just past centre to get all four wheels back in line and leaving the corner behind him.

'And that, my friends, is Tokyo Drift!' he shouted, above the snarl of the engine. There was a time when a younger Kinshobi had witnessed the birth of what the youngsters he was chasing called drift racing. On the winding mountain roads or *tōge* around Tokyo they would race their lightweight, souped-up cars, sliding them smoothly round corners. The only way Kinshobi had been able to keep up with them was to learn the art of what became known as the Tokyo Drift.

Kinshobi's perfect line through the corner had put him several metres nearer to the girl on the futuristic tricycle, but in order to close the gap still further he'd need to employ another advantage – his intimate knowledge of the city. With the foresight of one of his winning sudoku strategies, in his mind Kinshobi mapped the streets ahead of the girl, then made his move – another sublime drift, to the right this time, into the city's jewellery quarter.

Brooke noticed the police car peeling off on the thirty-centimetre rear display in the middle of her Urban Jet's dash. She touched the screen and a translucent Japanese menu appeared. Three touches later, one of which executed a blaring J-pop soundtrack, and she was looking at a three-dimensional, fully rendered top-down map of Tokyo, with a chunky yellow arrow representing her position, hovering in the centre between a line of skyscrapers.

The cop who had been following her for the last forty

minutes was no fool, but neither was she. No one put that much effort into a chase and then just backed off. Brooke had been driving on the edge of her ability, in a vehicle far more manoeuvrable than the supercar that had been chasing her, yet the guy at the wheel had still managed to keep up. So why had he just given up? The answer was obvious. He hadn't. It was a ploy. Brooke fully expected the Gallardo to appear from a side street in front of her at any minute. She wasn't about to be that predictable. Easing off the throttle and slowing the Urban Jet to a sedate 40 kilometres an hour, Brooke took a left turn, followed by another left. If she kept a steady pace she wouldn't draw any attention, and by using her satnav she could double back and still make it to the Invader in time to meet Jackson.

One angry police motorcyclist millimetres from the back of his head. A bus and a lorry side by side just centimetres in front of him. Jackson was beginning to wonder if the robot-powered rickshaw was such a good idea after all.

Whatever the officer was saying, the Japanese commands blasting from the motorbike's front-mounted speaker system were deafening at this range. Jackson presumed they included something about the risk of being shot if he didn't pull over. He'd formed a protective fist round his handset with the fingers of his right hand and now he gently twisted his wrist to the left. Inside the handset three tiny slivers of silicon, so small they were barely thicker than a human hair, precisely mirrored the angle of his wrist. In turn, minute sensors registered a change in the electrical field in which each sliver was suspended, converting each adjustment into a string of numbers that were then fed to a dedicated processor occupying less space on the handset's motherboard than would a grain of rice. Finally, the subtle movement of Jackson's hand, reconstituted as a complex algorithmic string of numbers, was transmitted from the phone to the robot in front of him, via an encrypted data link, causing *Tread* to pivot ever so slightly left. The whole process had taken less than a hundred milliseconds, roughly four times faster than the blink of Jackson's eye that coincidentally happened at around the same time. The effect on the rickshaw, however, was very noticeable; its metal structure lurched to the left and the rubber of one of its seventy-centimetre-tall tyres rasped the edge of the pavement.

'Do you see any pedestrians?' shouted Jackson over the eardrum-ripping howl of the motorcycle's siren.

To his amazement, when he shot a glance over to Marty, the boy's head was down, punching the keys on his phone. He looked up and, without losing a big smile on his face, snapped his head out to the left and glanced up the pavement. 'Two!' he shouted back. 'Why?'

Marty was still leaning out of the rickshaw when Jackson jabbed his right hand towards the kerb, causing *Tread* to veer violently on to the pavement. Jackson was forced to use all his strength to keep his passenger from falling out, as the force of the spindly wheels mounting the kerb at different times bounced both boys out of their seat like two rag dolls. For a heart-stopping second, Jackson thought they might be catapulted straight through the canvas canopy above them, before they slammed back on to the rickshaw's hard seat with spine-crunching force. Not that any of this seemed to bother Marty, who, to Jackson's surprise, let out a kind of cowboy's 'Yehaa!'

Shop windows, a neon blur. The deep leathery furrows on the amazed face of a man sweeping his shop doorway flashed by. Jackson swerved *Tread* and the wireframe chariot he was pulling round a number of obstacles, with split-second reflexes honed by years of playing video games. In the adrenalin-charged moment, where any rational appraisal of his chances would have to include the likelihood of a spectacular crash, Jackson applied full throttle, locking his wrist back. *Tread*'s brushless electric motor responded by sucking as much current as it could from the robot's advanced lithium-ion polymer batteries. Within seconds, the rickshaw had passed the bus on its right and *Tread* was turning back on to the road.

To Jackson's surprise, Marty cheered with excitement again as they swerved in front of the bus and lorry that were still side by side on the one-way street and *Tread*'s straight-line acceleration threw them both back in their seat. Jackson had to hand it to Marty. When they'd first met, he'd figured him for a nerdy bedroom blogger, not the adrenalin junkie he was proving to be on this journey.

'We've left that cop sucking in bus fumes!' Marty shouted triumphantly as he stared out of the back of the rickshaw. He then turned back the way they were heading and started to motion left.

'We're not far from the Invader now. This next left will take us to the car park behind it. My friend should be waiting for us there. You should call Brooke and get her to meet us there. His van is big enough to hide us and the robots.'

So that's what he was doing on his phone, thought Jackson. *Sorting out an escape plan. Impressive.*

Jackson was steering *Tread* a sharp course left when he commanded the robot to stop abruptly, throwing him and Marty forward and almost completely out of the rickshaw. As they recovered and sat back down, they could see a shimmering cavalcade approaching from down the road, the outline of Brooke and the Urban Jet silhouetted in front of a background of sparkling white headlights and blue flashing lights. Within seconds Brooke passed them at what Jackson guessed was around 150 kilometres an hour. Despite displacing enough air as it rushed past to make the rickshaw rock, the Urban Jet's electric engine made virtually no noise at all, save for a high-pitched whirr that sounded like most people's idea of a hover car from a science-fiction movie. The same couldn't be said for the snarl from the Lamborghini as it passed just moments later, or the roar of the tight formation of five or so black superbikes that shot past like a swarm of angry hornets.

Jackson was still watching the high-speed procession of vehicles when his handset pulsed. He looked at the phone in his hand, its curved edges and glossy white surface giving it the appearance of a large wet pebble. In the middle of it was a small stop-frame animation – a cut-out of Brooke's face pulling all kinds of funny expressions. Drawn over the face, in a kind of virtual felt tip, was a beard, eye patch and head scarf, which was intended to make Brooke look like a pirate. And below her chin a hand-drawn 'X' made of two spanners.

'Animated Caller ID! I love it!' yelled Marty, a look of childlike marvel in his eye.

Jackson lightly tapped the top edge of the phone with his thumb and the call connected. Then, with the phone still in his hand, he traced a shape in the air, two concentric quarter-circles, symbolizing sound waves. Instantly the phone switched to speakerphone mode. 'I'm afraid the Invader is a no go!' It was Brooke's voice. 'I made it there, but I just couldn't shake the cop in the Lambo! Dude thinks he's Jack Bauer or something, he just won't give up!' As Brooke paused to manoeuvre or breathe or both, Jackson and Marty could hear the faint whine from the siren on the Lamborghini that was close behind her. 'Get Marty to come up with another meeting place. I've gotta concentrate on losing this speed freak.' Then the call was disconnected.

'I know exactly where we should meet,' said Marty. 'Let me see the satnav on that fancy phone of yours and I'll set us up.'

Jackson drew an 'N' for 'navigation' in the air and the phone's milky plastic surface was suddenly decorated with vivid blues, yellows and reds that formed the outlines of downtown Tokyo. He then handed the phone to Marty.

'Wow! I've never seen a screen on a phone like this before!'

'It hasn't got a screen, as such,' said Jackson. 'Turn it over.'

Marty did as instructed and was amazed to see that the map of Tokyo extended across the phone's entire surface.

'The whole surface is a nano-particle display covered in a layer of graphene, the world's thinnest conductive carbon.'

For a moment, the Japanese boy just stared in wonderment at the device in his palm before he instinctively touched the screen and started to scroll around the streets. Jackson squinted as he looked at Marty, trying to decide what it was about him that he found strange. A Japanese boy who dressed as a character from a 1980s American movie – that wasn't exactly normal. But there was something else, a feeling he got from the boy that was hard to pin down. Then he realized what it was; it was as if the young blogger was two people in one. There was the person he'd introduced himself as: a nerdy budding writer with the kind of innocent inquisitiveness he was showing right now towards the prototype phone in his hand – shaking his hand and beaming as he manipulated the graphics on its cutting-edge active surface display. But he was also the streetsmart operator who could call up a man with van and could persuade a beefcake fishmonger and a group of angry rickshaw owners to step aside with a few softly spoken words. Yet Marty's impressive street knowledge and that uncanny ability to defuse explosive situations were the reasons Brooke and Jackson had been able to stay ahead of the deadly game they were in – a game in which the Yakuza, no less, were now players.

I'm doing it again, Jackson told himself. As if seeing Brooke in a police chase wasn't enough to convince him that he needed help. Then his thoughts were gone as quickly as they'd arrived as Marty looked up from the phone.

'Tokyo Bowl! Tell Brooke to meet us there.'

CHAPTER 6

Sergeant Kinshobi pushed the white leather stick shift from sixth to third gear, causing the Lamborghini to bark ferociously. As the car's rear end slid round yet another tight corner, its elderly driver was confident that his superior driving skills and intimate knowledge of this part of the city meant he could catch the fleeing fugitive in front of him. The matrix of roads, intersections and little-known short cuts formed a grid in his head like the rows and columns of his beloved sudoku puzzles. He knew it wasn't the quantity of pre-filled squares that set the difficulty of a puzzle, but their position on the grid. In his mind, the *givens* were the dead-ends ahead of him, the one-way streets and crossways that would be snarled up with traffic and pedestrians even at this ungodly hour. He then scanned the routes either side of them, in just the same way he'd consider the sudoku squares, trying every possible combination until the solution came.

Kinshobi made the first move in his master plan – he accelerated from 130 kilometres an hour to just over 200 kilometres an hour – a process that took the 5.2-litre supercar one and a half seconds. Twenty seconds later and he was alongside the girl on the space-age trike. He could see the surprise in her bright, piercing-blue eyes. But the girl didn't wait more than a nanosecond to react – just as Kinshobi expected, she turned hard right, performing the kind of tight manoeuvre his sports car couldn't, heading off towards the tightly packed streets of the Shinbashi district. What Kinshobi guessed she didn't know was that Shinbashi was the busiest railway terminus in the world. While there were several ways into the maze of winding one-way streets and impassable railway tracks – there was only one way out.

Marty had chosen what he called a discreet route to Tokyo's famous baseball stadium, so their unconventional mode of transport didn't catch too much attention. When they'd arrived, he'd directed Jackson on to the pavement round an arm barrier that led down into an underground car park.

'They use it for coaches during the big matches,' said Marty, climbing from the rickshaw and stretching his neck and back. 'And Tokyo's skateboarders use it as a skatepark!' He picked up and waved half a broken skateboard deck before throwing it back on the floor.

'Did skaters do those?' Jackson pointed towards several thick stone columns and a long wall, all of which were covered in graffiti. As he looked more closely at the colourful spray-can art that adorned the concrete around them, he could see it was quite different from the kind of street art scrawled on many walls where he lived in Peckham. Back home it was all tags, basically signatures scrawled with paint pens and some larger-scale words, which, like the Japanese lettering in front of him, he could never decipher. But mixed in with a jumble of Japanese characters were lots of savage-looking animals, including several snakes, tigers and dragons wound around the stone pillars, and a particularly vicious-looking dog sitting on top of a cartoon tombstone that was dripping with blood.

'No. That's Yakuza!' said Marty. 'The different animals show affiliations with the different Yakuza groups in the city. The boss of a certain area has an animal or some such symbol tattooed on his body. They are copied on the walls here as a mark of respect.' Marty walked over to the image of the dog. 'In Japanese culture, the dog is the symbol of the criminal. Whoever this belonged to was proud of his criminal status.'

A tingling feeling jumped between a few of the vertebrae in Jackson's spine as he looked at the bared teeth of the dog, blood dripping from their sharp tips like something from a vampire nightmare.

'If you step back, you'll notice that all of the creatures are smaller than the dragon in the centre.'

Jackson took a few paces backwards until he could take in the whole of the main wall. From here he could see more clearly that all the graffiti creatures either side of a five-metre dragon in the middle of the wall were considerably smaller than it – and they were all facing inwards, looking at it.

'It's a Komodo dragon. They really exist, you know. An actual, living, poisonous dragon! How cool is that?'

Under normal circumstances Jackson might have shared Marty's very obvious glee at the idea of a poisonous dragon. Perhaps it was the eyes of the meticulously detailed monster, two fiery-red embers smouldering inside pitch-black sunken sockets. Or was it that smile, lined with razor-sharp teeth and tipped with a forked tongue? The kind of smile a wounded antelope sees before it's ripped apart by a drooling hyena.

'What's so special about it?' Jackson asked, unable to take his eyes off the creature.

'It's the symbol of the *Oyabun* or boss. The leader of all Yakuza,' said Marty.

That's what it was about the dragon that Jackson found so unnerving. Once he'd learned the significance of the artwork, instinct had told him that the leader of the pack of graffiti creatures had to be Yakimoto. The name echoed in his head and he almost said it out loud, before stopping himself. Marty didn't need to know everything. Besides, if Jackson mentioned the name of the man who had killed both his parents to Marty, he might not be able to stop himself laying bare every painful detail of his life's tragedy.

'So, the man who that is a tribute to has the same dragon tattooed on his body?'

'For sure,' Marty replied.

'Why here?' Jackson asked.

'I beg your pardon?' Marty replied, once again punching the keys on his handset.

'Why choose this place for the artwork? Are the Yakuza based around here or something? An underground car park in a sports stadium isn't exactly the obvious choice for a tribute to a crime boss.'

Marty looked up from his phone. 'Yakuza are mainly in Shinjuko district, but tributes like this are all over Tokyo, if you know where to look. Perhaps they're just fans of baseball.' He smiled, trying to make a joke out of the whole thing.

Jackson's handset pulsed again. It was Brooke.

'I've managed to dump the cop. According to the co-ordinates you sent me I'm about three minutes away.'

Brooke traced a series of ninety-degree turns through the only part of Tokyo she'd seen that wasn't bathed in the glow of neon. She was pushing the Urban Jet hard, leaning low into every corner and paying scant attention to red lights. She no longer had the pressure of the coolest and fastest police car she'd ever seen bearing down on her, and even if it had turned round and followed her into this tight network of narrow streets, it would never match the Urban Jet's agility. The other reason she wasn't letting up on the throttle was that she couldn't afford to waste any more time. She wanted to reach the stadium as soon as possible, sort a place to hide out and get back to finding the twins. Marty was key to that strategy. Finding him was just about the only stroke of luck they'd had since arriving and his scoop about the missing gamers their only lead.

Brooke looked at the display in front of her. The moving map showed that her route through the maze would soon deposit her alongside a cluster of railway lines that pointed the way to the Tokyo Dome.

Grandmother will turn in her grave, thought Kinshobi as he smashed clean through a section of tall wire fencing that surrounded a corner of the Shinjuku Gyoen National Garden, ragged strands of metal clawing at the exotic car's paintwork.

During *sakura* season, when the cherry-blossom trees were in bloom, he and his *obaasan*, or grandmother, would join thousands of other Tokyo dwellers for *Yozakura*, the night-time flower festival. And here he was, racing a sports car along the cobbled footpaths where he and his grandmother used to stroll.

He drifted the car a perfect quarter-circle across a gravel square until the Tokyo Metropolitan building was in the centre of his windscreen. *One minute and I'll be there*, he told himself. Moments later he could see the Shinto shrine. The bright orange paint on the *torii* gates that led to the wooden building flashed as the beam from his car's headlights caught them. Kinshobi felt a twinge of apprehension as he passed through the gateway – if he were to hit any part of the shrine, the Shinto gods would surely punish him.

Through the gates without a hitch and now a hard right just metres from the shrine's front door. Now the car was hurling Kinshobi towards a set of wide stone steps that led out of the park. Each gear change was like the detonation of a bomb. Third gear – six thousand revs. Fourth gear – seven and a half thousand revs. Fifth.

It was the final move in Kinshobi's elaborate play. He couldn't know for sure if the steps were sufficiently high to provide a launch pad that would get him over the turnstile, because he'd never tried to jump a car out of Shinjuku Gyoen before. The Lamborghini left the top step at 125 kilometres an hour. It landed on the three remaining steps and Kinshobi performed a final handbrake turn that left the battered squad car stationary in the middle of the road, facing down a narrow one-way street.

The driver's-side door was so crumpled, the sergeant had to kick it several times to open it. Outside the car, he unclipped his gun from its holster and, using the door for cover, levelled his weapon at the apex of the corner in front of him. *By the time she sees me, she'll have two choices*, he thought. *Stop or die.*

'Sergeant Kinshobi! Come in, Sergeant Kinshobi!' The voice crackled from the police radio that was fitted in the centre of the white leather console between the driver and passenger seats. Kinshobi shot a glance inside the car, not wanting to interrupt his focus on the corner ahead.

'Sergeant Kinshobi, this is Detective Inspector Yoshida of the Central Anti-Organized Crime Unit. I demand that you answer this call!'

The Anti-Organized Crime Unit was the top of the Tokyo Metropolitan Police food chain. Kinshobi knew that the officers of this elite unit outranked virtually all others – he had no choice but to answer. He crabbed sideways into the car, keeping his pistol in his right hand and fishing for the transceiver's handheld microphone with his left, while staring through the windscreen at the corner.

'This is Kinshobi!' he said.

'Sergeant, I have been informed that you are in pursuit of a suspect.'

'That is correct, sir. I am about to apprehend her.'

'Sergeant. It is imperative to my own investigation that you do no such thing!'

Kinshobi couldn't believe what he had just heard.

'Detective Yoshida, I am moments away from apprehending a brazen and dangerous thief, who has cut a reckless path across our city. Are you telling me I am to simply let her get away?'

'That is correct, Sergeant. I need her to think that you've given up. Then I want you to make sure she gets to wherever she's going. From a distance! I don't want her to know you're following her. Can you do this, Sergeant?'

Kinshobi was silent. *So how much had this Yoshida been paid to let the girl off the hook?* he wondered. *What was she? A gang member's sweetheart? A Western politician's daughter?* It sickened Kinshobi to the pit of his stomach that like many others in the Tokyo Met force, this detective was obviously in someone's pocket.

'Need I remind you, Kinshobi,' said the detective impatiently, 'if you do not follow this order, you will face disciplinary procedures.'

Disciplinary procedures meant no golden handshake and quite possibly no pension.

'OK, I'll do it!' said the sergeant reluctantly.

'Let me know when she reaches her destination,' said the voice on the radio, before disconnecting.

One minute fifty seconds. The Urban Jet's moving map predicted this next sweeping bend and then a junction at which a ninety-degree turn would put Brooke on the final stretch to the Dome. She tucked low into the corner, the machine's impressive rollover characteristics enabling her to hug the inside curve. As she powered out of the corner in order to make the green light at the intersection ahead, she didn't notice the battered squad car pull out from between two parked cars and begin to follow her.

Marty clapped as the Urban Jet glided silently down the entrance ramp to the car park.

'How was that test drive?' he said with a smile.

'I'd buy it!' said Brooke as she lifted herself out of the cockpit and jumped to the ground. 'But I'd like a new one! This model's got one too many scratches on it.'

Jackson smiled. He hadn't forgotten the decision he'd made to show Brooke he could now be depended on. 'Marty and I have been talking about what to do next,' he said, as he finished locking *Tread* into his case.

'Hopefully, your plan doesn't involve another police chase,' said Brooke, hauling *Fist* and *Punk* out of the back seat.

'My friend should be here soon. I'm working on finding you a place to stay outside Tokyo,' Marty told her. And, as he was speaking, the faint hum of an engine could be heard coming down the ramp. The hum became a drone, then a roar, as six motorcyclists entered the underground level, followed by a blacked-out Mercedes and a van.

The vehicles glided to a halt but the motorbikes

continued, and like a swarm of hornets the identical bright-yellow Suzuki sports bikes began to circle Jackson, Brooke and Marty. The riders were dressed in black too – trainers, tight black jeans and vests that did little to hide colourful tattoos that stretched from their wrists to their necks, one or two rising up their throats and continuing inside their black helmets. Jackson didn't need Marty to explain who these men were; their tattoos said it all. As they circled he saw dragons, serpents, samurai swords and daggers – the unmistakable marks of the Yakuza. He also spotted weapons. Two riders carried firearms – one a pistol and the other a snub-nose machine gun. A couple more had knives, and one a baseball bat, slung nonchalantly over his shoulder.

Jackson glanced at Brooke. They were unable to speak in the din of the circling sports bikes as the machines whined in unison, but they didn't need to – both of them were slowly moving their hands into their pockets to retrieve their phones. Brooke would use hers to wake up *Fist*, and Jackson, *Punk*. But Brooke had only touched a finger to her phone when a deafening stuttering sound erupted behind her and a volley of bullets tore a jagged line in the concrete at her feet. The machine-gun shots were followed by the rider with the bat, gliding towards them, his hand outstretched. Brooke and Jackson had no choice but to place their phones in his hand as he cruised along in front of them.

As the driver's door of the Mercedes opened and a thick-set man in a suit got out and walked towards the rear of the car, the motorcyclists stopped, turned off their engines and put the bikes on their stands. The driver opened the rear passenger door and a taller man in a much better-fitting cream-coloured suit slowly emerged. Jackson could only see the top of his head, which was completely bald, as he was helped from the car. But when he eventually stood up, there was no mistaking who it was. Yakimoto.

The Yakuza gang leader's long, jet-black hair might have all gone, but those distinctive angular features, the blade-like cheekbones that gave his face the look of a snake, were unmistakable. And Jackson had seen those round, blue spectacles before. The thick, raised scar on his right cheek was new, but Jackson was only too aware where it had come from. It had happened during Jackson's first encounter with the Yakuza leader at one of his diamond mines, when Jackson had been tracking Lear. Yakimoto had travelled to the remote mine in Canada following news that rare and priceless blue diamonds had been discovered there. In reality, it was an elaborate ruse, set up by Devlin Lear to trap Yakimoto. Lear hoped to exact revenge on him for killing Jackson's mother during a sting operation in which she'd been involved several years before. But Lear's plan had failed – in a vicious fight he had been thrown to his death and Yakimoto had escaped. But not before *Punk* had punctured the Yakuza leader's face with one of his spikes.

Jackson noticed that Yakimoto was walking with the aid of a walking stick. In fact, the formidable fighter who had fought to the death on the edge of the diamond mine had been replaced by the weaker-looking figure hobbling towards him and pausing to cough deeply into a red handkerchief. Then it hit him. Something his father had said to him about the diamonds that Yakimoto had made off with. 'They're radioactive!' Lear had cried. 'They're rotting him from the outside in!' As Jackson stared at the infamous gang leader before him, the horrible reality of what had happened suddenly became clear. In order to lure him to the mine, Lear had needed Yakimoto to think that rare blue topaz diamonds had been discovered in his own Canadian mine. To do this Lear had irradiated common white diamonds inside a nuclear reactor, a process that turned them a topaz-like blue. Then he'd planted the stones in the mine. Lear's words, spoken just before he fell to his death, hadn't really registered with Jackson at the time. But now Jackson could see that those long black locks hadn't been shaved off. They'd fallen out, along with all trace of hair anywhere on his face and head. Jackson was looking at a man who was suffering from the deadly effects of radiation poisoning.

Marty was in front of Jackson and Brooke with his

back to them. Jackson couldn't see his face, but watched as the boy bowed low when Yakimoto passed him, dipping about forty-five degrees at his waist.

Jackson observed Yakimoto, half expecting him to nod to Marty and confirm his own suspicions that the blogger was responsible for leading him and Brooke into this trap. But Yakimoto failed to acknowledge the boy and walked straight past. Once again, Jackson was left feeling guilty and confused about Marty, not to mention concerned for his safety. He understood why Marty might think that showing his respects to the gangster boss with such a deferential bow might give him a chance of survival, but Jackson knew otherwise. This stone-cold killer didn't have a merciful bone in his body.

As Yakimoto approached, Jackson wondered if he should just let his fists unload all his rage. At least he'd go down fighting. But something was stopping him. It wasn't the reluctance to act that had taken hold of him on the boat and led to all the tension between him and Brooke. And it certainly wasn't self-preservation. The way he felt now, however suicidal it might be, he would give up everything for the chance to plant just one blow on that hairless skull. It was the Kojimas. He'd given this predator their scent. It was Jackson's fault Yakimoto had gone after the twins and if there was even the smallest chance they could still be saved, assuming it wasn't already too late, he would do whatever was required.

Yakimoto reached Jackson and Brooke. Two of the riders had joined him on either flank, an automatic pistol and a snub-nose machine pistol in their hands.

Yakimoto coughed again. It was a deeply unhealthy, consumptive cough that sounded like he was raking his lungs for phlegm.

'Keeping well, I see,' said Jackson.

Yakimoto's head snapped up with a speed that caught Jackson by surprise. The man's bloodshot eyes stared into Jackson's as he wiped his mouth with the handkerchief. Then, without warning, his arm shot out, the back of his hand slapping Jackson on the cheek. The force of the slap almost knocked Jackson off his feet, but as he recovered he felt a fury bubbling up from his core. It was as if a trigger had been pulled inside him, unleashing a fizzing electric arc that jumped between his shoulders and shot down his biceps, terminating in his hands which were forced into fists.

'Cool it, sugar!' whispered Brooke. She had noticed Jackson tense up and knew exactly what his response would be to such provocation from this symbol of all his misery.

'You poisoned me!' Yakimoto spat the words at Jackson with such fury that he convulsed with another series of deep, raw coughs.

'Yeah, well, you killed my parents. I guess that makes us even!' Jackson couldn't believe the words that were coming from his own lips. Here was the ghoul that stalked his dreams, the face behind the kind of fear and paranoia he'd never known he was capable of feeling. He should have been terrified, but he just couldn't let himself cower before this monster, like so many others did.

Yakimoto smiled and held out a hand to one of the henchmen. The other man placed his machine-gun pistol in his leader's open palm. Yakimoto swooped the weapon down on Jackson's head, its steel muzzle cracking him on the forehead. Brooke screamed as Jackson fell to the floor. He didn't lose consciousness, but he came close, the power of the blow sending an instant shuddering pain through his temple. As he brought his hand up, Jackson could feel blood starting to flow from a gash on his forehead.

Yakimoto, more animated now than had seemed possible when he'd stepped out of the car, sprang forward and put his face close to Jackson's.

'I should kill you and your girlfriend right now,' he hissed. 'But that would deny me the pleasure of watching you suffer, like your friends.'

That was it, thought Jackson. The first confirmation they'd had that Yakimoto was behind the twins' disappearance. But did it mean they were alive or dead?

The familiar rage tightened Jackson's arm and chest muscles. 'If you've hurt the Kojimas . . . I'll –'

Another swipe from Yakimoto's coiled-back gun

connected with Jackson's head. 'Who are you to threaten me?' barked Yakimoto, grabbing Jackson's collar and pulling his dazed face to within millimetres of his own.

'Sorry, but I have to take issue with you about the *girlfriend* comment!' It was Brooke. 'Mine and Jackson's relationship is strictly platonic. Not that Jackson is unattractive, of course . . . and his extraordinary ability with numbers is quite disarming. But when it comes to romance, I prefer the rock-star look – you know, leather jacket, stubble!' If Brooke's plan had been to divert Yakimoto's attention from Jackson, it worked. He unclenched Jackson's collar and stood up, walking slowly towards her with a smirk on his face.

'The brilliant Brooke English,' he said. 'Since our paths crossed, I've done a little research into the robotics development you and your father have been doing. As you know, we Japanese are no strangers to the art of robot design, but the work you're doing is really quite exceptional.' He brought a hand up to her face and stroked it with the back of his fingers. 'I wonder, if I were to let you go . . . would you consider working for me? I could think of some interesting uses for the kind of toys you dream up.'

'Kind offer,' said Brooke, pulling her face away with a jerk. 'But I'm guessing that working for a murderous filthbag might take the edge off my job satisfaction.'

'So be it!' said Yakimoto, the smirk still on his face. He

then snapped several words in Japanese to his men, who in turn picked Jackson up from the floor and dragged him and Brooke towards the Mercedes. Jackson was thrown on to the back seat and immediately joined by the tattooed motorcyclist with the baseball bat, then Brooke.

'Are you OK?' asked Brooke, trying to look round the henchman between them.

'You be quiet!' snarled the man. As he spoke, he flicked a wrist and the blade of a knife sprang from his hand.

Jackson nodded to Brooke, to show her that apart from blood congealing on his forehead he wasn't too badly hurt.

He watched with bleary eyes through the tinted windows as Marty pointed out the robots and their cases, which the men proceeded to load into the van. Jackson didn't blame him at all for doing as he was told by Yaki-moto's bruisers; he just hoped Marty wasn't repaid for his cooperation with a bullet.

Jackson glanced back at Brooke. She was being quiet, just as instructed, but not, he thought, in the way the man between the two of them had meant. She was completely still, her eyes were closed and the palms of her hands were together, almost as if she was praying. If Jackson wasn't mistaken, it looked as if Brooke was meditating. Jackson had seen her like this before – during the development of her phone's mind-control interface. He watched her closely and could just make out the edge of her Bluetooth earpiece, behind her ear. She must have slipped it in when no one was looking. Jackson had always thought that Brooke's latest innovation was like some superhero technology from a comic book. By simply composing herself, or chillaxin', as she put it, Brooke could alter the rate of her alpha and theta brain waves. In turn, this delicate change in the electrical activity inside her head was picked up by a tiny electrode on the modified earpiece, which then triggered an action in her handset.

Jackson watched as Yakimoto walked to the Mercedes. The driver helped him into the passenger seat before seating himself and starting the engine.

As the motorcycle outriders led the other vehicles towards the exit ramp, Jackson noticed that the enforcer beside him had started to fidget. His hand went to the pocket on the left-hand side of his suit, as if he was feeling an intense itch. He wasn't too distracted by it, because he was still nodding dutifully to Yakimoto who was talking to him and the driver, but Jackson knew the man was reacting to some kind of subtle sensation. And he knew what it was. It was one of the handsets he had confiscated, heating up in response to Brooke's mind-control command.

Jackson looked across at Brooke. She was maintaining her cool, watching the man through one open eye, but remaining almost trancelike.

For Brooke it was 'Mission Accomplished'. She now knew exactly where her phones were located.

As the convoy prepared to leave the car park, Brooke made her move, dipping her hand into the enforcer's pocket and managing to retrieve one of the phones as he leaned towards her.

Jackson watched through the rear windshield behind him as *Fist* erupted through the roof of the van. In response to Brooke's unseen manipulation of the phone, her robot's four powerful memory-metal arms and ballistic-plastic fingers tore through the vehicle's metal bodywork as if it were paper. Within seconds, the robot was running on its four hands like a mechanical monkey and leaping through the air in the direction of the Mercedes. Jackson felt an instant surge of hope as at the same time he braced himself for the impact *Fist* would bring to the Mercedes. But to his amazement, only a metre from the car, *Fist* faltered. One of his arms seemed to fold inwards, causing him to stumble on to his back and skid awkwardly along the tarmac before smashing into a line of scooters. Jackson turned to Brooke in order to make sense of what was happening and was stunned by what he saw. Her face was ashen and she was staring with wide eyes at her thigh. Jackson followed her gaze and saw Yakimoto's hand gripping the handle of the enforcer's flick knife, the blade of which he had just stuck in Brooke's thigh.

'I'm afraid we now have a problem,' Yakimoto said, taking his hand away from the knife handle and wiping it with his red handkerchief. 'You see, the men that work for me are lost souls. Take Hiro here.' He motioned to the man sitting between Brooke and Jackson. 'He is *gurentai*, what you call hoodlum. Is it fair to say, Mr Hiro, that you would be in prison, or possibly even dead from some shoot-out with the police, if it wasn't for my guiding influence?'

Hiro bowed and grunted a monosyllabic reply, which Jackson took to mean 'Yes'.

'Men like Mr Hiro here must have respect for the man who leads them. Without respect, who knows what the thousands of *gurentai* under my command might get up to. Before you know it, the hoodlums would be ransacking Tokyo – the lunatics taking over the asylum!' Yakimoto laughed and Mr Hiro reciprocated with a couple of deep grunts. 'My point, Miss English, is that for the sake of discipline, I can't let your attempt at embarrassing me go unpunished. The gamer, I can make use of.' He stabbed a finger in Jackson's direction. 'But you and your American insolence, I can do without! Mr Hiro, make sure you dump her body somewhere it won't be found.'

CHAPTER 7

As Yakimoto's convoy rolled towards the exit ramp, leaving Brooke and Mr Hiro behind, Jackson saw every detail as if time had been slowed down.

First, there was Brooke's expression. Not one of horror as Jackson might have expected but a warm smile, as if she cared more about how Jackson might be feeling than she did about her own mortal danger.

Then there were the motorbikes. One second they were two abreast, leading the car with Jackson and Yakimoto towards the exit – the next they were swatted aside, slammed against the concrete walls like little black flies by a long white limousine, power-sliding sideways.

The wheels on the Mercedes squealed as it stopped abruptly and, with Yakimoto shrieking at the driver, immediately started to reverse.

Crunch!

In his panic to do something, the driver had forgotten all about the van behind. And now, as he fumbled for the correct gear, the limousine flashed into view again, swiping across the front of the Mercedes – this time with so much force it caused the car to spin a full 360 degrees and collide into a concrete pillar.

Yakimoto blurted something in Japanese and Jackson saw his driver reach inside the glove compartment to bring out another stubby-looking machine pistol. He then opened his door, climbed out and started firing at the limousine, which was circling the car park at speed.

Jackson glanced through the shattered glass around him in an attempt to spot Brooke. She hadn't moved from where he'd seen her last, but, to his amazement, Mr Hiro, the man tasked with killing her, was lying at her feet, reeling around the floor in pain. Jackson was staring at the bizarre scene, trying to work out how a badly injured Brooke could have felled the formidable gangster, when a small black figure streaked past the glass. Moments later the body of the driver fell past Jackson's window. Jackson looked down at him and could clearly see he was out cold.

Jackson's attention returned to the car when he heard the front passenger door open. To his relief, Yakimoto had gone. Jackson was about to open his own door when he was startled by the sound of gunfire behind him. Two Yakuza men had left the van – one stood in a defensive martial arts stance, while the other had a machine gun in his hands and was letting off short fiery spurts in opposite directions, evidently looking for a target.

Then, right before Jackson's bleary eyes, something

small and metallic glinted as it shot across the car park and struck the gunman. He immediately dropped his weapon, stood bolt upright and, clutching his shoulder, fell to the ground, screaming in pain. Next a small figure appeared on top of the van. Jackson blinked several times, because he could swear that the figure was that of a miniature ninja, looking down on the remaining enforcer.

Jackson was familiar with ninjas – he had dressed himself as one for the profile picture on his blog, *math-fu.com*, and alongside zombies they were perhaps his favourite mythical fighting figures.

It was hard to see through the Mercedes' shattered back windscreen, but the little black ninja's arms were moving in quick, tight circles. *Nunchucks*, thought Jackson. Whirling round the mysterious figure's body were two wooden batons connected by a chain. A second later and the swinging sticks swept down, forming a solid circle like the propellers on the front of a plane, hitting the head of the Yakuza henchman and knocking him clean off his feet. Then, as quickly as the little ninja had appeared, he was gone.

Jackson was just considering if it was safe to get out of the car when his door was opened for him.

'Are you OK, Jackson-*san*?' said a voice. It was the little ninja, who was standing in the open doorway.

'Er, yeah. I'm fine, I guess,' said Jackson as he climbed from the car. 'But my friend . . .' He didn't need to finish his sentence. He could see Brooke across the car park. She was being helped up by two other identical miniature ninjas, one of whom had taken the black scarf off its head and was wrapping it tightly round Brooke's injured leg.

As Jackson and his ninja saviour walked towards Brooke he could see that the long, shiny black hair and delicate facial features of the person binding her leg belonged to a young girl.

'*Konnichiwa*,' said the third ninja, bowing to Jackson as he reached Brooke.

'Er, hi!' replied Jackson. 'And thanks for . . . you know . . . saving our lives and everything. But who are you?'

'Can't you see the family resemblance?' said Brooke, breathless with the pain from her leg. 'It's the Kojima sisters!'

Jackson stood open-mouthed, looking at the three girls, when he heard the sound of the van revving up behind them.

As the van shot forward, it was clear that the Yakuza henchman driving still had a tiny shiny flying weapon embedded in his shoulder. Everyone dived out of the vehicle's way and, as it passed, the rear doors swung open and a second Yakuza figure pushed something out before the black van sped up the exit ramp.

As Jackson walked over to investigate it, he could hear moaning. It was Marty, curled up in a ball.

CHAPTER 8

'Let me get this straight,' said Jackson. 'Three nine-year-olds took out six armed Yakuza enforcers?'

'And the driver,' added one of the identical Kojima triplets as she flicked her wrist and released a throwing star which flew across the room to embed itself in the centre circle of a small, round wooden target.

The Kojima girls had brought Jackson, Brooke and Marty to their dojo. At first, the girls had been suspicious of Marty and had wanted to leave him at the Bowl. But Marty had pleaded his innocence, explaining a number of different ways in which Yakimoto could have tracked him, Brooke and Jackson – including the cop who'd been chasing Brooke. He said he'd been violently bundled into the van and presented evidence of his struggle in the shape of a large lump and bruise on his forehead. But it was when Brooke vouched for him – explaining that he had information about the disappearance of other top gamers that might help in the search for their brother and sister – that the girls had conceded. Jackson was also willing to give Marty the benefit of the doubt. It was true that he'd shown an uncanny ability to get them out of trouble, but for every reason Jackson came up with to doubt the boy's integrity, there were far more that confirmed him as a useful and loyal ally.

The dojo, which was about the size of a small village hall, was where the girls practised their karate and other martial arts fighting skills. It was owned by their father and run by their own personal martial arts coach. According to the sisters' chauffeur, Mr Sato, who had driven the limousine during the triplets' astonishing intervention in the car park, the Yakuza would use all of their considerable resources to hunt everyone down. They would be safe at the dojo for a couple of nights while they worked out what to do next.

'It's a funny thing,' said one of the girls. 'We would never have found you if Yakimoto himself hadn't decided to go to the Dome.'

'As we were explaining on the way over here,' said her sister, 'our chauffeur, Sato-san, learned of your arrival in Tokyo in the same way Yakimoto did – from his contacts at the docks. We were planning to visit you at your hotel, when your capsules were raided.'

'We lost track of you then.' It was one of the other girls. 'Lucky for you, Sato-san guessed your robots would be taken to the Keishicho headquarters in Kasumigaseki district. We decided to go along for the ride, only to discover that you'd just broken them out.'

'We drove around the district for a while, but there was no trace of you anywhere,' said the first sister. 'We were actually heading back home when one of Sato's informants called to say he'd spotted Yakimoto's convoy entering the Tokyo Dome. We knew he wouldn't go anywhere with all those soldiers unless he was up to something.'

'How do you think Yakimoto knew where we were?' asked Marty.

'Probably one of the police officers who was chasing you. Yakimoto is a very rich and powerful man and his connections in the city run deep. We have found it safest to assume that where Yakimoto is concerned Yakuza and police are one and the same.'

Brooke limped towards the target in which the throwing star was embedded. 'Mind if I have a go?' she asked, motioning to it.

'Be my guest,' said one of the girls. Brooke carefully wriggled the shiny metal star out of the wood target and took several paces backwards. 'Next time I meet Yakimoto, remind me to have one of these in my back pocket.' She flicked her wrist and the flying star arced towards the target, sticking in the bottom corner.

'Well, it's an improvement on the wall!' said Jackson.

'I'd love to do a virtual wind-tunnel simulation on one of these bad boys,' said Brooke as she pulled the small four-pronged weapon from the target and placed it in the palm of her hand. 'Do you think it's stabilized purely by the gyroscopic nature of its flight characteristics or could Bernoulli's Principle be providing lift on the surface of these spikes?'

The Kojima sister stared dumbfounded at Brooke.

'Whatever,' said Brooke. 'I want another go!'

The Kojima sister giggled. 'Our karate *sensei* – our teacher – has a saying: *time is a circle.* Instead of trying to do more things faster, Brooke, we try to do less, slower.'

'What my sister is saying,' said one of the other sisters as she brought out a tray with a teapot and cups on it from the tiny cupboard-sized kitchen, 'is that it's time for tea!' She placed the tray on the low table in the middle of the main dojo space, and the third sister followed with a plate of little animal-shaped biscuits.

Jackson and Marty had devoured half of the biscuits before they even realized the girls were looking at them.

'Sato-san will be back shortly. You might want to leave some room for the food he's bringing,' said one of the girls, smiling and pouring the tea.

'Of course. Sorry!' said Jackson, blowing fragments of biscuit on to the floor as he spoke.

'What about Yakimoto?' asked Brooke, sitting down next to him. 'Any ideas where he might have gone?'

'Sato-san's limousine was no match for the sports bike Yakimoto made off on,' said another of the young girls. 'And, besides, he was too worried about us to chase him. Best guess is that he's in Roppongi now. That's where he operates from. He just about runs the whole district.'

'I love that,' said Brooke. 'Your driver was worried about what exactly? That you three would attack Yaki-moto's poor gang-busters some more?'

Laughter rippled round the table.

'May I see that ninja star thingy?' asked Jackson.

Brooke handed him the shiny star-shaped piece of metal she'd been fondling.

'In Japanese it's called *shuriken*,' said one of the girls. 'In English it means "sword hidden in the hand".'

'You could have killed them with those, right?' said Brooke.

'*Hai*,' replied the three girls in unison, nodding at precisely the same moment.

'So why didn't you?' added Jackson, locking one of the young girls into a stern, serious stare.

'There is an old Samurai saying,' said the girl. 'Easy to condemn. Harder to pity.'

'They didn't intend showing me too much mercy,' said Brooke, pointing to the thigh that Yakimoto had stabbed and shifting it gingerly. The leg was obviously still painful, but she was showing no signs of the agony that had contorted her face and body when the adrenalin of the car-park rescue had worn off. On their way to the dojo, Mr Sato had taken them to a pharmacy. It was shut when they'd arrived, but he'd woken up the owner, and with the aid of a thick wad of yen notes persuaded the man to treat Brooke's wound. It was a deep cut that required twelve expertly administered stitches, but the pharmacist seemed to think Brooke would be fine without visiting a hospital.

'I don't know if I could have shown the mercy you did to the men behind kidnapping your brother and sister!' said Jackson.

'Did you get anything out of the ones who didn't run away?' asked Marty.

'Lie,' replied one of the sisters, shaking her head.

'I wanted to,' said the middle girl. '*Shuriken* can be very persuasive if used on a pressure point.'

'But Sato-san wouldn't let us. He was keen to get us all out of there, in case more Yakuza or police arrived.'

'So, what do you know of the whereabouts of the twins?' asked Marty. His theory had been the hot topic of discussion in the car on the way from the pharmacy.

'Not much more than you. Mr Tucker, our father's head of security, made similar discoveries.' The girl paused for a moment. 'Before he went missing himself.'

As an uneasy silence fell on the group, the familiar pang of guilt hit Jackson like a sucker punch to the stomach. Several weeks ago, when Jackson and Brooke had been in Boston, this man, who was part of the Kojima security team, had investigated Yakimoto at Jackson's request. Now he was dead. But what was Jackson to do? He couldn't bring the man back. But he could concentrate on finding the twins.

'So we agree that Marty's theory that the disappearing gamers are connected in some way is our best lead?' asked Brooke.

'There's also something Yakimoto said, when he ordered you out of his car,' said Jackson, addressing Brooke. 'Something about being able to use me, because I was a gamer.'

'But what use could Yakimoto have for a load of computer gamers?' asked Marty.

'Find the answer to that question,' said one of the triplets, 'and you find our brother and sister.'

Mr Sato arrived, carrying several bags, and moments later all seven of them were sitting in a circle on the dojo floor, tucking in. Usually, Jackson would baulk at the idea of eating raw fish – but he'd rarely been this hungry. When they'd finished eating, Mr Sato handed everyone brand-new bedsheets he'd managed to purchase from the supermarket and insisted that they all go to sleep. Jackson and Marty unrolled two martial arts practice mats the girls had given them and rolled them out on the store-cupboard floor, while the girls bedded down in the main space of the dojo. Mr Sato insisted on sitting outside in his car, keeping watch.

Jackson was close to total exhaustion, but while Marty

soon slipped into a deep sleep, signified by deep rhythmic snorts, he was unable to clear this evening's events out of his mind – in particular, Yakimoto's admission that he could use Jackson's gaming skills.

After staring at a shelf of moonlit cleaning products for a quarter of an hour, Jackson rose slowly from his mat and crept into the dojo. The girls were sound asleep as he quietly crept into the tiny kitchen and booted up his tablet computer. Jackson wasn't sure what he was looking for and had just entered 'Yakimoto' into his search engine when he felt the presence of someone nearby. He peeked over the top of the tablet so its glow didn't impede his vision in the dark dojo and almost yelped when he saw a small figure standing in front of him.

'Sorry, I didn't mean to scare you,' said one of the triplets.

'Not a problem,' said Jackson, slightly embarrassed. 'Sneaking up on people – I guess it comes with the ninja territory.'

'May I ask what you are looking at?'

Jackson turned his screen round and showed the girl the page of search results.

She smiled. 'I can see why my brother and sister like you so much. You are tenacious, like a Kojima. May I?' She motioned towards the device in his hand.

'Be my guest,' said Jackson, handing her the tablet as she sat down beside him.

The girl's dainty little fingers danced around the virtual keyboard and after a few seconds a server login screen appeared.

'My father keeps all his files online,' she said as she speedily entered a Japanese username and password and clicked through several layers of folders, eventually resting her finger over two folders labelled in Japanese.

'What do they say?' asked Jackson.

'This one says *Interijensu*. It means "intelligence". My father's head of security, Mr Tucker, compiled all the information from his first investigation into Yakimoto's Yakuza in this folder.'

'And this one?' asked Jackson, referring to the second folder.

'*Chiisai ryuu*,' said the girl. 'It means "little dragons". That's what Tucker called the five of us. This holds the information he uncovered after my brother and sister went missing.'

She opened the 'Little Dragons' folder and then stood up, returning the tablet to Jackson. 'Tucker called Japan his home, but he was an American. Born in New York, I think. His notes are mostly in English. I hope you find them of interest. I am afraid I am very tired, but you can wake me if you like for help with any Japanese you run into.' She then bowed and walked back to her makeshift bed on the other side of the dojo, before slipping inside her sheet.

Jackson was dog-tired too, but the thought of what

the files might contain had an effect on him like drinking strong espresso coffee.

The 'Little Dragons' folder was mainly made up of Internet news stories. Jackson instantly recognized some of the same pictures Marty had shown him on his netbook when they'd first met.

Kenji Takahashi, the Cyber League Cup winner, whose parents had told Marty he'd just vanished in the night. And the girl called 'Baby Face' for whom her friends launched an online banner campaign, asking for information about her disappearance. And there were the names of other missing children that Mr Tucker had copied from blogs and forums, adding his own notations in English. Jackson could make out about ten names in the Japanese text. What he presumed was the description of each missing person's case, was followed by a few of Tucker's own words in English. He had added phrases like 'Has run away before' and 'Happy kid' in an obvious attempt to try and decide which of the missing children were potentially connected to the missing Kojimas. He had also drawn lines on a map of Japan in an endeavour to find some kind of pattern between the cases. Jackson looked at the JPEG of the map and the multicoloured lines added by Tucker in some kind of paint program. It was impossible to say without taking the time to do a proper analysis, but the multicoloured criss-crossing lines appeared to dissect the mainland at random.

The final file in the folder was a PDF of an English-language newspaper interview with none other than Detective Yoshida. The PDF was text only, unlike the other article Jackson had used to identify Yoshida outside the bakery, when he'd watched the man removing the robots from the Capsule Inn. This interview related to Yoshida's investigation into what he said he suspected were connected cases of kidnapping. Jackson recalled that Marty had also mentioned this article. From what Jackson could remember, Marty had said that while most police interviewed believed that all the missing kids were just runaways, one detective considered the Kojimas' disappearance as a kidnapping. But Jackson had never thought Marty had meant Yoshida. After all, in the other article, next to a picture of him, Detective Yoshida was quoted as saying that the twins were behind their own disappearance. And yet here he was advocating a completely different theory. Jackson had caught him in the lie and it was evidence of the cheating, dirty cop he was.

Jackson closed the 'Little Dragons' folder and turned his attention to the one labelled *Interijensu* or 'Intelligence', which according to the Kojima sister contained the research Tucker had done for the twins.

He scrolled down the list of cached websites and text files, choosing to start with several JPEGs that turned out to be photographs of Yakimoto. The pictures of the man getting in and out of cars and at various city functions were all taken before his run-in with Jackson and Lear, because he still had his distinctive long jet-black hair. Jackson clicked through more online newspaper stories. Most were in English, with one or two in Japanese, but the message was clear: the Yakuza ruled certain areas of Tokyo with an iron fist. The articles were decorated with pictures of gang members and one or two of their victims lying in pools of blood on the street. One magazine news feature, written in English, was about the arrest of two Tokyo police officers under suspicion of colluding with the Yakuza. Next Jackson perused a selection of pages detailing various companies, which Jackson could only assume were in some way connected to Yakimoto and his Yakuza. Jackson didn't relish the thought of plodding through several years' worth of company accounts and 'import/export manifests', whatever they were, and was relieved to find a document that appeared to summarize much of what he'd skimmed over.

Yakimoto Investigation Notes
Yakuza influence in Japan is strongest in the cities of Kobe, Hiroshima, Osaka, Kyoto and Tokyo, but extends into other Asian countries and they have strong links with organized crime in the United States.

In Japan, Yakimoto is widely acknowledged as *Oyabun* or leader of Japan's largest Yakuza crime family, the Yamaguchi-gumi. Many suspect he may be the *Kumi-cho* or supreme boss of all Yakuza in Japan. He has about three thousand men working under him in Tokyo alone. Many of his inner circle of enforcers were recruited from the city's *bōsōzoku*.

Jackson switched to an Internet browser and entered the phrase *bōsōzoku* into the search window. A reference to a Wiki page popped up:

> *Bōsōzoku* (暴走族) or 'Violent Running Tribe' is Japan's version of America's Hell's Angels and comprises several gangs of motorcycle enthusiasts famed for their love of speed and well-reported clashes with police.

There were several pictures of young men on motorbikes very similar to the ones who had arrived at the Dome with Yakimoto. The scowling riders looked mean in the pictures, but having witnessed the triplets deal with several of them earlier in the evening made them seem less scary.

Jackson flipped windows, back to Tucker's document folder.

In recent years, Tokyo has become Yakimoto's main theatre of operations – areas of the city he controls include Shibuya and the notoriously dangerous districts of Azabujūban and Roppongi. My research suggests Roppongi is where Yakimoto lives and works (see section called: Roppongi stake-out).

Jackson scrolled down about ten pages and located the section headed 'Roppongi stake-out' before shooting back up to Tucker's summary.

Illegitimate dealings: Yakimoto's branch of the Yakuza still take a regular income from the 'traditional' organized crime activities of protection rackets (extorting money from small businesses under the implied threat of violence), underground gambling networks, the distribution of illegal drugs and people trafficking.

People trafficking. The phrase stuck in Jackson's head. He remembered it from TV news and newspaper accounts a few years ago in England, when a shipping container filled with girls from Eastern Europe was discovered in Dover. The girls were being brought into Britain against their will. They hadn't eaten or drunk anything for a week. He'd been horrified by the idea that criminals thought nothing of packing human beings like sardines into a big can.

He carried on reading.

Legitimate business: Yakimoto uses a number of legal business concerns to hide some of the millions of dollars brought in by illegal means. He is a fan of golf and owns several courses in Japan. He can also be linked to several building and construction interests projects. He is also rumoured to have connections with several timber and logging interests, including an industrial engineering and electronics company operating out of Tokyo's Akihabara that produces hardware for the logging industry – although I have been unable to confirm this.

While it might have been an interesting insight into the dealings of an international criminal organization, there was little in Tucker's research so far that provided any clues as to the whereabouts of the twins. But the following mention of diamonds did pique his interest.

Yakimoto is known to have a keen personal interest in diamonds and over the years has acquired many rare and valuable stones. Eighteen months ago one of his holding companies acquired a majority stake in the Duovik Diamond Corp, which operates diamond mines in Sierra Leone, South Africa and Canada.

Jackson was instantly back on the edge of the Canadian diamond mine, seeing the fear burning in Lear's eyes as he slipped into the milky abyss.

This research, which indirectly had been commissioned by Jackson, was where it had all started, the disappearance of the twins being its heavy price. Jackson forced the thoughts aside and carried on reading. He scrolled through several maps of Japan and Tokyo, pausing to look at an aerial map section labelled 'Roppongi'.

About twenty locations were marked with four kinds of asterisks, which were explained on the next page down.

*   Yakimoto sightings
**   Known Yakuza hangouts
***   Yakuza underground casinos
****   Locations protected by Yakuza

Next there was a page of rough notes. Each sentence or two was preceded by a time stamp and described five days that Mr Tucker had spent observing life on the streets of Roppongi. Jackson skim-read the transcript, which mainly consisted of mundane observations as Mr Tucker watched various tattooed men going in and out of buildings. Some notes described in detail what groups of suspected enforcers ate and the tea shops and cafes they frequented. The only entry that registered on Jackson's radar was a reference to a Yakuza-run 'underground casino'. He'd seen the phrase a few times in Tucker's documents. Images of a neon gambling wonderland under the Tokyo streets sparkled in Jackson's mind, something as big and colourful as the towering casino hotels of the Las Vegas strip but inside a gargantuan subterranean cave. As he read on, however, he realized that the places Mr Tucker was describing couldn't be any less like Vegas. He had observed the goings-on in various gambling venues over several nights, which included amusement arcades and a coffee bar.

Roppongi stake-out

Monday (01.40). Jazzy pachinko arcade, Roppongi. As pachinko slot machines only pay out tokens for prizes, Yakuza run a general store outside where they secretly exchange prizes for cash.

Tues (22.55). Two Tokyo Met Police detectives drinking tea in Bar Matsuba with three Yakuza.

Thurs (02.55). Bar Matsuba. Think I saw Yakimoto. Hard to be certain through blacked-out windows. Mercedes flanked by motorcyclists arrived outside coffee bar. Man ushered in under umbrellas. Didn't get a clear look.

Fri (00.51). Heaviest presence of Yakuza yet. Ozu Arcade. The arcade has usual slot machines and Pachinko, but I saw a large area in the back with about fifteen tables packed with Yakuza playing Oicho-Kabu.

Jackson looked up from his tablet. One of the girls was snoring loudly. He'd been so engrossed in the material on the screen he hadn't noticed the noise before, but now he had he was reminded of how much he too needed to sleep. *Just ten minutes more*, he told himself, and then his head was back in Tucker's notes.

Oicho-Kabu? What is that? Jackson switched to his browser again and entered the two Japanese words. A Wiki site provided the answer again.

> Oicho-Kabu: Gambling card game known as Ninja Baccarat. Like Baccarat, the last digit of any total over 10 makes your hand. For example 15 = 5 and 20 = 0. The goal is for the last digit of the total to be as close to 9 as possible.

Jackson scanned through several paragraphs under the title 'Be a Ninja at Ninja Baccarat', which basically amounted to the rules of the game in more detail. Another sentence caught his attention. 'Like Blackjack, Oicho-Kabu is a game of chance and strategy.' Jackson had played Blackjack with his stepdad. It was one of what they called their 'Christmas games', which alongside thousand-piece jigsaws and endless games of Monopoly Mr Farley considered more 'constructive' than vegging out in front of the TV. Jackson always won their Black-jack sessions, accruing large stocks of pretend Monopoly money. His stepdad didn't know it, but several years ago Jackson had devised a card-counting system for Blackjack, which dramatically increased his chances of winning.

Jackson cast his eyes over the history of the Japanese card game and was about to move on when a sentence caught his attention:

> The word 'Yakuza' comes from this game. The worst hand a player can have is 'ya-ku-sa' (8, 9, 3). 8 + 9 + 3 = 20 which in the rules of Oicho-Kabu means 0.

Jackson's exhaustion was making the words on his screen oscillate and quiver as his tired eyes tried to focus. He scrolled quickly through the remaining files that covered more of Yakimoto's business dealings, but there was nothing in them to rouse him from his sleepy state. Finally, he turned the tablet off and made his way quietly into the store cupboard.

As he drifted into a deep sleep, three numbers formed in Jackson's head: *8, 9, 3. Yakuza. The worst hand you could be dealt.*

CHAPTER 9

When Jackson was shaken awake by Marty, the police officers had already entered the dojo.

Holding his finger to his lips, Marty motioned to the narrow slit of glass about four metres up the cupboard wall that constituted the small room's only window. Before Jackson could offer his conclusion that there was no way they could fit through it, Marty was leaning against the wall and cupping his hands for a foothold.

'One second!' whispered Jackson as he turned to the door.

The door to the cupboard was already slightly ajar and, as he peered through the gap, Jackson could see Brooke and the twins in handcuffs being led out of the dojo by uniformed officers.

'Do you think it's Yoshida?' he mouthed to Marty.

'Shut up and get up there!' Marty insisted. Jackson looked once more into the dojo and had to conclude there was nothing he could do for the girls. 'Damn it!' he spluttered under his breath, coiling his right arm up as if to punch the wall, in an uncharacteristic blind fit of anger.

'Jackson! Get a grip!' Marty was talking quietly but he snapped the words at Jackson. 'We need to leave, *now*!' Jackson reluctantly bent down to retrieve his tablet computer from under his pillow and slipped it inside his T-shirt. He then placed his foot in Marty's hands.

Within seconds, Jackson landed on his side with a slap in a courtyard. He wasn't sure which was the most painful – the metal latch on the narrow window frame that had almost kneecapped him on the way out or the courtyard's hard cobblestones. Moments later and Marty was beside him, picking them both off the floor and hurrying towards an alley that led to a busy street.

Jackson guessed it was around six in the morning because the sun had risen, but the market stallholders in the street were still setting up. 'I can't believe Brooke is in the hands of the police. If it's Detective Yoshida, he'll just hand her over to Yakimoto. She's as good as dead.' As he spoke, Jackson pulled away from Marty and started to walk through a greengrocer's that led out on to the same road as the dojo.

'Jackson!' Marty said forcefully, trying to keep up as Jackson charged towards the other side of the shop. 'If the police get hold of you, how are you going to help the twins?'

'I can't just let her be taken, not again!' he insisted.

Jackson thought with a shudder of the time he and Brooke had discovered the true criminal intentions behind MeX, the organization that had recruited them as robot operators. In order to silence them both, Brooke had been kidnapped from her Californian home. Thanks to a combination of Jackson's remote driving skills, honed on driving simulator games, and Brooke's own highly sophisticated self-driving Hummer, she'd been saved. But Jackson had sworn never to let it happen again and yet here he was, powerless to prevent Brooke being driven away.

Shrugging Marty off and leaning out of the shop's entrance, Jackson saw Brooke and the triplets gliding past in the back seat of a police car. He also saw a man on the front seat, his back turned to Jackson. He couldn't see his face but he instantly recognized that silvery-grey mackintosh. It was the one he'd seen Yoshida wearing outside the hotel.

Jackson used to spend a lot of afternoons like this. Stealing away to sit in a cafe window and watch the passers-by. He called it 'people crunching', making random calculations inspired by whomever and whatever he saw happening in front of him. There was something in the process of breaking down the traffic light sequence to a few discernible digits, or dreaming up an equation to predict the number of red cars he would see in an hour, that took him away from whatever was haunting him.

Jackson had done a lot of people crunching when his mother died. And when the attention he used to get from Tyler Hughes and other bullies became too much to bear, he would sneak out of school and take up position in one of the greasy spoons on Peckham High Street. Usually, he wouldn't leave until it shut.

The time at the top of his tablet screen read 18.42, but the cafe Marty had brought him to at lunchtime showed no signs of shutting. Marty had left Jackson in the cafe several hours ago. He'd gone to 'follow up some leads' and find them somewhere to stay, not trusting that his own house was safe from the Yakuza or Yoshida and his men. Jackson also wondered if Marty had grown tired of doing all the talking. He'd told Jackson to call him the instant one of the girls tried to make contact and Jackson had promised he wouldn't move from this spot. But the truth was he didn't want to. In a cafe window was exactly where he wanted to be, crunching the population of Tokyo.

A bus with the number 181 printed above the driver's window slowed to a stop on the opposite side of the road. Jackson found a space among the clusters of messy numbers he had already scrawled on the virtual paper of his tablet's drawing program. He added '181' using the nail of his index finger and then, scribbling with lightning speed, decorated the space with a pyramid of calculations.

181
1 x 8 + 1 = 9
12 x 8 + 2 = 98
123 x 8 + 3 = 987
1234 x 8 + 4 = 9876
12345 x 8 + 5 = 98765
123456 x 8 + 6 = 987654
1234567 x 8 + 7 = 9876543
12345678 x 8 + 8 = 98765432
123456789 x 8 + 9 = 987654321

But whereas back home the numbers provided the distraction he needed, for some reason, here in Tokyo a whole afternoon's crunching had failed to rid his mind of the horrible images that crowded it. The surprise and pain in Brooke's eyes when Yakimoto buried the knife in her thigh. The casual way he had ordered his man to kill her. The softness in her smile as Jackson was driven away. And the one detail he kept seeing – the man in the mac.

A taxi cab came to a rest outside the window. It was one of several cars waiting in line for the traffic lights to change. Glowing on its roof was an illuminated plastic sign featuring a picture of a man dressed as a genie zooming along on an oversized laptop, which had clearly taken the place of a magic carpet. Jackson couldn't understand the Japanese writing that accompanied the image, but it was obviously meant to suggest that the laptop was fast. Then the last three digits of the phone number that was written along the bottom of the advert jumped out at Jackson: 893.

Jackson scooped up his tablet computer, stuffed it in his rucksack and ran outside. The traffic was starting to move when he tapped on the window of the cab. The driver motioned for him to jump in and Jackson opened the back door, then leaped into the cab as it started to roll with the traffic.

'Roppongi,' said Jackson.

CHAPTER 10

Jackson didn't allow himself to question what drew him to Roppongi. When the cab dropped him off it was raining hard, but he didn't even attempt to cover himself up, and while others waited for the lights to tell them it was safe to walk, Jackson just drifted across the wide expanse of tarmac where several wide roads converged. Somewhere deep inside he registered that jaywalking in this place was a reckless act, but he didn't care. He could feel an anger so intense, there was no room left to feel the sting of the cold rain or hear the horn blasts from the cars flashing by. When Jackson reached the pavement he headed for a tight knot of alleyways, soaked in neon and flanked by wooden and brick shacks that were serving up every type of food imaginable. He could taste duck and pineapple in the air, along with seafood and freshly baked dough, as he walked through the steamy clouds created by the open-fronted restaurants on either side of him. When Jackson reached the street the driver had directed him to, he glanced up and down, looking for the

ATM he'd been told was there. Having spotted a bank, he walked up to the cash machine suspended inside its glass frontage and inserted his credit card. Moments later Jackson was walking away with one hundred thousand yen in his pocket, made up of five-thousand yen notes.

Two streets later and the taxi driver's instructions delivered Jackson to the pavement opposite the Ozu Arcade. The glow from the front of the building was so bright it made him squint. To his mind, its garishly gold pillars and triangular portico design gave the building the appearance of a grand religious temple rather than the pachinko pinball arcade the Kojimas' head of security had described.

Jackson stood on the pavement, rivulets of rainwater gathering on his chin and forming tiny tributaries that ventured inside the neck of his T-shirt. There wasn't much to suggest that the arcade was the Yakuza hot spot Tucker had described, other than two black Mercedes parked outside, a make and style of car Jackson had come to recognize as the Tokyo gangsters' preferred mode of transport.

He felt his brow begin to tighten and his hands close into fists as he recalled the horror of his last encounter with the owner of one of those vehicles. Then he stepped into the road and walked towards the glistening pachinko parlour.

As Jackson entered the building, he was greeted by a

low-hanging haze of cigarette smoke and the shrill cacophony of thousands of tiny metal balls making their way through the mechanisms of several hundred pachinko machines. Some players had evidently been playing for hours because they had stacked their winnings beside their chairs. Jackson counted five big plastic tubs beside one old lady, each filled to brimming with the pea-sized shiny balls. As he passed her, a cascade of the chrome balls spewed from the mouth of her machine into the tin tray below.

Jackson kept walking until he reached a section on the back wall, covered by a red velvet curtain. Pushing the curtain to one side, he walked into a different area almost as large as the one that housed the pachinko machines, but dimly lit and full of tables with chequered plastic covers. Japanese men in shirts and T-shirts sat round half the tables. Most of the men held a handful of small cards, which were decorated with black and red symbols.

The only person to notice that Jackson had entered the room was a well-built man in a creased white shirt, who was eating a big bowl of noodles while reading the newspaper. His sleeves were rolled up to avoid the slop and Jackson could clearly see the indelible detailing of various tattooed creatures as worn by the Yakuza. Jackson's arrival had taken him by surprise and, in his haste to rise from the table, he forgot to sever the noodles so that several thick, wet strands hung from his mouth like a dripping beard. He motioned emphatically for Jackson to leave as he stuffed the noodles into his mouth with a hand, and then barked something in Japanese that probably meant 'Get out!' But Jackson stood his ground and, as the man manoeuvred himself out from behind the table, stopped him in his tracks by holding out the wad of Japanese notes. The man considered the bunch of notes, then looked at Jackson in disbelief as he pointed to the tables where the other men were playing.

After scratching his chin, at which point he found a rogue noodle strand and popped it into his mouth, the man signalled for Jackson to wait and then walked over to one of the tables. He whispered to one man who, unlike the others, was wearing a tie loosely knotted over the most garish pink shirt Jackson had ever seen. The fabric positively glowed in the smoky darkness of the room and its big flared collar was like something from a vintage costume-hire shop. The player looked up and checked Jackson out, before saying something to the two other men round the table that made them all guffaw. Then, to Jackson's surprise, Noodles motioned for him to come over to the table.

'So you have money, *gaijin*,' said the man in the pink shirt.

There was that insult again. The one used by the boys at the Invader, that meant foreigner.

'And you want to play Oicho-Kabu? It is a strange choice for a tourist?' As the man spoke, Jackson spotted the telltale marks of the Yakuza, the swirling tail of a serpent curling up the side of his neck and ending in a sharp, pointed tail behind his ear.

'I want to play the game of the Yakuza,' said Jackson, without blinking.

For a moment the man was silent, then he and the other two men burst out laughing again.

'And why would a skinny punk tourist like you want to play with Yakuza?'

'Because I think I can beat you!' said Jackson.

For the third time, laughter rocked the table. The laughter caught the attention of some of the men at other tables and they wandered over to where Jackson was standing. Several of the men appeared to be just businessmen in drab suits, here for a little after work gambling, but some of the men who were gathering round the table wore black or white vests and T-shirts, their inked skin plain to see. There was no doubting it, Jackson had wandered into a viper pit.

'Hey, kid, maybe you've played Kabu on the Internet or something, but it's different here – we don't give credit.' The comment came from a large red-cheeked man sitting at the table.

'That won't be a problem,' replied Jackson, pulling up a chair. 'Because I've never played the game.'

Jackson's comment was greeted with silence. Then the loudest detonation of laughter so far.

'What do you mean – you've never played it?' said Pink Man, a surprised look on his face.

'Look, are you going to show me how to play this game, or should I take my money somewhere else?' said Jackson, standing up as if ready to walk away.

'No. Please, sit down. I will happily liberate you from your *kane*,' said Pink Man.

Jackson sat back down.

'Please, shuffle!' the man continued, handing Jackson the deck of cards. They were stiffer than the standard playing cards Jackson was used to and about half the size. Jackson shuffled the pack of forty cards and placed them on the table. One of the other men, whose bright-orange polo shirt looked at odds with his ugly pockmarked face and badly scarred cheek, assumed the role of dealer. He picked up the cards and dealt one card to each of the players, laying each card face down.

'You can look!' said Pink Man, pointing at Jackson's card while bending his own card up, hiding its identity so only he could see it. Jackson had skim-read the rules of the ancient game when he'd first come across it on the Net and decided it was the kind of game he'd be good at. But here, surrounded by a crowd of thugs and shady businessmen, his confidence was being tested.

'Consider that card a gift!' said Pink Man. 'A window

through which you can glimpse the future of the rest of the game.'

Jackson followed the other players in picking up the single card. Unlike regular playing cards, the Kabu card had no number on it. The small, rigid card featured a series of angular black stripes, similar to the stripes worn by a sergeant-major. Jackson counted two slanted lines, like the sides of a tepee tent, with a single line down the centre. This gave him the card's value – 3. Next, Polo Shirt dealt four cards face up: 2, 5, 6 and 1.

'Pick a card and place a bet?' asked Pink Man.

Jackson studied Pink Man more closely. The detailing on the scaly serpent's tail was exquisite. Its oyster-grey colouring, with glints of white and jet-black shading, made it look as if a piece of silver jewellery was spiralling up from underneath the man's starched shirt collar and tickling the base of his ear. But Jackson didn't need a tattoo to tell him this man was Yakuza. He could see the man was a killer by the emptiness in his pale, dead eyes. Jackson focused back on the cards.

A 3 in his hand, which didn't count towards his final hand, and four other visible card values of 2, 5, 6 and 1. This meant there were a lot of high cards – 7s, 8s and 9s – still left in the pack. So, when it came time to bet, Jackson chose the second lowest card – the 2 – to place his money on, handing over five thousand yen. Red Cheeks and Pink Man played the same amount, choosing the 1 and 6, respectively.

Four more cards were dealt face down and Jackson was permitted to look at the new card beneath the one he'd bet on. The 2 was matched with a 5 to make 7 – a medium value. Now Jackson glanced at the other two players to judge how confident they looked about the cards they'd been dealt, assigning each a value in his head from zero to nine. Pink Man was positively beaming with confidence in his bet, so Jackson gave him a nine. Mr Red Cheeks appeared less excited by the options the cards had presented him with, so Jackson awarded him a two on his confidence index.

The dealer now asked Jackson if he wanted a third card. Jackson ran an algorithm in his head, combining the cards he could see with the 'confidence values' and his prediction for the high cards he thought were still to come.

'No,' he said confidently.

Jackson watched as Pink Man calmly pondered his options for a moment before taking a third card, the card that would have been Jackson's. The dealer, Polo Shirt, turned it over to reveal an 8. The scowl on Pink Man's face said it all. The dealer then flipped his cards, revealing a 1 and a 4. With Pink Man's middle card being a 7, his final total was 21, giving him an abysmal score of 1. Red Cheeks' score had come to 6, with a 2 and 3 being matched to his card. Jackson had won.

As Jackson scooped up his own money and his winnings from in front of the two other players and the ugly dealer, all three men glared at him.

'Beginner's luck!' he said, raising his shoulders.

Jackson lost the next round, a loss that was made worse by the fact that he'd doubled his bet to twenty thousand yen.

'Don't take it too hard, kid,' said Red Cheeks, constructing two neat piles of notes with his winnings, the glowing stub of a cigar sticking to his bottom lip as he spoke. 'We'll make sure you've got enough change left over for the bus back to wherever you came from!'

'Where *did* you come from?' asked Pink Man, looking intently into Jackson's eyes as they continued with the next round.

'It doesn't matter where I came from,' said Jackson. 'What's important is that I've found what I'm looking for.' As Jackson spoke, he continued to analyse the cards and faces round the table, assigning each a value and lining them up for algorithmic conversion.

'And what is that?' asked Pink Man.

'I guess I want to rub shoulders with some gangsters,' said Jackson casually.

'Do you hear that, guys?' said Pink Man, addressing the men around him. 'We're one of the stops on the Tokyo sightseeing tour now.'

The new dealer, Red Cheeks, turned over his last card and once again Jackson was announced the winner.

Now it was time for Jackson to assume the role of dealer, and if as a player his mathematical prowess had given him a slight advantage, as dealer his arithmetical skills would prove even more effective. In the first few rounds, Jackson had soon worked out that during a round of cards, the dealer saw more card faces than the players; it was just one of the quirks of the Oicho-Kabu card game. This, in addition to Jackson's uncanny ability to apply a numerical value to each player's confidence, meant he stood the best chance yet of faithfully predicting what cards were likely to come up next.

'Tell me, *gaijin*,' said Pink Man as Jackson handed out the cards in the way he'd watched the others do, 'what is this fascination of yours with Tokyo's *Ninkyō Dantai* – our chivalrous organization?'

Pink Man was talking again, noted Jackson. There it was, the telltale sign that he wasn't sure of his cards.

'*Chivalrous?*' said Jackson, dividing his attention between the conversation and his analysis of the game. 'Is that what you call yourselves?'

'You haven't answered my question,' said Pink Man.

Again. More talk. Subtract one from the confidence stakes.

Jackson knew he needed to resist the temptation to say what he really thought, that he wanted to beat the Yakuza at their own game. 'I dunno, I guess I wanted to see if you gangsters are as bad at cards as you are at choosing a shirt!'

The two other players and a few spectators round the table burst out laughing at Jackson's comment, until Pink Man silenced them with a grimace.

'You should watch your mouth, boy!' he spat across the table at Jackson.

'And you should watch your cards,' replied Jackson, pointing to his own cards and their winning value of 9.

For his first role as dealer, Jackson had played it safe, betting only five thousand yen. But seven quick-fire rounds later, half of which he won, including another winning stint as dealer, it was his turn to deal again.

Jackson dealt the cards as if going through the motions, trying his best to keep a neutral expression on his face so as not to give anything away. Polo Shirt was clearly unhappy with his cards because he kept moving around, in contrast to the stillness that had accompanied the three times he'd won previously. Red Cheeks had all but pulled out of the game a few rounds back and Jackson could tell he'd lost interest and focus. Pink Man, however, was as sharp as the blade Jackson expected he kept somewhere on his person. He'd been harder to read in the last few rounds, so Jackson assigned him a medium value of five in the confidence stakes and focused instead on his dealer advantage, the cards he could actually see.

With the mental maths done, Jackson made his move. He bet his entire wad of cash, which with his winnings was a staggering two hundred and twenty thousand yen – well over two and a half thousand dollars – on his calculation that a 3 would come up last. To everyone's amazement, except his, the final card of the game was decorated with just three stripes. He had a perfect score of 9. The game was over. Jackson had beaten everyone.

'Thank you, gentlemen!' he said, gathering his cash into piles in front of him. Feeling a presence behind him, Jackson glanced over his shoulder. The enormous Noodles leered down at him, uncomfortably close.

'You've forgotten about my fee,' said Pink Man from across the table.

'What fee?' asked Jackson.

'The fee for teaching you Oicho-Kabu, of course. Whatever you've got there should cover it!'

'You've got to be kidding. The way you were playing, I should charge *you*!' said Jackson.

Pink Man chuckled without any hint of humour. He then nodded to Noodles who leaned forward and scooped up the money in front of Jackson.

Jackson's eyes narrowed and the muscles in his neck and shoulders tensed. He gritted his teeth and prepared to unleash the fury fizzing inside him.

'Thank you for your generosity in allowing my friend to play.' It was a familiar voice. Marty.

Stepping forward from behind Jackson and putting a hand on his shoulder, Marty whispered earnestly in his ear. 'I must insist, Jackson, that we leave. Now!'

'You know what?' said Jackson, turning back to the players. 'You can have the money!' Marty began forcibly pulling Jackson backwards towards the exit. 'It's saturated with your evil stench anyway!'

Jackson had never seen Marty so angry. His friend kept up a verbal tirade about how dangerous Jackson's behaviour was until they exited from the Metro. Marty told Jackson that he was relieved he'd been able to find him before he'd come to any real harm. Luckily, Marty said, the cafe owner had seen Jackson get into the taxi. He'd called the taxi company and traced Jackson to the arcade by asking people if they'd seen him. 'You stand out, Jackson,' he said. 'Kids like you don't often venture into that part of town!'

Marty had sorted out a hotel room for the two of them to stay. He'd mentioned something about it being anonymous because the hotel belonged to a friend from college. Jackson wasn't interested. He was just allowing himself to be swept along in Marty's whirlwind.

'Do you even care about the danger you just put *me* in?' said Marty, slamming the hotel room door behind them.

Jackson thought about the question. His answer was an emphatic 'No'. He didn't care. Not a jot for his own safety or indeed that of his only friend here in Tokyo, Marty. It was a startling realization, that he had become this reckless, but it didn't change anything because caring had to come from somewhere – it needed an energy source and Jackson was running on empty. It had taken the card game to show him that whatever had fuelled his inner drive to reach Tokyo, then kept him going these last few days, he had used it all up. And, worst of all, he felt exhilarated by the feelings of bitterness and hatred that now drove him. He'd actually enjoyed staring danger in the face back there. But at the same time, he knew, if he didn't get a grip it would destroy him.

'I think we'd better have some sleep,' said Jackson, slipping his jacket and shoes off, then climbing on to one of the two single beds in the cheerless room.

Jackson closed his eyes. He could sense Marty moving around the room, gargling some water from the sink beside his bed and using the toilet, before he eventually lay down himself.

Jackson was back at the Oicho-Kabu table. 'Try and place a bet now!' said Pink Man, the blade of a chrome flick-knife between his teeth, the faces of Red Cheeks and Polo Shirt either side of his, glints of madness in their eyes. There was a huge pile of money in front of Jackson, but as he attempted to push the pile forward he realized he couldn't move his hands. He looked down and was horrified to see Pink Man's tattooed snake alive in his lap, wrapping itself round his wrists and ankles, and squeezing them so tightly it felt as if his bones were about to break.

'Time to make you one of us!' said Pink Man, dipping the point of the knife into a pot of ink on the table. Now the other two players were on him, holding him down and forcing his head sideways. Pink Man began to dig the blade tip into Jackson's cheek. He wanted to cry out but Red Cheeks had his hand over Jackson's mouth. Then he heard it. A siren, blaring from outside.

Jackson woke with a start, his hand darting instantly to his cheek. No ink or blood, just sweat. He could hear the dying echo of the siren as it moved along the street below.

He looked across to the other bed. Marty was snoring loudly.

Jackson sat up and fluffed his two pillows against the headboard. He then leaned forward and grabbed his jacket, pulling his thin tablet computer from an inside pocket. He sat back and turned on the device. Then he touched the *Whisper* icon.

'Did they call?' Marty was rubbing his eyes as he staggered towards the tiny toilet cubicle.

'No! But it doesn't matter!' said Jackson, blurting the words out excitedly. 'Marty, I think I've cracked it! It's *Whisper*!' He was gabbling his words. 'I mean, I had a feeling the game was trying to tell me something!'

Marty joined him by the side of his bed. 'Jackson, you're talking nonsense. Slow down.'

'Sorry!' Jackson breathed deeply and then continued to speak, without taking his eyes from the screens of his tablet and Marty's laptop, both of which he'd lined up on the bed in front of him. 'When I started my *Whisper* session a few hours ago, I noticed the same thing that's been happening for weeks – lots of player chatter about raiding parties attacking villages and stealing stuff. It's happened to me, several times, packs of high-level bandits hitting fast and hard, working as a tight unit and making off with valuable game assets. Then it hit me, Marty, you asked the question yourself when we were at the dojo. *What use could Yakimoto have for a load of computer gamers?*'

'Well?' asked Marty.

'Gold farming!' said Jackson. 'The wholesale selling of virtual game assets – valuable spells, swords with special abilities and entire characters complete with the best armour and weaponry – all of them can fetch hundreds if not thousands of dollars on the online black market!'

Marty looked impressed by the idea.

'The answer to your question is simple. Yakimoto could use a load of gamers, just like the ones you discovered are missing, to set up the mother of all gold-farming outfits. A slave labour camp dedicated to the business of making and exchanging cyber gold for real money.'

'That's an impressive theory, Jackson,' said Marty, pacing up and down the room. 'But, if such a place exists, how would it be possible to find it?'

'IP addresses!' said Jackson, smiling. 'I've come up with a way of using *Whisper* player accounts to find out where players are located in the real world. Look at the data on your laptop. It's a list of account IP addresses.' The laptop screen was full of eight- to ten-digit numbers in columns. 'As you know, any device that connects to the Internet – a phone, a laptop, a games console, has its own unique Internet Protocol or IP address. You could say that the string of numbers, usually organized in four clusters, is your computer's postcode.'

'I get it! So if you can find the IP addresses of the gangs in *Whisper*, you might be able to find out where they are?'

'Theoretically, yes. The only problem is being in the right place at the right time when one of the raiding parties strikes. I've got some names of raiding-party members from forums where their victims have made complaints.' Jackson opened a .txt file on the laptop with three player names in it. 'But the IP addresses associated with these accounts are not enough. I need at least treble that to stand a chance of spotting a pattern in the numbers. But, if I could be there in the right village or town at the exact moment a gang of fifteen or twenty raiders attacked, then I could record their player names and track their IPs!'

'So, you just keep moving around, between the towns and villages in the game. You're sure to come across them, right?'

Jackson smiled. 'In the kingdom of Delvia alone, if you count all the cities, towns, villages and trading posts, there are over a thousand. And that's only one of three playable kingdoms.'

'Well, that's that then,' said Marty. 'You've got no chance of being in the right place at the right time and witnessing another attack.'

'That's not exactly true,' said Jackson. 'I have a chance of witnessing an attack – it's just that the chance is a remote one. However, there is a way that mathematics can help me improve that chance.' Jackson switched windows on the laptop to a search engine and entered two words.

'Data mining!' he said, pointing at the screen and scrolling down the page of results. 'It's an area of mathematics that can help find meaningful information in the mass of data that swirls around all of us. It's used by credit-card companies to track card fraud, or by intelligence agencies to find who the leader of a terrorist group is. You can even use it to define geometric clusters in eight-dimensional space!'

Marty said nothing, but his brow was creased under the weight of his confusion.

'Look, here!' Jackson was pointing at a search result that read 'Free Neural Network Program'. 'A neural network is a type of data-mining computer program that is specifically designed to look for patterns. In theory, if I can gather enough information about the locations the *Whisper* raiding parties have already attacked – like how well the towns are defended and the type of valuables they had in them – I can use a neural net to reveal patterns within the data that might enable me to predict the gang's next target.'

Marty couldn't hide the scepticism in his face. 'Does this involve you playing some more *Whisper*?'

'Of course!' said Jackson.

It was that game show again. The one where the contestant, dressed as a salt-shaker, threw stuff at his food-like friends as they rolled around a revolving plate. But even the surreal scenes on the hotel room TV and Marty's laughter couldn't break Jackson's focus. He was surrounded by pieces of hotel-branded notepaper, each covered in calculations and rough drafts of diagrams. It all terminated on the laptop screen where he'd fed all his variables into the neural-net program he'd downloaded. In front of Jackson was a complex web of intersecting lines joining four vertical columns of circles.

'I think I'm on to something,' said Jackson, punching in some final numbers.

'What on earth is that?' said Marty, standing beside Jackson's bed and looking at the webbed structure on his laptop screen.

'It's a neural net representing the raiding parties' behaviour in *Whisper*. The circles, or nodes, in the left-hand column each represent villages that the gangs have

VILLAGE NOT ATTACKED

NORTHWICK
KELTHAM
PORTISHAM
AXEFORD
CLIFFS END
TERRORHAM
WINDSHIRE
SOUTHLAW
DIAMOND COVE

IDEAL TARGET VILLAGE

1x1xEE

VILLAGE VARIABLES

GUARDS
2334
2252
2432

DEFENCES
233X
5222
3X25

APOTHECARY
124
3122
215

ARCHERS
X131
A23
24223

GOLD STORES
25121
2232
4X22

GARRISON
1X34
1X45
1224

CANNON
3332
21213
5122

BLACKSMITH
2232
15111
3222

AUCTION HOUSE
222
3344
5555

MINE
4251
1555
3312
1513

VILLAGES ATTACKED

SHANDOR
GALLIPODY
VEXOR
WEST HIGHTHORN
EVERSHIRE
SANDLAW OUTPOST
THORNY OUTPOST

already attacked. Like most of the information I've used to create this network, I found news of village attacks from reports in forums and blogs. The same goes for the tallest of my columns: Village Variables.' Every circle in the tallest column was labelled with a single word or phrase, each one clearly a description of a different village feature – Guards, Auction House, Apothecary and so on.

'And the numbers?' asked Marty, pointing at clusters of numbers in each of the circles.

'I've given all the variables in each village a rating from one to five. Look, the village of Shandor, which was attacked last week, has no wall round it and no moat, so I've given it a defences value of just two. Gallipody sits on a mountainside, a little better defended, but not too much, so it gets a value of three.'

Marty shook his head. 'Sorry, Jackson, I'm getting double vision staring into your crazy web! What's all this about?'

'It's about this!' Jackson pointed to the single circle, in the third column. 'The raiders' ideal target village is . . .' He clicked a button in the program labelled SCAN and the village name of 'Northwick' came up.

'The neural-net program can see patterns in the number clusters on screen,' continued Jackson. 'It simply uses these patterns to predict the village our bandits are most likely to attack next.' Jackson moved the laptop to one side and grabbed his tablet, on which *Whisper* was running. 'We'd better get to Northwick!'

'I just don't understand,' stuttered Jackson, slamming the tablet on the bed and moving to the window. It was lunchtime and raining hard. The bright neon HOTEL sign fastened to the wall outside made the beads of water on the glass look like luminescent blue pearls.

'Maybe you got the timings wrong,' said Marty from the armchair. He'd watched with Jackson for the first half-hour or so before turning his attention to another game show.

'No!' said Jackson. 'The timing for their attacks is one of my most reliable variables. The reports on the Web made that very clear. They generally attack villages at key times in the day.'

'Sorry, dude!' said Marty. 'But it's like I said, we need to be patient and wait for someone to make contact. I think you might have exaggerated how good this neural-net thing of yours really is!'

Exaggerated! said Jackson to himself. 'Marty, you've got it!' He jumped back on the bed and scooped up the laptop.

'What have I got?' asked Marty, his focus on the TV unwavering.

'People exaggerate!' said Jackson, feverishly poking at the laptop's keys. 'The values I assigned all my variables were based on forum and blog descriptions of how many soldiers were guarding a village and how many weapons or gold pieces were stolen. But the players who witnessed the attacks will have *exaggerated* – it's only human nature!'

Jackson busily adjusted the numbers in circles, dropping those in the 'Guards' and 'Gold' columns by one digit each. He then hit SCAN again and a different village came up.

'Diamond Cove!' he shouted. 'It's Diamond Cove they're attacking!'

Marty joined Jackson as he directed WizardZombie to mount a Griffin and fly at full speed towards the coast.

The feathered animal swept vertically down the side of a tall cliff and, pulling up, deposited Jackson's character on a chalky ledge overlooking the seaside village of Diamond Cove.

The commotion in the village's quayside was obvious. The bodies of slaughtered fighters lay everywhere and the last few defenders were being dispatched by a Dark Shaman called Thievius. Jackson and Marty watched as the wizard-like character smashed a staff on the wooden jetty where several dwarfs were attempting to fight the raiders. The staff, which was decorated with a jewel-encrusted skull, emitted a bright-green circular pulse which killed all the fighters instantly.

Jackson quickly changed windows on his tablet device,

bringing up a blinking white command prompt in a black box.

'What are you doing?' enquired Marty.

'I'm executing a simple application I coded last night. It can run in the background while *Whisper* is still up and harvest players' IP addresses.'

'Clever,' said Marty.

The two of them watched as the raiding party, which consisted of nineteen players, finished loading the goods they'd stolen into a ship and eventually sailed away.

'Well,' said Jackson, closing *Whisper* and opening his application full screen. 'Let's look at the numbers behind our raiding party!'

To Marty, at least, the nineteen number groupings didn't share much beyond the fact that they all started with '164', the part of their Internet address that even he knew signified they were located in Japan.

Jackson, however, had no trouble in finding a logic to the rest of the numbers.

'The mean IP address is: 164.47.253.121,' he said triumphantly, copying the numbers, changing windows to a mapping application and pasting them into the search window. A full-colour map of a forested area west of Tokyo loaded full screen on the tablet. In the centre of the large wooded area was a small turquoise arrow, pointing down.

'That's it! If the Yakimoto gold-farming theory is

correct, and the Kojima twins are part of it, that arrow is pointing to their location!'

'That's genius, Jackson!' said Marty.

'Now who's exaggerating!' replied Jackson.

CHAPTER 11

A *short* ride and a *brisk* hike through the woods, that's how Marty had described the journey from their hotel to the location on Jackson's tablet screen.

The reality was that the cab had taken two and a half hours to reach the forest and a further half-hour until Marty requested the driver to drop them off. As for the hike, they'd been at it an hour. It was unforgiving terrain, the tall trees knitted together so snugly that the boys couldn't even walk in a straight line. And the fallen branches and leaves that covered the ground were slippery from the day's rain.

The wound on Jackson's forehead, from the butt of Yakimoto's gun, was throbbing and he could already feel the skin on his left ankle beginning to rub raw. To make matters worse, it was showing signs of getting dark, and if there was one place Jackson didn't want to be lost in at night, it was a forest that Marty had delighted in telling him on the way was famous for being haunted.

Jackson was just attempting to struggle through the

branches of a fallen tree, when he noticed Marty standing with a hand up ahead.

'Shh!' whispered Marty, beckoning for Jackson to tread quietly.

'This must be it,' he said as Jackson reached him, pointing to Jackson's tablet that he'd been carrying, and then down a slope towards a large concrete complex.

The two of them kneeled as Marty opened his rucksack and searched for the binoculars he'd packed. Having fished them out, he handed them to Jackson.

Jackson put the binoculars up to his face and was surprised to see what looked like a concrete castle.

'What do you see?' whispered Marty.

'It's definitely a war bunker of some sort. But it's big, probably the size of a factory. I'm guessing it was some kind of military headquarters in the Second World War.'

Then as his eyes adjusted to the dimly lit image he began to notice details that didn't fit with the old structure. There was a freshly cut ditch that traced the complex's high concrete walls and certain sections of the roof were covered in green plastic sheeting. Then Jackson thought he caught a glimpse of a man with a gun in his hand. The figure appeared for a fraction of a second beneath one of the plastic covers, but Jackson lost him as he moved the binoculars.

'Wait a minute!' he said. 'I think I saw a guard!'

'You saw a guard, did you?' asked Marty calmly.

'I think so!' said Jackson, speaking without taking his eyes away from the binoculars.

'That's funny,' said Marty. 'Because I can see a guard too!'

'Really? Where?' Jackson's attention was still focused on the image in the binoculars.

'Behind you, Jackson!' said Marty, a hint of laughter in his voice.

'What are you talking about?' said Jackson, finally dropping the binoculars from his face and turning round.

Jackson's mouth dropped open. To his horror, he was greeted by the sight of three armed guards, one holding a large machete knife and the other two pointing shotguns at him.

Even more astonishing was the fact that Marty stood between the men, grinning.

CHAPTER 12

'What on earth is going on? Who are you really?' cried Jackson, looking in horror at the boy he'd thought was his only friend in Tokyo.

Marty just laughed as the guards frisked Jackson, taking his wallet and phone from his pocket before kicking him down the hillside.

'My name is Miki. Miki Yakimoto!'

'Wait a minute,' said Jackson, picking himself up from the dirt at the bottom of the slope. 'You're . . . Yakimoto's son?'

'Yes, I am.'

'So you're behind all this?' asked Jackson, just metres from the rubble bridge that led over the deep ditch and up to a metal door set in the complex's concrete wall.

'I am indeed,' replied Miki. 'I'm actually quite pleased you left me no option but to let you bring us here. I've missed the place.'

One of the guards pulled a walkie-talkie from his belt, pushed a button and hailed someone inside.

How could I have been so stupid? Jackson asked himself. But at the same time he had to admit that he had always suspected that something wasn't quite right about Marty – about *Miki*.

'What I don't understand,' said Jackson, 'is why volunteer all that information about the missing gamers? Without that, I would never have worked out this place existed.'

Something behind the heavy wood and steel gate clicked and an electric motor whined as the door slid slowly open.

'Because the Kojimas' bodyguard had already found out about them,' replied Miki, signalling to one of his men to push Jackson forward. 'When I told you and English about my mysterious missing gamers theory, I thought I'd just be confirming what the two of you already knew. The fact you didn't made me seem all the more trustworthy. Quite brilliant, when you think about it, don't you agree?'

It was all too much to take in. The armed guards smoking in the small courtyard. The clunk of the metal behind. The revelations of Miki's deviousness.

'So you didn't really visit that missing kid's house?' asked Jackson as he was led into a corridor.

'Yes, I did. But it was only after my men climbed in through his bedroom window and we brought him here that his parents reported him missing. The best lies, Farley, always contain an element of the truth.'

'And meeting Brooke at the Invader?'

'That was easy. Nothing goes through the port of Tokyo without us knowing. We followed you to your hotel and everywhere else after that. When I was told Brooke was sniffing around for information on the missing twins, I just popped up and made myself useful. Would you believe I created the marvellous *Marty* on the day you arrived in Tokyo. I needed something to disguise me – didn't want someone tipping English off that her knight in a shiny Puffa vest was Yakuza. I saw a movie memorabilia shop and Marty's clothes were on a mannequin in the window.'

'So why did you wait with us in the Kojimas' dojo? Why didn't you just have us all picked up?' asked Jackson.

'Because I needed to be sure how much the Kojima girls knew. With that bodyguard of theirs, they had been poking their noses into my father's affairs. I hung around to find out what they'd discovered.'

'So, where are you holding the girls?' asked Jackson.

A broad smile spread over Miki's face and he signalled to the men to stop in front of a wooden door.

'Let me ask you a question. What does Detective Yoshida look like?'

'Why are you asking me that?' demanded Jackson.

'Just answer the question.'

'Short grey hair, round spectacles, mackintosh. Why?'

Miki chuckled. 'Where did you get that description from, man?'

Jackson thought for a moment. 'From a Web story I was reading when he came to take the robots from the hotel that Brooke and I stayed at.'

'So, you saw a picture of a grey-haired, four-eyed, raincoat-wearing cop labelled "Yoshida"?'

'Yes!' replied Jackson firmly.

'You sure about that?'

Jackson brought up the mental image of the news article. The picture of the grey-haired detective smoking a cigarette had been near the bottom. It did have a tag line below it – something about the Kojimas planning their own disappearance – but now Jackson came to think of it, there had been no actual mention of Yoshida by name in the whole article. Knowing that Yoshida was investigating the Kojimas' disappearance, Jackson had just assumed he was one of the detectives referred to in the newspaper.

'Let me put you out of your misery,' said Miki. 'The police officer who took your robots was not Yoshida. It was another detective. One who works for us. We weren't sure what exactly you had in your hotel room; you could have booby-trapped the place for all we knew, so we used a dirty cop. Cops are expendable and they can get access to places, like your hotel room, without raising any questions.'

'But I don't understand,' said Jackson. 'If you wanted the robots, why let your cop take them to the police pound?'

'When we use the police, we still have to go through the motions. He was due to deliver them to one of my father's warehouses the next day.'

'So why did you let us go to all the trouble of breaking them out?'

'Curiosity, I guess. You and Brooke were very insistent that you could get them back. I guess I was intrigued to see how they worked. What better robot masterclass than watching you break them out of one of the most secure buildings in all of Japan?'

Once more, Miki nodded to a guard who proceeded to push Jackson through the door and into another concrete-lined corridor, lit by wall-mounted lanterns.

'But I still don't understand why you helped me to escape at the dojo,' said Jackson. 'Why send your dirty cop for just Brooke and the girls?'

'Haven't you realized it yet – I didn't send anyone!' said Miki.

'But I saw him, your dirty cop, in the car with Brooke and the Kojima girls –'

'You saw a Tokyo detective wearing a raincoat. All the detectives in this city wear those raincoats, man – it's like their uniform. Your friends lucked out! The cop who picked them up doesn't work for us.'

For a moment, Jackson forgot about his own predicament, his mind shooting back to the police car outside the dojo, pulling away with the girls inside. Miki's revelation raised more questions than it answered. If Brooke and the triplets had been picked up by a good cop, how had he found them and why had he taken them away? *And why hadn't Brooke called to say she was OK?*

'As it stands,' Miki continued, 'the cop and your girlfriends have dropped off the end of the earth. That's why I didn't call my father to come straight away – I was hoping they'd contact you! I have to say, though, Jackson, your little stunt in the pachinko arcade had me worried. Before I received word that you'd popped up there I was convinced you were on to me. You had me rushing around Tokyo like an idiot. I was tempted to let those guys rough you up a bit for that! But you redeemed yourself when you found this place. Really, Jackson, you have no idea how grateful I am that you managed to highlight that little security flaw in my father's enterprise. Thanks to you, my father's tech team are spoofing all our IP addresses now, giving them false numbers so no one will ever be able to trace them again. Watching the way you worked out the location of this place was so amazing, it almost made me wish I'd paid attention in maths class.'

They came to the end of the corridor, where a metal door hung open at the centre of a concrete cell.

'Make yourself at home, Farley,' said Miki as his henchman pushed Jackson into the dark, dank room. 'I suggest you get some sleep. You'll be no good to us tired. Your first work shift starts in four hours. Sleep tight!'

As the flicker from the lanterns was reduced to a faint sliver between the door and floor and the putrid smell from the slop bucket clawed at Jackson's nostrils, he should have felt wretched. But standing there, in the darkness, Jackson was imbued with an overwhelming sense of hope. There was a very good chance that Brooke and the Kojima girls were safe.

CHAPTER 13

'I need to speak to Detective Yoshida,' said Brooke.

She was talking to the police officer standing a couple of metres behind her. He was watching her every move as she worked at a computer terminal. The officer, one of three stationed in and around the safe house where Brooke and the Kojima girls were staying, was supposed to be guarding them in case of an attack by Yakimoto's men. But, to Brooke, having someone glancing over her shoulder every minute of the day made her feel less like a victim of Yakimoto's evil deeds and more like a prisoner.

After being rushed from the dojo to the first safe house, a hotel suite in a posh Tokyo tower-block hotel, the girls had been told by Detective Yoshida that he was extremely concerned. He'd received information that the Yakuza were so determined to find them they were leaning on every dirty cop in the force. For the second night, he'd taken the decision to secretly move locations and thin his team down to only his most trusted officers.

As far as Brooke was concerned, all the cloak-and-dagger stuff had one big advantage – the girls' parents had not been contacted. Detective Yoshida believed that Yakimoto might well be monitoring Mr Kojima and J.P. in the hope they would lead them to the girls, so he'd insisted no one should attempt to contact them.

Since they'd arrived in Tokyo, Brooke had kept in touch with her father. The professor wasn't stupid and her doctored camping photographs had only bought Brooke a few days. When she'd come clean and explained they were in Tokyo, on the trail of the twins, J.P. had been furious. 'This is another reason why I no longer want you building robots that can do damage!' he'd shouted down the phone. 'They make you think you're invincible! They encourage you to go off on hare-brained adventures!' He'd also insisted that she tell him exactly where she was and stay put while he came to fetch her and Jackson. This Brooke refused to do, emphatically, explaining that she and Jackson were the twins' only hope and that if he came to Tokyo, or even called the police, he'd be endangering them all. It was an ultimatum Professor English had no choice but to accept. Brooke cemented the deal by promising to call her father daily.

J.P. might not have been so accepting had he known his daughter was now in custody. Though she was being kept safe from Yakimoto's henchmen, Brooke still faced criminal charges for theft of a motor vehicle, attempted bank robbery, two counts of speeding and dangerous driving, and withholding evidence. The latter charge related to Jackson and Marty, whom Brooke had refused to talk about, convinced the two boys had a better chance of saving the twins without police interference. The truth was that she didn't know where they were as Yoshida's ban on phone calls meant they hadn't talked since they'd been at the dojo.

Brooke's dealings with the detective had been a little strained. He was a serious man who didn't appreciate her penchant for sarcasm. She was also frustrated by his continued insistence that she should not contact Jackson. He'd explained the Yakuza could monitor phone lines as easily as the police force. Brooke was a material witness and victim of an attempted murder by Yakimoto, so Yoshida just wasn't prepared to risk them finding her.

Brooke was important to Detective Yoshida. Her witness statements and those offered by the Kojima girls were enough to have the head of the Yakuza arrested and put away, something Yoshida had been trying to do for most of his career. He needed her and the girls, so Brooke had used this fact to politely persuade the detective to allow her Internet access so she could help in the search for Jackson and the twins. The safe house's desktop computer was deathly slow and, annoyingly, her sessions were chaperoned, but she had been allowed access to part of the file the detective kept on Yakimoto.

It had taken Yoshida over ten years to collect the

information in the folder he stored on the Tokyo police server, part of his attempt to build a solid case against the crime boss. One thing was abundantly clear from the mix of photographs, interviews and company records – Yakimoto had tried his hand at just about every criminal exploit imaginable. Some of Yoshida's recent documents suggested that the Yakuza boss's latest racket was people trafficking. Brooke couldn't help but conclude that the concerns she'd shared with Jackson, about the twins being sold to a slave labour camp, were well founded.

The detective also had an interesting theory that Yakimoto's ambitions in this area were maturing. Evidence suggested that as well as selling people abroad, his organization was also suspected of running its own labour camp somewhere in Japan. Where, and for what reason, wasn't clear.

Another part of the hundred and fifty or so pages of the Yakimoto file that caught Brooke's attention was a small section about one of the many companies the Yakuza boss might have links with. Brooke wouldn't have given the company's name, Tokyo Mokuzai Kougaku, a second glance if it hadn't included a translation beside it in several languages, including English. As an engineer herself, she was intrigued to find out what exactly 'Tokyo Timber Engineering' produced.

The company brochure, presented as a PDF file, consisted of ten pages' worth of company profile and product listings, with each paragraph presented in Japanese, French, German and English. The main research and development centre for Tokyo Timber Engineering was based in Akihabara, or Electric Town. By coincidence this was the part of the city where Jackson and Brooke had stayed in the Capsule Inn and the city's main hub for all things electronic. But while the company's headquarters was based in the city, the brochure made a great deal of fuss over their test facility in a forest called Aokigahara.

> We know logging! We have been in the forestry business for ten years – not just designing and building agricultural and logging machinery, but using our own inventions to work our own ten-kilometre square forest, which is part of Japan's famous Aokigahara wooded area.

Brooke read on to the list of the company's products, including Log Loaders, Automated Wood Harvesters and Chippers, and the rather painful-sounding Delimbing Attachments. But the paragraph that really got her attention was headed 'OX: Optimized Exoskeleton'.

> The OX system is a revolution in forestry technology. Available in a number of different load-outs, the basic 5.2-metre-high power-assisted suit can make short work of most logging and farming chal-

lenges. Using state-of-the-art technology, the OX will enhance the productivity of your workforce. Standard specifications include:

- 3D Laser scanning (enables automated identifi-cation of tree types)
- State-of-the-art electromechanical muscles
- Our patented range of saw blade and grappler hand fixtures.

Not logging? We offer a range of OX modifications for even the most diverse industrial applications, including an electromagnetic hammer system and laser-cutting attachment.

Human Assisted Robotic Lifters like the OX are the industrial machine class of the future. Please call our Akihabara office for more information.

The description was accompanied by a small photograph of an OX in action. The chest and head section contained a metal cage inside which a Japanese operator sat smiling, his checked lumberjack shirt slightly at odds with the space-age helmet and visor he was wearing on his head. The description underneath the image read:

OX unit and operator, Aokigahara

Brooke examined the photograph and realized she'd seen an OX before. It was several weeks ago, when Jackson had asked her to identify three white vehicles lined up on the edge of the Duovik Diamond Mine in Canada. She'd only seen them via a video link but she knew they were some kind of powerlifters. The one in the picture in front of her was the same design except it was gunmetal grey as opposed to white and it had an open cockpit instead of the large, glass half-sphere that protected the diamond mine drivers from the freezing -40 °C of Canada's north-west territories.

Brooke also remembered that one of these powerful machines, operated by Yakimoto, had almost killed Jackson.

'What is it? Have you found something?' said Detective Yoshida as he entered the room. He was pushing six feet in height, quite tall for a Japanese man, although at least an inch of that was his haircut, the uniform hairs standing straight up on his head like the bristles of a brush. Brooke thought his furry head, round face and the dark-brown rings around his eyes gave him the appearance of a panda.

'You could say that,' she replied, pointing to a series of numbers on the computer screen. 'I think I've had a bit of a breakthrough.'

The detective nodded encouragingly.

'Your theory about Yakimoto operating his own labour camp ... how confident are you about that?' asked Brooke.

'It was something I was excited about a few months ago. I interviewed a few witnesses, one guy who said he'd been offered low prices for transporting some goods that were made in a Yakuza slave factory. Another witness who swore he'd seen someone trying to run away from a van in a petrol station before a guy with gang tattoos bundled him back in and drove off. But I didn't get any further leads from these interviews.'

'What if I had a location for you?'

'I'd be surprised, Brooke. Those were just two of several leads that didn't go anywhere.'

'Well, look at this.' Brooke pointed at the sentence below the picture of the OX on the computer screen.

'Aokigahara, you mean? It's the location of a forestry project. The company in that brochure, Brooke ... I can't say with any certainty that Yakimoto is even involved with them.'

'I can,' said Brooke, smiling. 'We know for sure that Yakimoto owns a diamond mine in Canada, right? Well, I've seen those powerlifters at his mine. Heck, Yakimoto drove one that killed Jackson's father and almost killed Jackson!'

The detective squinted at Brooke as he thought for a moment.

'All that proves is that Yakimoto has bought some of these . . . OXs from this company.'

'OK, how about this?' Brooke switched programs on the computer to a window stacked high with clusters of six-figure numbers.

'I'm sorry, but what am I looking at?' asked the detective.

'*Tread*'s location!'

The detective's wide brow was furrowed. He didn't seem to understand what Brooke meant.

'You're looking at a hexadecimal dump of geotagging data stored inside compressed picture files taken by *Tread*,' said Brooke.

'You're still not making any sense,' said the bemused detective.

'Jackson would be able to explain exactly how this process works better than I can, but basically when *Tread* takes a picture or video he stores it as a file. Inside that file, along with the details of the image, he also keeps a numerical reference of where the picture or video was taken. It's called geotagging: each picture kinda remembers where and when on the planet it was shot.'

'So, all those numbers represent pictures taken by your robot?' asked the detective.

'Yes. Yesterday I connected to *Tread* via my handset and uploaded some code that would trigger a photograph from his camera every ten minutes.' As she spoke, Brooke brought up a series of digital images on the screen. Every one of them was blank. 'As you can see, *Tread* is locked in his case so the images themselves tell me nothing, but the geographical tag inside each JPEG file shows that he was moved by Yakimoto's people from Tokyo to . . .' She highlighted and copied the last two sets of figures and then changed applications to a browser, where she pasted them into the search bar. A map sprang up, showing a red marker that hovered over a mountainous area south-west of Tokyo.

'Fujisan!' said the detective.

'That marker isn't on Fujisan,' said Brooke, zooming the picture in still further. The map closed in on a large area of green at the foot of the famous Japanese mountain. 'It's Aokigahara! *Tread* is in Yakimoto's forest project. And what do you say the twins are there too?'

'And Jackson,' said the detective.

Brooke looked confused.

'I just heard from a contact of mine in Roppongi. It seems our concerns for Jackson were well founded. It's Marty. His real name is Miki. Miki Yakimoto.'

'Yakimoto's son?' gasped Brooke.

'Yes!'

'Oh my God! I introduced Yakimoto's son to Jackson!' Brooke dropped her head, the guilt of her mistake weighing heavy.

'Don't worry about it now!' said Yoshida. 'Thanks to you, we've got a chance of finding him and the twins.'

'You think he'll be there too?'

'From what you've told me about his gaming skills, I'm sure of it, Brooke.' The detective placed a finger on the computer screen where the marker hovered in the middle of the forest.

'Aokigahara. The haunted sea of trees.'

CHAPTER 14

Pain pulsed through Jackson's back and thigh muscles as he attempted to rise from the straw mattress.

He hadn't been woken by anything in particular, not even the ache from his forehead which he'd grown used to. But the strange fusion of unfamiliar sounds, the metallic clank of door locks, the booming laughter of some guards passing by and an occasional fitful shriek from the Japanese boys in the cells around him – that was hard to sleep through.

Jackson examined his cell. It was about two metres by four metres in size with nothing to break up the cold, damp concrete of the walls and floor but the toilet bucket, the rotting mattress, which was held together by string, and a small square of barred window that was too high to reach and right now showed nothing but pitch black outside.

Jackson was struck by the words of the email he'd received from Yakimoto: *Forget about the Kojima Twins. They are gone. Stop your meddling or you'll be gone too.*

Was this place what he'd meant by *gone*? If so, it wasn't so bad. Even as they'd raced towards Tokyo, Brooke and Jackson had both shared an undeclared foreboding that the twins were already dead. But if Yakimoto had wanted to keep Jackson alive for his gaming skills, surely the Kojimas were a precious commodity too. As the bolt on his cell door scraped through its iron housing, rather than feeling scared, Jackson couldn't wait to meet the prison's main population and start his search for his friends.

As the door swung open, Jackson was surprised to see a scrawny-looking boy entering in front of a man who was clearly a Yakuza guard. The Japanese boy was quite a lot smaller than Jackson and had shaggy black hair, knotted so it looked a bit like an Afro. He was barefoot and wore ripped jeans and a dirty T-shirt with I ♥ BOWSER written on it. The brightly coloured transfer on the boy's chest, of Nintendo's famous dragon-like turtle character, seemed bizarrely at odds with the surroundings. The boy passed by as if Jackson wasn't even there and just curled up on the mattress as the guard motioned for Jackson to follow him out.

The guard pushed Jackson along a corridor with jabs in his back from a fist. Much like the cell, the corridor was constructed in concrete with the same square portholes too high to reach, still showing black outside.

They passed through a maze of tunnels, dotted with

strong wood and iron doors identical to the one that secured Jackson's cell. Jackson had the impression that he was being led to a mess hall. He wasn't sure what time it was but his stomach told him it was morning. When they eventually emerged from tunnels, they entered an area that looked as if it had been a dining room for whoever resided there in the past, but while the rows of benches and tables were all occupied by boys, there was no food in sight. Instead, the great hall, with its concrete walls and high ceiling made of recently stripped tree trunks and branches, was full of computer terminals – too many for Jackson to count. There was no natural light whatsoever but the faces of the boys were clearly visible in the vivid glows cast by their monitors.

Jackson was directed to a corner of the hall by jolts in his back from the guard's fist. As he walked he noticed the games the rows of boys were playing. The jagged mountain ranges and floating Armour Abilities menu were a dead giveaway for *Whisper*. Some were playing *StarMarine*, a *Whisper*-like massive multi-player game set in space, and Jackson also noticed two popular first-person shooters, *Crusader2040* and *Bizerk!*

'This, you!' said the guard, stabbing a finger at a computer screen on a large wooden bench. Jackson sat down on a plastic crate that looked as if it had been used to transport milk or fizzy drinks bottles.

The guard took a piece of paper from his pocket and

looked at it for a moment. 'You are 5-1-2.' He then folded it, placed it back in his pocket and walked away.

Jackson looked at the computer screen. In the centre was a text box with a cursor blinking inside. He hesitated for a moment, visualizing the number the guard had given him. *Five hundred and twelve,* he thought. *Not exactly a lucky number. But, as the cube of the sum of its digits, not without merit.* There was a keyboard on the table in front of him. He pulled it closer and punched the three numbers into the keys along the top. The window changed and Jackson was looking at a circular menu, divided into eight segments. Each segment featured the name of a game. The four he'd seen on his walk into the hall were there, and four others, one of which, *HeroCorp*, he recognized and three others, written in Japanese, that he'd never heard of.

He clicked the *Whisper* segment and felt the table vibrate slightly as the computer, which was bolted to the underside of the table by a crude metal bracket, began to whirr. Ordinarily, at this boot-up stage, Jackson would enter his *Whisper* username and password, but instead, as the normal login screen appeared, another program loaded over it. The small box contained two text fields with Japanese words above each that Jackson deciphered to mean username and password. Almost as soon as the box had loaded, the fields were filled out automatically with account details he didn't recognize.

'It's their own code!' The quiet voice came from the

terminal to Jackson's right. It was another small, scrawny boy. It seemed that look was the one adopted by most of the inmates in this place. Jackson suspected it wasn't by coincidence but rather down to the working conditions, which, as evidenced by the hollow space in his own stomach, included working before breakfast.

'It's a bit of script that logs you into the game of your choice,' said the boy, looking around to make sure none of the guards noticed him talking. Jackson did the same. There were four guards in total, standing near the entrance to the hall, talking and smoking. He noticed that two of them had machine guns slung over their shoulders.

'It also monitors you as you play,' continued the boy. 'So that you don't make contact with any players outside this room.'

'So how do things work around here? The guard just gave me a number but didn't explain anything else,' said Jackson.

'I heard. 512. That's your number and from now on, it's your name. It's also the amount of boys they've brought to this place. God help us all!' The boy looked thoughtful for a moment before checking the guards and continuing, keeping his voice low so that Jackson had to strain in order to hear him. 'Sorry, I'm Shin. But you'd best get into the habit of calling me 308. The guards prefer things that way.'

Three hundred and eight, thought Jackson. *A heptagonal pyramidal number. Nice name!*

'You've just started a shift,' 308 continued. 'Gaming shifts last fourteen hours. If you put your hand up, a guard will escort you to the toilet block – but that's the only break you get. When your shift is finished there's a changeover and you have an hour or so in the yard to get fresh air in your lungs and some food in your stomach. They didn't use to do that, but so many of us became ill from the damp and heat in here that they thought it might improve our performance.' Another glance. 'After *Keimusho Taisō* – sorry, Yard Time – they put you in your cell. And five hours later it all starts again.'

'Are you kidding me?' said Jackson. 'I have to wait fourteen hours until I eat? I'm starving right now!'

'No, they'll put out something for you to eat while you play, in a couple of hours. Then again in the afternoon. Yard Time, though, is the only chance you'll have for a proper meal. If you can call the junk they give us *proper.*'

Jackson noticed that the *Whisper* welcome screen had vanished and his character, a level 72 Rogue Knight called LordVangelis, stood waiting for him to take control.

'Miki, he's the boss around here, expects all of us to acquire in-game goods worth at least a couple of hundred dollars in each session.' The boy then shifted his focus back to the monitor screen in front of him. Jackson looked up and noticed a guard walking towards them, down the line of benches.

'What if you fail?' said Jackson, looking forward and trying not to move his lips.

The boy frowned and his shoulders dropped a couple of centimetres. 'You disappear,' he whispered without looking up.

Jackson had been playing for about twelve hours solid. To his frustration, the guards had changed shift and the four replacements had chosen his side of the hall to get together for a group chat. He'd checked those faces he could see in the dim light of the terminals and the ones of gamers being taken out and brought in, but he hadn't seen anyone who looked like the twins. He was burning to ask if the boy to his right knew of the Kojimas' whereabouts, but having seen one player on the table opposite picked up by his weedy arm and hit about the back of the legs by a guard with a stick, he was in no doubt of the consequences of being seen talking.

Some talking was allowed, but only for quiet commands and confirmations spoken into the headsets that were connected to every terminal. Jackson had put his on so he could hear the game, but he couldn't join in as the game chatter was in Japanese. The language barrier, however, didn't prevent him from recognizing the short, serious conversations for the game strategy they were. It was obvious that the chat channel wasn't a place for idle talk.

Despite his inability to decode the tactical talk on the gaming channel, Jackson couldn't miss the raiding parties. Three of them had spawned and formed up in a field on the edge of a nondescript village. In itself this was strange as it wasn't usual to see this many high-level characters in one place at the same time. Certainly not outside the big cities.

Jackson had directed LordVangelis to follow a level 60 Fallen Demon operated by 308, who had indicated the character was his with a couple of nods to his own screen. The boy had led them over to a party who were in the process of mounting up and flying off on a mission. It was the biggest swarm of flying mounts Jackson had ever seen. The party of twenty, which consisted of eight Rogue Knights like Jackson's character and a mixture of powerful Wizards, Druids, Warlocks and pure fighting classes, flew deep into a group of tunnels run by one of the game's biggest mountain mining guilds. There they attacked a clan of dwarfs, killing around thirty of them and stripping them of their weapons, tools and precious stones. Jackson didn't allow his character to take part in the massacre, a fact that didn't go unnoticed by 308.

'You must join in!' the boy insisted, in a low whisper in case the nearby guards heard. 'Or the other boys will report you!'

It was one thing that the thuggish party Jackson was forced to be a part of was dealing out such harsh treatment to innocent players, in order to fulfil the guards' quotas for in-game assets. But to think that his fellow prisoners would report him for not being as unscrupulous as them, was horrible.

During one raid on a treetop village, Jackson caught sight of a player name he'd seen before. It was Thievius, a level 79 Dark Shaman, whose murderous behaviour he'd witnessed before, in the hotel room with Marty. Now the player, who had adopted the role of leader of the pack, was using a spell to summon five Dragon Whelps. The baby dragons set about randomly ransacking the treehouse homesteads and spitting fire from their jaws, for no reason other than to ignite laughter among Thievius and a handful of other party members. When the party flew off, they left with nothing more than a few worthless provisions. The village and its inhabitants, however, were consumed in flames.

Jackson was fortunate enough to be handed a bag of gold pieces during a bank raid carried out by the gang of twenty in the centre of one of *Whisper*'s larger villages, Windshire. The player behind the Elfin trader, who had simply chosen the wrong time to visit the city bank, transferred the gold he was carrying to Jackson's character without even asking. Jackson had positioned Lord Vangelis near the entrance to the building and was wrestling with the problem of what exactly he should do while the rest of the party, including 308's character, picked fights with the sole intention of stripping the corpses of all their possessions.

The gold coins meant Jackson would certainly reach his quota. He'd traded *Whisper* currency like this himself online and estimated the bag of fifty coins was worth around a hundred and twenty dollars. What he wasn't so sure of was whether his fellow marauders had noticed his reluctance to get involved.

A box appeared over Jackson's screen. Again the text was in Japanese but it was obvious that it indicated the end of his shift. Jackson massaged his neck with his hand. He was stiff all over and hot – the heat in the games hall had to be somewhere in the upper eighties – but apart from a ferocious hunger, he would never have guessed he'd just been gaming non-stop for fourteen hours.

Jackson stood up and tucked in behind 308 as a queue of boys filtered slowly out of the hall.

As the line of boys snaked through the tunnels, they passed others moving in the opposite direction, obviously on their way to start their shift. Jackson checked every face, looking for the features that would reveal the twins beneath the greasy, unkempt hair, layers of grime and, as was the case with some of the older boys, the first hints of facial hair. But he was out of luck.

In some ways, the large mass of uniformly dressed children moving in long trains down the corridors reminded Jackson of school – except the grey attire of these children was the result of weeks soaking up sweat and the same dirt. And something else was different. No one was talking, or even smiling. If this was like a school – it was a school for zombies.

Random prods from the rifle butts, sticks and elbows of guards stationed at corners and in doorways kept the line moving at an even pace until it emerged into a large open courtyard.

The sky was the first thing Jackson noticed. It resembled one of those nights from a horror film, where streaks of fast-moving cloud compete to keep a full moon from unmasking itself. Then he noticed the smell. Pork. Two whole pigs were roasting on a spit over a fire in the centre of the courtyard. As the line of boys filed past, they picked up metal plates on to which a bare-chested guard placed slivers of meat and crackling, and two small boys served up fist-sized dollops of rice from a huge cauldron. The scene could have been straight out of medieval times, if not for the colourful tattoos on the arms, back and neck of the butcher guard and the dirty GUNS 'N ROSES logo on the T-shirt of one of the rice boys.

About five places up from Jackson, a tall boy leaned forward and whispered something to the butcher guard.

Both of them then turned and checked Jackson with a glance, before the line moved on.

'That didn't look good,' whispered 308 over his shoulder.

When Jackson reached the guard, who held a huge knife in one hand and a three-pronged skewer in the other, the man just stared coldly at him. Jackson moved to the cauldron of rice, and again his plate remained empty. He was opening his mouth to get the attention of the servers when he was ushered away by 308.

'Don't say a word!' warned 308 as they found a spot on the cobbled floor and sat down.

'What the hell just happened?' asked Jackson.

'The guards aren't the only ones you need to fear here,' said 308, scooping up a ball of rice with his fingers and placing it beside a chunk of grizzled meat on Jackson's plate. 'Your fellow players can be just as cruel. It's simple, really. This place is all about making money for boss man, Miki. And 297 is good at it.'

308 motioned to the tall boy from the queue, who was now eating in the corner of the courtyard. He was surrounded by about ten other boys who were sitting around him chatting and laughing. 308 continued to talk through mouthfuls of food. '297's player name is Thievius. He's one of the most successful players in here. He gets perks from Miki and the guards if he or his crew exceed their quotas, like extra rations and less time in the

gaming hall, more time in the yard. And he's not happy if someone lets the side down.'

'You mean me!' said Jackson, scraping his plate clean of every fragment with his fingers before resorting to licking it like 308 was doing.

'I expect your reluctance to get involved didn't go unnoticed. You need to make sure you recover your share of game swag tomorrow or you might not get away with just a warning.'

'What d'you mean by that?'

'297 doesn't just play brutal. He is brutal out here too. He and several members of his crew know karate. You filled a space on his crew that was created by the last kid who couldn't keep up. It was a girl. They threatened to rough her up a bit, but when her brother got involved things turned nasty and he ended up with several of his fingers broken. Ain't much use for a kid with broken fingers around here. Last I heard they'd shipped him out. Funny thing, but the kids in question are actually a bit of a big deal here in Japan. Talk about a fall from grace.'

Jackson froze, barely able to comprehend the importance of what he'd just heard. 'Tell me . . .' He stumbled to find the quickest route to the answer he needed. 'You mean the Kojima twins?'

'That's right!' 308 said casually. 'I guess I thought you wouldn't know them. You're English, right? How the hell did you land up in here, anyway?'

The boy's question evaporated before it even reached Jackson's consciousness. 'What do you mean *shipped him out*?'

'Dude. Like I said, it's all about the money. If you're not earning it for them by playing, they'll get it by selling you to somewhere else.'

'*Selling* human beings?'

'Rumours are the youngsters get sold to child traffickers abroad. The rest of us, well, put it this way, the supply for body parts on China's black market will never outstrip the demand. You might have broken fingers, but as long as your organs are healthy the Yakuza will put a price on them.'

Jackson felt slightly sick, and it wasn't down to the charred boar fat he'd just swallowed. 'What about the girl?' For some reason, he felt it was wise to hide his desperation to find Miss Kojima.

'She's working on another crew. Seems her brother's plight sharpened her focus a little.'

308's words could have sounded callous in another situation, but the last twenty-four hours had taught Jackson that this place would strip out every sinew of humanity in a person, as easily as the butcher guard had reduced one of the pigs to a pile of steaming bones.

This living nightmare of a place was also sharpening Jackson's focus. *I can't afford to think about Master Kojima now*, he told himself. *Find Miss Kojima. Then find a way out.*

CHAPTER 15

It was too dark to see Mount Fuji as the highway stretched out ahead, but Brooke knew it was there. She could see the jagged shadows of trees through the passenger window of the unmarked police 4x4 and sense the thick forest encroaching on either side of the road.

'You definitely packed my red holdall?' she fussed.

'Yes!' said Detective Yoshida emphatically from the driver's seat. 'How many times do we need to go through this? Sergeant Endo and I packed every one of the bags you indicated. Including all the boxes of components you forced us to shop for in Akihabara.'

'You're positive you packed the micro servos? I can't do anything without micro servos! And the motherboard attachments for the digital compasses – tell me you remembered to put those in one of the boxes!'

'And the electron-beam lithography system and the wafer fusion furnace,' chimed the detective. 'And the rate sensors. And the Li-Po cells . . .'

'And the package from your friend at the University of Tokyo?' enquired Brooke.

This time, Detective Yoshida answered Brooke's question simply with a glare.

'I have to say, Detective,' said Brooke, 'I'm very impressed that you're able to recall my shopping list.'

'How could I forget it, Miss English? You've made sure that each of your meticulous orders is seared, painfully, into my brain.'

'Like I said, we have to expect we'll be up against several armed gangsters and possibly an OX powerlifter. My little shopping list could just help us balance the sides.'

'And *like I said*, Miss English, assuming I let you participate in this mission, it will be on the understanding that it is purely reconnaissance. All we need to do is confirm the location of Yakimoto's facility. We'll leave any rescue missions to a Tokyo police SWAT team. Do we understand each other?'

'Affirmative, captain!' said Brooke, saluting the detective.

The vehicles turned into an unmarked tarmac road that led deep into the forest. Ten minutes later they arrived in front of an unusual-looking modern building.

From the way the Kojima sisters had described their father's Aokigahara retreat, Brooke had imagined a cramped chocolate-box holiday chalet. But the unusual wood and glass construction was like something from a science-fiction film. The giant wooden trapezoid structure was balanced above the forest floor on four rectangular concrete pillars and accessed by a wooden staircase on the side.

'This is what you call *a little place in the woods*?' said Detective Yoshida as he helped his assistant sergeant unload the second vehicle they'd brought to carry everyone's gear.

'Does it not meet your requirements, Detective?' asked one of the triplets, concerned.

'Just thirty kilometres from our intended target. Quiet and remote, if not a little grand. It's perfect, Ms Kojima!' said Yoshida, bowing courteously.

'Great!' said Brooke, helping another of the sisters wrestle a large black nylon holdall towards the building. 'We'll take our things inside and then you girls can give us the tour!'

The building consisted of five large bedrooms in the upper section and a spectacular glass spiral staircase that led down to the main open-plan living space.

Being set so high up on pillars, and with tall glass walls at either end, it was a little like being in a huge tree house.

The sisters took everyone outside. There was no garden, though the forest that surrounded the house for some fifty kilometres on all sides ticked that box, but there was a large outbuilding, about a quarter of the size of the main house and constructed in the same quadri-lateral style, minus the concrete legs.

The inside of the outbuilding, which itself was larger than most conventional four-bedroom houses, was divided into two halves. The first half was an immaculate garage, big even by Brooke's standards. As the group walked on to its pristine, shiny red-painted floor, Brooke took stock of the vehicles inside. There were five Kawa-saki quad-bikes – 'One for each of us,' one of the sisters pointed out – and a beat-up Toyota Landcruiser and an Audi A8 Quattro, the kind of executive car she imagined the girls' father liked to be driven around in. But Brooke was most intrigued by the low-profile outlines of two other vehicles, which were visible beneath two tailor-made bright-red covers. Brooke identified them instantly by their shape as two Italian supercars.

'The twins' famous identical Ferraris?' asked Brooke. '458 Italias, if I remember correctly.'

Everyone who had heard of Japan's most revered professional gaming team knew about the Italian sports cars they'd bought with their first tournament prize money. And the road they'd had constructed, so they could legally drive them.

'Yes,' replied one of the girls. 'The test track is behind us.'

'Unbelievable,' said the detective, scratching his head.
'Cars and games, that is all my brother and sister care

about,' said one of the sisters as she opened a set of sliding *shoji* double doors that offered access to the other half of the building. 'But this is where we play.'

As the Kojima sister slipped her shoes off and walked into the blacked-out space, lanterns that hung from the high-vaulted ceiling came on automatically and revealed a sizeable dojo. Everyone else removed their footwear and followed her in. Like the main house, the entire length of one wall was glass and gave a dramatic view of the full moon, clearly visible above the snaggy edge of the treeline, the perfect blue circle repeated in the room's deep-brown polished wood floor. Brooke made straight for one wall that was decorated with weapons, targets and punch-bags.

'What's with the bamboo stick? This doesn't look too harmful!' she said, taking one of a pair of one-and-a-half-metre long sticks down from the wall on which they were positioned in a cross formation.

'Is not stick,' said the first Kojima sister, taking the second bamboo weapon down and pointing it at Brooke. 'It is *shinai*. Means to bend or flex. It's a type of wooden sword we use for a martial art called kendo.' Brooke instinctively pointed the weapon in the direction of the Kojima sister. 'In the right hands, it's a very useful tool.' The girl twisted her bamboo sword in a fast spiral, flicking Brooke's out of her hands and sending it clattering to the ground.

'You practise kendo as well as karate?' asked Brooke.

'Karate. Kendo. Tae kwon do. Wing chun kung fu. We

practise many fighting styles. Whatever gives us an edge.'

Another of the other sisters spoke up. 'We believe that an understanding of many fighting disciplines will help us to be as successful in our tournaments as our elder brother and sister are in theirs.'

Brooke looked at the girls and then glanced around the impressive, purpose-built martial arts practice facility. If this is how their father supported his children's interests, it wasn't difficult to see why the twins and their three sisters were so unusually talented at doing what they loved. But as Brooke knew only too well, this kind of parental support also brought its own kind of pressure – a pressure to perform at the highest standard. Brooke and her father were cool now, but there had been a time when she was younger, when her own remarkable talents for engineering had become obvious, that her father pushed her too hard. Sitting a university degree in mechanical engineering at eight years old and gaining a PhD in Applied Robotics at eleven was something Brooke was very proud of. But she would have liked to at least have the choice of doing all the dumb dressing-up and dancing-class type of stuff most girls her age were doing. That's what her shocking-pink hair and pierced lip were all about – a little bit of rebellious Brooke that her father couldn't control.

She looked at the girls, who had congregated below a wall on which hung an extensive collection of ancient-looking fighting weapons. *Still*, she thought, *if your dad's gonna force you to do an extracurricular activity, it's gotta help if it involves butt kicking and cool weapons!*

'What about these?' she said, pointing to the savage metal, wood and leather objects mounted in neat lines on the wall. 'Surely you don't use these in tournaments?'

The impressive miscellany of knives with curved blades, spears and ornate swords, with sparkling engraved brass and leather hilts, stretched all the way from the floor to halfway up the high-vaulted ceiling.

'Most of those are antiques,' laughed one of the girls as she walked forward and grabbed a pair of thirty-centimetre-long dark wooden sticks joined by a chain. As she continued to speak she proceeded to swing the sticks around her head and body, the sticks a blur as her arms tucked and crossed in a series of blisteringly quick but precise movements. 'These *nunchaku*, for example, are over a hundred years old.'

'Bomb-diggity!' exclaimed Brooke, transfixed by the whirling nunchucks. 'Those things could really do some damage!'

'Cool, huh!' said the girl, flailing the sticks in one hand above her head, while performing kicks and blocking techniques with her other hand and legs. 'In Japan they are used in Okinawan kobudo, an ancient weapons-based martial art from the islands of Okinawa, and as part of karate. They are designed to disarm an opponent, but can be used to attack as well.' The girl let out a guttural cry and leaped at a punch-bag that was suspended from the ceiling, landing a cascade of blows from the sticks to the red leather bag.

Brooke rushed towards a blackboard that was mounted a few metres further along the wall. It was decorated with a lot of Japanese writing that she didn't understand and several drawings of stick people performing what were obviously martial arts techniques.

'May I?' she said, grabbing a piece of white chalk from a tray beneath the matt blackboard. '*Hai!*' said one of the girls, bowing.

'Do that twirly movement above your head again, please,' demanded Brooke as she began to scrawl arrows, curved lines and numbers on the board, while watching the nunchucks demonstration.

'Girls, it's important we all have some rest,' ventured Detective Yoshida. 'The next few days are going to be hard on us all. I think we should turn in now.'

'Not a chance, pops,' said Brooke, endeavouring to cover a clear section of the blackboard with geometric shapes and symbols. 'You can go get your beauty sleep in a minute. But first be a darling and fetch me my bags. Oh, and don't forget the package from your friend at the University of Tokyo.' Brooke nodded in the direction of the Kojima girl who was still forming blurred circles around her body with the nunchucks. 'I think I might have found a use for that shape-shifting polymer!'

CHAPTER 16

News of that night's karate fight had travelled around the complex like wildfire. And, according to 308, the boss had something very special lined up for tonight's *kumite* or 'sparring fight' between the guards.

Jackson's gaming shift was nearly over. It was only his fourth since arriving at the prison, but the gruelling gaming marathon was already starting to feel familiar. He'd grown used to the shooting pains in his neck and back brought on by the crooked crate he was forced to sit on and the constant inclination to lean forward and fall asleep. And he was only too aware of the constant pressure to deliver the virtual goods, which for everyone else in the raiding party meant robbing unsuspecting players – something Jackson still wasn't prepared to do. Yesterday, he'd narrowly escaped a beating from Thievius and his goons because by sheer gaming skill he'd managed to level-up his character, LordVangelis, to 80. When put up for sale on the online black markets where Yakimoto's people sold the gaming prison's produce, a level 80 Rogue

(217)

Knight could sell for as much as five hundred dollars. Jackson had bought himself a few days' grace, not to mention the first meal that wasn't borrowed from 308's plate, but he knew Thievius was watching.

'Is there anyone in here who *doesn't* know martial arts?' said Jackson, whispering his question in 308's direction but looking across the hall to Thievius's terminal. Jackson guessed the boy was a couple of years his senior. He wasn't that muscly, but he had a kind of predatory confidence about him that made most of the other inmates keep their distance. Even now, Jackson didn't allow his gaze to rest for too long in the boy's direction for fear he would lurch, panther-like, across the tables.

'You English kids play soccer at school, right?'

'Well, I didn't, but most do, yeah.'

'Well, in Japan, we do martial arts like you do soccer. Mainly ju-jitsu, but some other styles, including karate. Not all Japanese children show an aptitude for it, but I think it's fair to say, Jackson, that a large proportion of the boys in here could kick your British ass without breaking a sweat.'

'That's great news,' said Jackson, feigning enthusiasm.

'But don't mistake their fledgling fighting styles with the kyokushin karate practised by the guards.' Like Jackson, 308 was continuing to play *Whisper* while engaged in the hushed conversation. As their party sat on a hillside, spying on a blacksmith's forge in the valley below where they suspected a large stash of weapons was kept, 308 continued to talk, keeping his voice low. He explained that guard fights, like the one planned for this evening, happened once every few months when one of the guards thought he was ready to join the elite class of guards. These men, kyokushin karate masters, had the most comfortable quarters and the pick of guard duties.

'Kyokushin is a vicious full-contact fighting style,' said 308. 'Yakimoto's best men all practise it, regularly engaging in knock-down multi-man sparring. To progress to the elite level, a kyokushin fighter must fight and beat a hundred men.'

'What, so there'll be a hundred fighters in the courtyard tonight?'

'A hundred and one, you mean? It's the only time all the boys in here are gathered in one place. Can you believe Miki thinks it's good for morale?'

At last, thought Jackson, this was the chance he needed to find Miss Kojima. He'd looked for her every day in the glow of the monitors and during the changeovers between gaming shifts. He'd performed quick circuits of the courtyard during Yard Time and even caught a stick to the neck when he'd intentionally wandered off in the opposite direction to his cell. He must have checked a hundred faces in the melee of the corridor in between shifts before the guard on duty for his block came looking for him. But tonight everyone would be in plain sight.

If, as 308 had told him, Miss Kojima was still an inmate, Jackson was going to find her.

It was hard to tell the faces apart. It was the dirt and dust of the old bunker complex; it penetrated every pore until everyone, even the guards, became a similar pale hue. Finding Miss Kojima was proving more difficult than Jackson had imagined.

Thankfully, just as he'd hoped, it looked as if all the inmates were in the courtyard, sitting on the cobbles round a square that was marked out with candles. Jackson and 308 had made it to the yard early and secured places on the front row, Jackson hoping this might give him the best vantage point. But he hadn't banked on how densely packed the crowd would be, not to mention how dark it was. There was also the fact that Jackson had never met Miss Kojima in person. He'd known her and her brother for two years and taken part in several important missions with the twins as part of Devlin Lear's top-secret robot defence force, MeX, but they'd only met over a hi-res video feed – Jackson had never seen Japan's most famous gaming girl in real life.

The kick hit Jackson between his shoulder blades, instantly winding him.

'Hey, *gaijin*, you're sitting in my place!' sneered Thievius, balancing on his left leg, his right leg bent at the knee and held high above his waist, chambered for another attack.

Jackson knew there was no point in trying to answer back. He wasn't sure he could have formed the words anyway as he was so winded he couldn't breathe. He knew that whatever he said would provoke his raiding clan leader.

Jackson motioned to 308 and the two of them shuffled up the cobbles, making room for Thievius and the four boys who were with him, who Jackson recognized from the gaming hall as fellow clan members.

'You can't sit there either,' Thievius continued. 'My friends and I need room to stretch our legs.' The boys around him closed rank and one of them, a sturdy-look-ing boy with a round face and pug nose, sniggered behind his hand.

Jackson sighed. He had been in this kind of situation so many times before. In his mind, the concrete walls of the courtyard could have passed for the tower blocks of south London that surrounded his old school playground. And the dirty grey clothes worn by Thievius and his boys could be his school uniform. He'd left Peckham Academy over a year ago, but he could remember the beatings and humiliation he'd suffered at the hands of Tyler Hughes and his gang as if it was yesterday.

The only language bullies understand is violence. It was the voice of his stepdad, in his head. *Hit him back and he'll leave you alone*. Like catchphrases in a game show, the advice sounded good, but it didn't stand up too well to empirical testing. When he'd attempted to hit Hughes back, his pathetic attempt at a punch only resulted in a cacophony of laughter from Hughes and the crowd who'd gathered to watch; that and the worst beating he'd ever suffered.

Several months later Jackson had finally dealt with Tyler Hughes, but it was his brain, rather than his fists, that he'd used to fight back. Now, Jackson was a very different person from the scared boy he'd been in the Peckham playground. He still wasn't that strong physically, but the last eighteen months of fighting international super villains, even if it was with the help of robots, had galvanized his fighting spirit. The truth was, however suicidal it might have been, Jackson had to focus his energy on *not* getting up and attacking Thievius. He was no longer fearful of bullies. What did bother him was the possibility that Thievius might ruin his best chance of finding Miss Kojima. He wished he could just lean forward and silence him in the way he'd silenced Tyler Hughes, with the threat of revealing humiliating facts about his father. This was an entirely different situation, but still, there had to be some way to silence the karate-kicking clan leader.

'Just so I understand,' said Jackson, standing up and turning to look at Thievius and his friends. 'Is your problem with me really about my reluctance to destroy innocent players? Or is there something else about me you find threatening?'

The boys flanking Thievius were at first shocked by what Jackson had said, then amused, poking and pushing Thievius in order to provoke as explosive a response from him as possible. Thievius just stood still, with his arms crossed over his chest, Jackson's comment inspiring a broad smile.

'I have to admit,' said Thievius calmly, 'you might be on to something. There is a quality about you, *gaijin*, that I find . . . unusual.'

'Could it be the way he smells?' said the boy with the round face.

'Perhaps *unusual* isn't the right word. You have to forgive me, my English isn't too good. What I think I mean is – pathetic.'

More time wasted, thought Jackson. He was aware that his back was now turned to the majority of the audience. Time spent debating whatever it was Thievius wanted, was time that could be spent scanning faces for Miss Kojima and checking the new arrivals who were still streaming into the courtyard.

'Tell you what,' said Jackson. 'I don't really care what you think. I'm paying my way in your precious little *Whisper* clan, without the need to terrorize other players. But if you've still got a problem with me, then that's just fine. Because you know what? I've got a problem with you!'

Jackson fired the comment at Thievius without even blinking. He could have been mistaken, but he might even have squared himself up a little to add emphasis. 'I've got a problem with anyone who hurts my friends.'

'Friends? What friends?' asked Thievius.

'The Kojima twins!' said Jackson.

Thievius was surprised to hear the famous gaming duo's name from a foreigner.

'You see, you might think you can get away with beating up people half your size,' Jackson continued, 'but you can't!'

Thievius, who hadn't dropped the smirk from his face the whole time, stepped forward, curving his neck down slightly so he was just millimetres from Jackson's face.

'Cool. So what are you going to do about it?' said Thievius in a low, controlled tone.

He was so close Jackson was given a foul-smelling reminder of what the boy had to eat last night.

'I'll fight you!' said Jackson unflinchingly.

'You'll do what?' 308, who'd reluctantly stood next to Jackson the whole time, couldn't help but choke out the question in amazement.

'I'll fight him,' said Jackson. 'If I win I take over leadership of the clan.'

'If you win?' laughed Thievius. He placed his forehead on Jackson's, then shunted it quickly forward, causing Jackson to stagger a couple of steps backwards. '*When you lose*,' he said, his smile transforming into a scowl and his eyes flashing with menace, 'I'll take yours and 308's meals for a week. Of course, that's assuming you're still alive! Here then, tomorrow night.'

'Fine with me,' said Jackson, regaining his composure. 'But I want you out of my face until then.'

Thievius put his arms up and stepped back in mock surrender. 'Whatever you say, *gaijin*.'

'Come on,' said Jackson to 308. 'We'll find somewhere else to sit.'

'What was that?' asked 308, struggling to keep up with Jackson as he darted between the rows of boys. 'D'you have some kind of death wish or something?'

'No, I just needed to buy myself some time,' said Jackson, nudging his way through groups of boys who were gathered against the yard wall, and then along the rows of those seated on the floor, examining every face in the hope of spotting a familiar one.

'For God's sake,' said 308, stopping abruptly. 'Would you just tell me what is going on?'

Jackson stopped and narrowed his eyes in 308's direction. 'I came here to find the Kojimas. I'm too late for Master Kojima, but according to you his sister is still here. This gathering is my best shot. I haven't time to explain any more. Are you gonna help me or just stand there talking?'

'I gotta say, Thievius is right, 512, you're definitely *unusual*!' 308 pointed. 'You carry on this way. I'll try and cover the late arrivals.'

Jackson continued with his search. The yard was packed now, and once or twice he received an elbow in the side or a shunt in the back in response to his barging through the tightly packed groupings of fight spectators. At one point he caught sight of a face that could have belonged to Miss Kojima – a soft oval in shape with the thin arched eyebrows he remembered, and eyes that at this distance could be his friend's unusual emerald green. But the face belonged to a boy with short, matted raven-black hair, who quickly vanished behind a throng of taller boys pushing their way to the front.

Jackson figured he'd covered about half the spectators and was making his way to a section of the crowd that appeared to be made up of particularly small boys when a hush swept through the yard.

Flanked by two armed guards, a man in a white karate suit walked into the square in the centre of the yard through a gap in the crowd. The two guards moved to the edge of the square and kneeled on the cobbles at the edge where the first row of boys sat. Jackson recognized the man in the karate outfit as one of the guards from the gaming hall called Tomo, short for Tomoko. He also spotted the black sash round the man's waist. He was already a black belt, so whatever level he was attempting to reach tonight was very advanced.

The man started a series of movements – punches, chops and kicks – that he performed almost like a kind of dance routine. Jackson found the display quite compelling to watch, but forced himself to ignore it. Now the crowd was calm and more people had dropped to the ground to make themselves comfortable, he would be able to have a better look at their faces. He looked in the direction of the boy with the oval face, but he was nowhere to be seen, then he spotted the delicate features of a girl. He recognized the face instantly – green eyes, shiny black hair. But it wasn't Miss Kojima. It was Baby Face, one of the missing players Marty had told him about. Jackson recalled the line from the banner ad her friends had used to try and find her: WHERE IS BABY FACE? Jackson corrected himself. Marty didn't exist. The scumbag's name was Miki and more than likely he'd been the one responsible for targeting the girl for abduction.

The girl looked frail, like a scared kitten. He tried to suppress the pangs of desperation that started to rise from his stomach like acid reflux. He would concentrate on finding Miss Kojima and then work on getting her and everyone else out of here.

Jackson felt a tap on the shoulder and turned to see 308. 'No luck, I'm afraid,' he said.

'Nor me,' replied Jackson.

The guard finished his *kata* or practice routine and bowed to the audience, dipping his head, in the deferential way Jackson had noticed so many Japanese people doing, to the four sides of the square. There was a smattering of applause, mainly from the guards around the courtyard, but some from kids for whom even the brutality of the prison wasn't enough to stamp out their good Japanese manners. Suddenly the yard was gripped by an electrifying silence. Once again, two guards walked towards the square, but this time, walking between them, were Yakimoto and Miki.

But soon the silence turned to an almost simultaneous intake of breath. What fuelled the sudden mix of fear and astonishment in the air wasn't the sight of the Yakuza father and son, but the Komodo dragon that Miki had on a lead in front of him.

The animal swaggered into the courtyard on four muscular legs. It was about three metres long, including a scaly tail that was the same length as its body. Its long, yellow, deeply forked tongue lapped at the cobbles and the feet of a wave of front-row boys who scrabbled to move out of the terrifying creature's way.

The lizard was a bizarre sight, but Jackson was gripped by another sensation rather than fear. It was the fire of pure rage, ignited by the sight of Yakimoto and Miki, a feeling that burned in his very core and threatened to explode at any second. *Stop it!* he told himself as he considered the option of rushing them both. *You'll either be karate chopped or shot. Either way, it will achieve nothing.*

As Yakimoto started to speak in Japanese, Jackson prodded 308 who began a whispered translation.

'Good evening,' announced Yakimoto. 'As you may know, all of the guards here are trained in a form of karate called kyokushin. To reach the level of master, a kyokushin candidate is required to fight a hundred men.' Yakimoto paused for a moment to yack up something disgusting into the red handkerchief that seemed to be permanently attached to his hand. It was a sign of Yakimoto's radiation poisoning and it warmed Jackson's heart to see it. *Just what the doctor ordered*, he told himself with a smile. *A little bit of light relief in this horror show.*

'For those of you who have been here a while, you may have witnessed Mr Siku here, attaining the level of Master two months ago.' Yakimoto pointed to one of the guards standing beside him. The man bowed as Yakimoto continued. 'The only problem is that Mr Siku hurt so many of the hundred men we found for him to fight, killing one poor soul, that we are in danger of attracting too much attention to our little gaming club.'

Jackson half expected to hear a reaction from the crowd to the idea that the hell on earth in which they were forced to work as slave labour was being described as a club. But no one said a thing.

'So, thanks to Miki and some of the technicians who work in my logging company, we have come up with a solution.' Yakimoto turned to his son and nodded.

Miki bowed to his father, then handed the end of the Komodo dragon's lead to Mr Siku, who pulled the snarling beast past a row of terrified boys before leading the animal out of the courtyard. Yakimoto retreated to a point just inside the entrance, leaving Miki with a mobile phone in his hand. Miki poked a few keys and then, holding the phone in front of him, he gently twisted it towards him. If Jackson didn't know better, it would have looked as though Miki was using the phone as a controller, in the way he and Brooke did.

To everyone's complete amazement, a large, white shiny sphere rolled into the fighting square and stopped. The sphere was about forty centimetres high and constructed of several asymmetric plastic sections, indicated by seams that cut into its smooth surface at various angles. An irregular band of black ran round the centre of the sphere and, with it positioned next to the karate guard, the implication of the object's colouring was clear. It was a karate machine.

Continuing to translate, 308's incredulity was obvious from the excitement in his voice.

'This is the KX100,' said Miki. 'It is an automated fighting robot. It has been programmed with the full range of kyokushin karate techniques and is designed to simulate the experience of fighting a hundred men.'

A muffled wave of astonishment rippled across the courtyard.

Miki formed a shape in the air with his phone and the robot at his feet suddenly started to move, various interlocking sections sliding into position like the pieces of a spherical puzzle, until it eventually became still and sounded a short electronic tone.

A thought struck Jackson. This was why Marty, aka Miki, had been so fascinated by Brooke's mobile phone and robot interface during their time in Tokyo. Jackson had thought it strange at the time that despite the stress of their situation – stealing robots and being chased across the city – Miki had been more interested in their tech. Now it was clear why: he was involved with building his own robot, the KX100.

Holding the handset up to his mouth, Miki said a phrase in Japanese. '*Mawashi geri!*'

In response to the command, a horizontal section of black plastic in the middle of the ball-shaped machine began to spin and the whole robot jumped about half a metre vertically in the air. Simultaneously, a section of black plastic shot out and spun round 108 degrees. In less than a second, the ball was complete again and sitting back on the cobbles.

At the same time as the robot's blisteringly quick movement, 308 translated in Jackson's ear, 'Roundhouse kick!'

The crowd was shocked by what they saw, this time ignoring the consequences they knew could follow if they chatted too much as they talked excitedly among themselves.

'*Uraken shomen uchi!*' said Miki, holding his handset in front of his mouth.

The KX100 rolled half a turn forward and again sprang into the air, this time almost twice as high. At the apex of its jump, a piece of the robot's white plastic body uncoiled itself and snapped quickly forward in a quarter arc. The entire movement, including the robot rolling backwards to where it had started, took around two seconds.

'Back fist strike to the face,' said 308.

'And now a combination. *Shiko dachi. Oi tsuki. Hiza ganmen geri. Shutō hizo uchi.*'

As the moves were performed in a blisteringly fast sequence, 308 quickly translated. 'Sumo stance. Lunge punch. Upwards knee to face. Knife-hand strike to spleen.' Two stunted sections of the robot's outer casing shot out, lifting the entire machine off the ground in a configuration that even Jackson instantly thought looked like a fat sumo wrestler. After a series of what were obviously short punches and possibly a knee-kick from chunky inner sections of the robot, another bounce, lower than the first two, set the machine up for a mechanical karate chop to what would be a target's chest area.

'These are just some of the techniques this guard must defeat in a hundred bouts, if he is to advance to the level of Master.' Miki bowed to the man in the white karate suit and he bowed back. 'While today's fight should serve as a reminder that you would be wise to do precisely what my father's guards tell you, I trust you will also enjoy the spectacle.'

Miki walked backwards to join his father and then poked his phone's keyboard a few times. The KX100 did a similar set-up routine to the first one, its various inter-connected sections spinning and locking into position. Then a short beep sounded and a single glowing blue line appeared on part of the robot's black belt.

'That's *ichi*,' said 308. 'I guess that means it's man number one!'

Jackson found it hard to continue his search for Miss Kojima during the *kumite*. For a start, the crowd was animated. The boys were much louder and moving with more energy than they normally did. It was horrible, but Jackson could tell that the brutal ways of the prison were changing them. But he himself had to admit that the guard versus the KX100 was quite a spectacle. As 308 told Jackson that the robot was now showing 'Man number 28', Jackson caught himself thinking how much Brooke would have liked the concept of a karate-kicking robot.

Jackson quashed the thought. He'd been forcing himself not to think of Brooke or the girls. He had no choice. Allowing himself to think of them, and how they might come to his rescue, softened him. And in this place, he absolutely needed to remain hard.

Ago uchi – jab to the chin. Kin geri – snap kick to the groin. Mae gedan barai – low sweeping block. The running commentary by 308 continued right up to the point when the guard performed a powerful crescent-shaped kick that snapped off part of the KX100's casing.

The fight, which by now had reached 'Man number 89', continued, the guard sweating like a pig, limping on one foot and wiping blood from a gash above his eye. But the courtyard was now quiet. The expectation was that Miki would not be pleased to see his creation damaged.

'Man number 90' started with the KX100 unleashing a barrage of spinning kicks, one that took the guard's good leg from under him. The robot followed up immediately with what Jackson now knew was a roundhouse kick. Because the guard's leg was weak and couldn't properly support his weight, he was kneeling. He took the full force of the kick in the side of his head.

Jackson couldn't help but watch as the guard's limp body spun a full revolution in the air. Suddenly, through the fine mist of blood and saliva that sprayed from the guard's mouth and nose, Jackson's eyes met those of the oval-faced boy.

The boy's eyes were wide with amazement. Not only had Jackson spotted him – but he had spotted Jackson. And while the short, scraggy hair and dirty complexion had fooled Jackson the first time – those sparkling emerald eyes and the warmth that now radiated from their centre told Jackson that they weren't a boy's eyes. They belonged to Miss Kojima.

'Quiet!' shouted Miki, the four guards in the square pointing their machine guns at the crowd and scowling.

The mixture of alarm and excitement that had swelled in the crowd was immediately extinguished.

'My commiserations to Tomoko.' As Miki spoke, two guards were dragging the unconscious man towards the exit. 'It seems he is not kyokushin Master material. I have to say, I am disappointed.' He bent down and picked up the segment of the KX100 that Tomo had broken off, turning it around in his hands and examining it. 'My father's team and I have spent a lot of time and money to perfect the KX100. It seems a shame it hasn't been properly tested. And so, a thought occurs to me – is there anyone here who thinks they have the skill to fight our machine?'

Another surprised murmur radiated from the spectators.

'I don't expect you to win. I just want someone brave enough to stand in this ring and go five rounds with the KX100. I will offer double rations and light gaming duties for a month to anyone brave enough to take up my challenge.'

Jackson was half listening to Miki's speech. His real attention was on Miss Kojima, who was now smiling across the ring at him. Suddenly he felt a sharp jolt in his back that made him fly forward. Tripping over the boys in front of him, Jackson tumbled into the ring.

'He will do it!' shouted Thievius in English. 'He just challenged me to fight! He is a great fighter!' The boys around Thievius chuckled.

'What is it you English say?' remarked Miki, looking down on the pathetic figure of Jackson sprawled on the cobbles before him. 'Well, well, well! What have we here?' he said in a mock English accent. 'You know the rules as well as everyone else, Mr Farley. Fighting among gamers is a punishable offence. And your punishment . . . is *ten* rounds with the KX100!'

Once more a murmur rippled through the crowd. Even Yakimoto, who had been standing in the shadows for the entire fight, reacted to the arrival of Jackson in the ring with a loud laugh. 'This I have to see!' he said.

'Stop this!' The shout came from behind Miki. He and Jackson turned to see Miss Kojima, pushing her way through the boys in front of her and walking into the ring. 'That machine of yours will kill him easily. If you really want to test your karate robot, you should test it on someone who knows karate – like that bully there!' Miss Kojima pointed her finger towards Thievius.

Miki smiled at Miss Kojima and then looked at Thievius. 'Is this true? Do you know karate?'

Thievius shook his head frantically, but the boys who were always glued to his side all nodded.

'Perfect!' exclaimed Miki. 'The fight will last a hundred rounds. The KX100 versus 297, the boy with his karate, and his two new friends, the Geek-Fu – 512 from England – with our very own celebrity 333, the Kojima girl!'

Several members of the crowd laughed.

Miki turned to his father. 'I need a day to fix my machine. With your permission, Father, the fight will take place here tomorrow night!'

'I look forward to it!' said Yakimoto, sneering at Jackson and Miss Kojima, before bowing to his son and summoning his men to leave the arena.

CHAPTER 17

'That was, without a doubt, the dumbest game play you've ever made,' said Jackson as he and Miss Kojima moved with the half of the courtyard crowd that streamed down the corridor leading to the cells.

'Perhaps,' said Miss Kojima. 'But you looked so nerdy and useless when you fell at Miki's feet, I thought you might appreciate some help.'

They both burst out laughing.

'Not the kind of help that's going to end up with you being beaten up!' said Jackson as the two of them were carried along in the current of inmates.

'Don't you worry. Me and my brother have survived everything this place has thrown at us so far.'

'Wait a minute!' Jackson insisted, stopping dead in the corridor. 'Your brother is still here?'

'Yes! He is here!'

Jackson was thrilled by the revelation. As the force of the crowd pushed them forward again, Jackson fired questions about her brother at Miss Kojima. 'But I heard he'd been shipped out!'

'No, that only happens to the younger kids. God help them. He's working as a servant in the Master guards' quarters. They like to brag that their food is served and their washing done by a famous rich boy!'

'But what about his hands? I heard that Thievius had broken his fingers!'

The muscles in Miss Kojima's face tightened and Jackson could see the bitterness in her eyes.

'Don't mention his name,' she said. 'You see this!' she added, parting the hair on her forehead and revealing a large, congealed bloody lump. 'I almost killed myself running from that snake. I'd have made it out of here too, if I hadn't decided to slip off the wall and headbutt the ground.' They both laughed, before Miss Kojima became serious again. 'The animal broke all but four of my brother's fingers. I helped to splint and bandage them. He can clean and serve with them, although he must be in terrible pain.' Her expression softened into sadness. 'But I don't think he'll ever be the gamer he was.'

They reached a branch in the corridor. One way led to Jackson's cell area and the other to the section of the facility where Miss Kojima slept.

'Wait here,' she whispered, walking up to the guard

who sat on a box where the corridor divided, a pistol in his lap, white iPod headphones in his ears.

Jackson watched as Miss Kojima whispered something to the man. He smiled and nodded at her, then she turned and walked back. 'You're coming with me,' she said to Jackson, putting her arm inside his and leading him towards the left fork.

'Call it the perks of celebrity,' she said, smiling. 'That guard runs this part of the facility and happens to be a big fan of me and my brother. Can you believe that? He gives me special treatment, like turning a blind eye to you being in my cell. It's weird, he gets all excited about my gaming stories, but he can't see how wrong it is to keep us locked up in this place!'

'Bizarre,' said Jackson, looking at the guard as he passed him, the man returning a friendly smile.

'You've got six hours, Jackson, to tell me all about how you got into this place and how you and Brooke plan to help us escape!'

An escape plan, thought Jackson. *I knew there was some-thing I'd forgotten to bring with me.*

'Shape-shifting polymer!' said Brooke, touching parts of a tiny circuit board with a metal probe and causing the surface of a short section of black tubing on a cluttered workbench to ripple and form into different shapes.

The Kojimas' immaculate garage had been transformed into a shambolic mishmash of high-tech electronic equipment, coils, cables, upturned boxes, computer innards and the discarded remains of various foodstuffs and their packaging, including a small pyramid made of Diet Coke cans and an intriguing diamond-shaped octahedron made from eight slices of dehydrated pizza, that Brooke had cemented together with a glue-gun.

'So, specific voltages cause the material to form into a variety of shapes?' asked one of the three sisters, their eyes fixed on the black tube.

'Correct. From voltage change to shape shift, the process only takes a microsecond,' said Brooke. 'That's one millionth of a second, if you're interested.'

'Incredible! But how does this enable the weapon to work?'

Brooke cleared away some of the mess on the workbench, some knotted clusters of brightly coloured cables connected by dog clips to various voltmeters, a packet of doughnuts and some ribbon cable that ran between the circuit board and an oscilloscope. Now the shape of Brooke's Automated Nunchucks was easier to see. The weapon consisted of two of the black polymer tubes, each thirty centimetres in length and a similar thickness to a stick of seaside rock. They were connected together by a section of thick, black nylon cable. The outside end of one of them was connected by a length of yellow USB cable to a laptop computer.

'I have programmed various shape-shifting routines to respond to different user inputs. For example, if the tiny magnetometers and accelerometers inside each stick sense me attempting to flick them horizontally, the polymer will change shape. With a shift in shape comes a shift in weight.' Brooke pressed a few keys on the laptop. 'In order to demonstrate, I've just slowed the reaction time down.'

The girls watched open-mouthed as a thickened lump pulsed along the surface of one stick and then the next.

'And that shift in weight is enough to enable the weapon to propel itself?'

'Yes, and increase whatever energy the user puts into it by several orders of magnitude.'

'*Sugoii, sugoii!*' said the girls simultaneously, the amazement in their eyes translation enough for Brooke.

'The shape-shifting skin is all new,' Brooke explained. 'But most of the really time-consuming stuff – the user-collision-avoidance sensor, for example – has been harvested from my other projects, like the self-driving car kit!'

'And that goes for this too?' One of the girls pointed to a selection of the sisters' throwing stars, which were laid out on a rubber mat at the end of the workbench. The stars were made of metal and embellished with various motifs – one had a dragon on it, another a tiger and the others Japanese writing.

'Don't touch them!' said Brooke, noticing the girl's hand hovering over one of the five-pointed metal stars. 'I've modified them. For the most part they are still your traditional *shuriken*, but I've improved their flight characteristics by modelling them in virtual wind-tunnel software and adding a baked ceramic coating to their leading edges.'

'We don't really know what you're talking about!' remarked one of the girls.

'Don't sweat it, girlfriend,' said Brooke. 'Just keep your hands off the merchandise until I've given you the masterclass. I've fitted them with a low-inductance, high-voltage capacitor. Touch one in the wrong place and you'll instantly frizz that lovely shiny hair of yours! Now hand me those phones of yours. I wanna start the modifications we talked about.'

The girls were digging in their pockets for their phones when Detective Yoshida and his sergeant entered the garage behind them. They had left in the early hours of the morning to get visual confirmation of the prison's location.

'We're almost done in here, Detective,' said Brooke, opening the back of one of the girls' pink handsets. 'You think you're going to be ready?'

'I need to talk to you about that,' said Yoshida. 'First, let me show you what we found!'

Sergeant Endo pulled his camera strap over his head

and turned his Canon digital SLR camera round so the girls could see the pictures he'd snapped of the forest facility on its playback screen.

'We used the highway to get close,' said Sergeant Endo, 'then hiked the last three kilometres through the woods.'

'That's what I wanted to talk to you about,' said Yoshida. 'I'm afraid I can't allow you and the girls to come on the assault. It's a job for SWAT!'

'You can and you must, Detective,' demanded Brooke, slamming the metal probe she was holding on to the workbench. 'Jackson's in there! We hope the twins are in there too!'

As Yoshida continued to talk, the sergeant cycled through several pictures on the camera's colour viewing screen. Brooke saw several close-ups of Yakuza guards holding a variety of guns, including AK47s, M16 assault rifles and a shotgun. One image showed no less than five armed Yakuza guards posted on top of a high concrete wall. Set into the wall below them was a wide metal door accessed by a bridge built of rocks and earth that provided passage over a deep trench. It was clear from other pictures that the trench traced the walls of the concrete complex.

'It look like medieval castle,' remarked one of the girls.

'Yes, but note the state-of-the-art security measures,' said Yoshida, pointing at various grey oblong-shaped cameras along the wall, the LED rings around each lens obvious to Brooke at least as offering a night-vision capability.

'And there's nothing medieval about these!' said the detective. The image on the back of the camera showed a line of three OX units. Two more close-up shots revealed that the two-legged logging machines had a number of different load-outs. One had a chainsaw for a hand and another had been left holding half a tree trunk in between two large metal pincers.

'I'm afraid, girls, there is no way I guarantee your safety. This is one mission you have to leave to me and my people.'

'No way, cowboy!' exclaimed Brooke. 'I don't know what my sisters here think, but we ain't the kinda gals who are happy to sit at home doin' our nails while the menfolk get all the glory. We've got the skills. We've got the gear. Like it or not – we're coming!'

'Young lady, you will stay here and that is an end of it!' The detective's usual calm had evaporated in the sudden heat of his frustration. 'Sergeant Endo, please consider these girls under house arrest. I'm meeting the SWAT team along the highway at sixteen hundred hours. It is your job, Sergeant, to make sure these girls go nowhere!'

Dead man walking. That's what Jackson read in the face of every boy he passed in the games hall. And he could no longer rely on Miss Kojima's upbeat mood to lift his spirits. Her shift had been changed so she would be ready for this evening's fight. She was exhausted and panicky. It didn't help that last night Jackson had explained that he wasn't sure whether Brooke was safe, and that they'd been duped by Miki. Jackson could see Miss Kojima now, five rows away, the odd worried glance towards him from behind her terminal screen all the confirmation he needed that tonight's fight was likely to end badly for both of them.

He could draw some consolation from the fact that Thievius wasn't his usual cocky self. None of his regular mocking looks across the tables, followed by a comment Jackson couldn't hear and a detonation of laughter from the boys around him. If Jackson and Miss Kojima recognized the lethal consequences of going up against the KX100 tonight, so did Thievius.

The gaming shift had never gone by so swiftly, and soon everyone was filing out of the games hall and heading for the yard.

'Jackson, listen carefully,' whispered Miss Kojima, falling in behind him. 'When I last saw my brother, he mentioned something about a way out of here, through the Master guards' quarters. He didn't have a chance to say more, but I thought it was worth mentioning.'

Jackson smiled. He wanted to point out there was the little matter of a battle with a killer robot standing between them and any break-out attempt, but he could see how distressed Miss Kojima was and thought better of it. 'That's great!' he said, over his shoulder. 'I'll think on it!'

Their arrival in the yard caused a wave of excited chatter to race around the audience. It looked as though most of the prison's population had turned out for the fight, guards sneering at Jackson and Miss Kojima as they walked to the edge of the clay square that denoted the space in which they would be fighting. But there was no sign of Thievius.

'Where is he?' asked Miss Kojima. 'He left the hall before us. He should be here!'

'I have no idea,' Jackson answered, shaking his head. In his mind there was only one scenario worse than him, Miss Kojima and Thievius going up against the KX100 – and that was just him and Miss Kojima fighting the killer karate machine.

The next flurry of anticipation came as Yakimoto and his bodyguards arrived, Miki walking behind them, the mobile phone in his hand directing the KX100 to roll slowly into the middle of the ring and stop.

'You should consider yourselves very fortunate,' said Yakimoto, walking on to the clay square of the fighting ring. 'Two fights in two days!' He spoke the last few words with such zeal he made himself cough up something into his trademark red handkerchief. 'I can only hope that you show your appreciation for all this entertainment, by stepping up your productivity over the next few days!' The audience suddenly stiffened. 'Anyway, thanks to my Miki, tonight we have a rare and exotic treat. My son assures me that his robot is fixed and ready to put up a good fight against some of your own kind, who think they have what it takes to win themselves special treatment.'

Define 'some', thought Jackson.

'You have all witnessed what can happen to even the most experienced of fighters when up against the hundred-man fighting machine. What you haven't seen is the state that some of the men were left in during the testing of the KX100.' Yakimoto turned to Jackson and delivered his next line while staring at him with mad eyes. 'Let me say that I have witnessed with my own eyes that left unblocked, even a simple punch from the KX100 can kill!' Jackson knew that he was supposed to be intimidated by Yakimoto's scowl, but he possessed such deep loathing for the man that he just stared back without blinking.

Yakimoto broke the trance between them as he turned towards the source of a commotion in the entrance to the yard.

Two guards entered. Between them was the limp figure of Thievius, his feet scrabbling to keep up as they dragged him into the ring and dumped him on the clay.

'So you see,' Yakimoto announced, 'attempting to escape from our little gaming resort is futile.'

Jackson never thought he'd be so relieved to see Thievius, or feel so sorry for him. He was kneeling and as he raised his head, Jackson could see a bloody swollen lump around his right eye.

'And now we have our three challengers in the ring,' shouted Yakimoto. 'Let the hundred-man *kumite* begin!'

Jackson sensed a change in the atmosphere of the crowd when they heard the whizzing and clicking of the servos and actuators inside the KX100 as it went through some kind of test sequence. He didn't blame them, but their obvious excitement didn't make him feel any better either.

Just as it had yesterday, the karate robot quickly performed a series of movements, several combinations of punches, some shooting straight forward and others hooking round from the side as various interlocking sections of the spherical fighter spun round with shocking speed. Finally, the machine sprang a metre straight up, performed a lightning-quick combination of three spinning kicks in mid-air before landing, then beeped and brought up the Japanese character that Jackson now knew meant 'one'.

Thievius dragged himself to his feet and automatically adopted a wide-legged stance. As he instinctively snapped his arms into a defensive guard he winced – his eye was obviously not the only part of his body that had felt the boot or gun butt of the guards.

In a flash the KX100 rolled forward towards Thievius. A section of its shiny plastic central casing shot out and Thievius instinctively dropped both arms, palms down to block it. But then, before it had even finished its gut punch, the agile machine sprang into the air, a projection of plastic flicking out from its top section and hooking down in some kind of hammer blow towards Thievius's head. The machine's tactic, to use a feint to get the boy to drop his arms, had worked brilliantly. Realizing his mistake, Thievius ducked and weaved to one side with amazing speed, but the mechanical arm still smashed down on his shoulder, sending him down to his knees.

As the KX100 landed back on the clay, the dazed Thievius was in the perfect position to receive a potentially lethal strike to his undefended head.

Without even thinking, Jackson started running. Two

strides and his right foot came up, swinging forward from the side in the kind of perfect goal-scoring form he'd be too nervous to find on the school football pitch, but could, here, in this life-and-death situation. Jackson's foot hit the karate machine with enough force to move it a few centimetres sideways, the spinning backfist strike it had just unleashed towards the side of Thievius's head missing its target altogether.

As Jackson limped back to Miss Kojima, who was cowering in the corner of the ring, a shooting pain oscillated from his instep and up his leg. But the pain was the least of his distractions. What had his full attention was the sound of the terrifying martial arts robot rolling straight towards him and his friend.

CHAPTER 19

Detective Yoshida should have known better than to trust the Tokyo Met police department for whom he'd worked most of his adult life. Perhaps it was because he was using SWAT that he'd let his guard slip. The men from Special Weapons And Tactics had a reputation for being untouchable. But one of them was on the Yakuza payroll. His fellow officers would have thought he was just trying his gas mask on for size when he pulled the black rubber mask over his head as the ten-strong team sat in the van at the side of the road. Seconds later and they were all unconscious, asphyxiated by two of the gas canisters they had planned to use in their forest prison assault.

When Yoshida arrived at the rendezvous most of the men were still unconscious. But one, a twenty-five-year-old sergeant on his first outing with SWAT, was alert enough to tell Yoshida to *run!*

Something in the young man's eyes told the experienced old detective to back out of the van. He'd moved just two steps when the vehicle exploded.

Yoshida was aware of two men checking for a pulse on his smouldering body, which had been blown ten metres and landed in a ditch. If the trained officer rather than the ghetto-born Yakuza thug had tested for a pulse, he'd have found one. Then they'd have put a bullet in the detective and left his ghost to join the others who wandered the haunted sea of trees. But bloated by their success, they missed Yoshida's vital signs of life and drove away.

Twenty minutes later, dizzy and bleeding from a deep cut in his shoulder where a piece of hot van shrapnel had embedded itself during the blast, Yoshida staggered into the forest. He couldn't call anyone – the Yakuza had stolen his car with his phone and radio inside. Yoshida wasn't sure what one man could do against a fortress full of armed Yakuza, but for the sake of the children held captive inside he was willing to find out.

Yoshida was trying to keep up as much pace as his weakened state would allow across the uneven forest floor.

Every time he stumbled on a branch or a rut, his head pounded and the wound on his shoulder secreted another painful splotch of blood. He'd hit the ground hard after the explosion and knew he was probably suffering from concussion, but the old policeman stumbled on in the direction he hoped would eventually lead him to Yakimoto's compound.

It was very dark now, almost pitch black, and if it hadn't been for a lustrous moon edging the trees with a silvery glow, Yoshida might well have blinded himself on a branch or slipped down a slope. His ears had become superbly sensitive, scanning for a trace of anything human among the cracks and rustles of twigs and leaves under-foot and the squawks and whistles of the forest's bird life. Then he heard it – either a man's guttural cough or the throaty snarl of a wild boar. Whatever it was, Yoshida slowed his pace and moved towards the sound's source.

He saw the glow of a cigarette's lit end first, then another cough that confirmed what he had come across was a man. From the sound of liquid splashing on to the floor, he was answering a call of nature.

Yoshida followed the silhouette of the man as he zipped his fly and walked up a short ridge, beyond which the detective could now see a glow. Cresting the ridge, being careful to remain hidden behind a clump of several thick tree trunks, Yoshida's eyes fell upon a basin about fifty metres below his position. It was a large area, distinct from the forest that surrounded it because the trees had been cleared away, and at its centre sat what looked like a concrete castle.

The man, quite obviously a guard by the shotgun he was holding in front of him, was making his way down the slope towards the complex when he stopped. Yoshida watched carefully and saw that he was lighting another cigarette. The detective took the opportunity to make his move and rushed the guard. It was more by fluke than design, but as the detective's shoulder barged the unsuspecting guard, the man's head was dashed against a tree, knocking him out, clean.

Yoshida worked quickly. Stripping the man of his guard's outfit – a black T-shirt, black jeans and plain black baseball cap – he then undressed himself and put the guard's clothes on. The guard started to murmur, suggesting he was waking up, so Yoshida used his own tie to gag him and his belt to secure the muscular gangster's hands behind a tree. Then, scooping up the shotgun, the detective set off in the direction of the compound's main entrance.

As he approached, he could see the large wooden gate in the middle of the front wall. It was a solid design, framed in steel and supported by three heavy metal spars that ran in diagonal. The only visible access to the complex was reached by a flattened pile of rocks that bridged a deep trench. As he came closer, to his amazement he could just make out the heads of wooden stakes, stuck in the bottom of the trench and pointed towards the tall concrete outer walls.

He counted three other guards, his police training telling him that the two chatting on his side of the trench were not a threat as they'd leaned their weapons up against the front of a pickup truck, while they were unloading from the other end. The third guard at the gate had an M16 assault rifle in his hands, but didn't look too alert as he was evidently listening to music by the look of the white wires dangling from his ears.

Keeping his head down, so the peak from his baseball cap hid his face, Yoshida strode past the first two men, tapping the barrel of his shotgun on the fabric peak in a kind of salute that further obscured his features. The men were too busy unloading a large metal barrel to pay him any attention.

As Yoshida walked across the rock bridge towards the main entrance, the guard in front of him was also uninterested, his head down as he leaned on the gate, rocking from side to side to the music coming in his in-ear headphones.

Yoshida couldn't believe it had been so easy as the guard pulled a walkie-talkie off his belt and mumbled into it, followed by the clunk of the gate's locking mechanism and its electric motor spooling up.

The gate was slowly sliding open when the man next to him pulled an ear bud out of one ear and asked him if he had some cigarettes.

'No, sorry!' replied Yoshida in Japanese.

'No worries, man,' said the guard, still bobbing up and down to the music in his ear. Then he thrust a hand forward for Yoshida to shake. Being careful to keep his face hidden as best he could below the brim of the cap, Yoshida grasped the man's hand with his own and shook. At that moment the guard looked down, intrigued by the warm, sticky liquid he sensed in his palm. Both men realized at the same moment that Yoshida's hand was covered in blood, blood that had dripped down his arm from the oozing wound in his shoulder. As the guard reeled back in shock, his eyes widened when he caught sight of Yoshida's face.

The detective was the quickest to react, swivelling the butt of the shotgun he was carrying up and into the guard's chin before the man had time to raise his own weapon. The guard fell backwards to the floor and, to make sure he stayed down, Yoshida brought his gun butt down hard on the guard's temple. *Well*, he thought, *it's gotta be better than blowing his head clean off with the other end!*

Yoshida heard the guards he'd passed a few moments ago shouting and then the electric gate motor stopped and restarted, the gate now beginning to close.

Yoshida made an instant calculation that even if he made it through the ever-tightening gap, his cover was now blown. Dropping to one knee, he grabbed the rifle that lay next to the injured guard and quickly placed it in the path of the closing gate.

He then sprang up and ran at the two guards who by now were running towards the front of the vehicle they'd been unloading in a bid to retrieve their weapons.

Boom! The sound of the shotgun was deafening. Hundreds of tiny lead balls from the exploding cartridge slammed into the truck, peppering its driver's door and bursting the front tyre. The detective's warning shot did the trick; both men hit the ground before they reached their weapons. The detective was still moving forward and was about ten metres from the two men as one of them started to get up again. He didn't want to kill the men, but he only had one more shot left and if he let them reach their weapons he was a dead man. Then he saw the bright-orange marking on the side of the barrels still on the back of the pickup. A bright-orange diamond shape, with the black outline of a flame in the centre. Whatever they'd been in the process of unloading was flammable.

As the man reached the front of the vehicle, Yoshida raised the shotgun and levelled it at the back of the truck.

CHAPTER 20

'Seven!' said Miss Kojima, translating the number on the front of the robot.

'Ninety-three rounds to go! You have to be kidding!' wheezed Jackson as he desperately gasped for breath.

He was continuing a strategy that had worked for him so far, namely that of running away from every attack the robot threw at him. He'd worked out that the KX100 used some kind of proximity sensors that meant it directed its attacks at the nearest threat. Whenever the machine rolled towards Miss Kojima, Jackson would close in, tripping its sensors and directing its attention to him, rather than his friend. He'd been caught out a few times, receiving a circular kick from the KX100's hard black centre section to the side of his thigh, and what from a human opponent would have been a back elbow strike when he'd tried to rush it from behind – that punch had winded him badly.

Every bit of Jackson's body was screaming at him to stop and rest – his lungs, his legs, his throbbing forehead.

But one thing was crystal clear – if he stopped distracting the machine and darting from left to right like a bad breakdancer, the robot would kill him and Miss Kojima. And judging by the pumping heart that felt about ready to burst in his chest, that eventuality was only a few rounds away.

Jackson half fell, half dived, to avoid a lunge punch aimed directly at his groin, and in the process flew straight past Thievius. Any hope he might have harboured that the clan leader would rally to help his fellow gamers had evaporated when the boy had stood by during one of the first rounds and watched Miss Kojima, curled up in a defensive ball on the cobbles, pummelled by the KX100's ferocious combination of knife-like chops aimed at her back and neck. She'd only survived because Jackson had rugby-tackled the robotic bully, rolling the machine into the crowd where it had mercilessly slapped a few spectators before rolling straight back and targeting Jackson.

Thievius clearly knew his stuff, but it was by no means easy for the svelte boy to block the machine's violent assault, and no one could miss the wince-inducing sound of slaps and cracks the KX100's plastic limbs made as Thievius expertly intercepted them with palm and forearm blocks. And Jackson had noticed him starting to limp, probably the result of the barrage of shin blocks he'd needed to protect his lower body. And while he was significantly fitter than Jackson, he too was struggling to suck enough air in.

Suddenly the shrill sound of an alarm filled the courtyard. For the first few seconds the crowd reacted with nothing more than a murmur, but then someone pointed to the sky beyond one of the courtyard's tall concrete walls where thick black smoke could be seen billowing up in front of a floodlight.

Someone yelled a Japanese word that Jackson worked out must mean 'Fire!' because en masse the fight-night's audience descended instantly into panic. The guards who had been keeping them back from the ring were swallowed up as the crowd surged forward, making for the door. Jackson couldn't even see Thievius or the KX100 any more; both had disappeared inside the throng of people. He quickly grabbed Miss Kojima's hand and the two of them were swept up in the push towards the exit

Detective Yoshida had underestimated the force of the explosion his shot would cause.

This, the second blast he'd been involved with inside an hour, didn't have the concussive force of the car bomb, but the chain reaction of several barrels of petrol igniting had produced a huge fireball.

The heat alone had floored him and the burning fuel and fiery molten plastic that had rained down from the sky had effectively set fire to everything around him. In less than a minute the wooden parts of the gate were consumed by flames, and the sharpened wooden spikes that filled the trench had ignited so that the walls of the structure were now surrounded by a burning pit of fire.

Yoshida rolled on to his back and spat out a mouthful of dirt. As he looked at the front of the complex, he could have been forgiven for thinking he was lying at the gates of hell. Then hell's own gatekeepers came walking through the smoke at the side of the complex – in the shape of a line of four armed Yakuza guards, firing at Yoshida from low-slung automatic weapons.

At his feet was the raging inferno of the complex gate, behind him the burning pickup truck and the first stages of a forest fire that could consume the whole district. He folded the shotgun in half, opening the two barrels to look inside, as if checking might change the fact that both cartridges were spent. Looking up, he saw the Yakuza men had stopped taking pot shots, choosing instead to walk slowly towards him and execute him close range.

So this is it, thought Yoshida. *This is how I am to die. Surrounded by fire and chaos.*

He didn't notice the blur of green shooting down the hill he himself had walked down not long before. But he couldn't miss the sight of a Kawasaki quad-bike, its tyres flaming as it ploughed straight through the line of men.

As a shocked Yoshida dragged himself off the ground, two of the men lay on the floor, one of them cradling a leg that was twisted entirely the wrong way, the other scrabbling around looking for his weapon. Yoshida didn't even want to think about the consequences for the other two who had been caught by the vehicle's bull bars and dragged into the burning pit.

'I think this is what you're looking for!' said Yoshida, picking up the man's machine gun and pointing it at him.

The rumble of three further Kawasakis announced the arrival of Brooke, the Kojima sisters and, to Yoshida's escalating surprise, his sergeant.

'Sergeant Endo!' he said. 'What wasn't clear about my instructions to make sure these girls went nowhere?'

'I'm afraid we gave him no choice, Detective!' said Brooke from the driving seat of one of the quad-bikes.

'They were determined to follow you, sir,' said the sergeant, who was riding pillion with Brooke. 'I figured staying with them was the best way of ensuring their safety.'

'Safety?' retorted Yoshida. 'On those things? With no helmets?'

'Forgive me, sir,' said the sergeant, climbing off the quad-bike and walking over to the two injured Yakuza men. 'But judging by the scene here, you haven't exactly been avoiding danger!' He pulled two sets of plastic hand-cuffs from his pocket and proceeded to secure the men's hands behind their backs.

'Do you have a radio, Sergeant?' said Yoshida.

'I do, sir!' replied Sergeant Endo.

'Then call for back-up and fire services! There are several hundred children trapped in that burning hell-hole!'

'My robots can help!' said Brooke. 'I've tracked them to a location at the back of the complex.'

'I'm sorry,' said Yoshida, 'but this situation is already out of control. With the fire raging and the gunmen in there, our only choice is to sit tight and wait for the cavalry to arrive.'

'Sit tight? And let my friends burn to death?' said Brooke testily. 'Sorry, amigo! If you want to stop me from helping my friends, you'll have to shoot me. This is what we do! Me and my dot.robots are more qualified to rescue those kids than you and your so-called cavalry!'

For a moment it seemed as if electricity would spark from the intensity of the stare between Yoshida and Brooke.

'All right!' said the detective. 'If you can locate your robots, try and use them to find a way out for those kids at the back of the complex!'

'Roger that, skipper!' shouted Brooke, revving the engine of her quad-bike. 'All right, girls!' she shouted to the triplets who sat on the other two vehicles. 'Wagons roll!'

CHAPTER 21

'Are you sure the Masters' quarters are this way?' shouted Jackson above the din of the crowded corridor as he pushed against the flow of the traffic.

'Just keep moving!' hacked Miss Kojima, choking on the fumes as she spoke.

All the corridors were filled with thick, acrid smoke and Jackson and Miss Kojima had to keep low to find enough oxygen to breathe.

It seemed as though the entire prison population was heading in the opposite direction to them, towards the main gate. Jackson hoped that the children he passed weren't just rushing to a fiery dead end.

The corridor led through a door into a wide room. As soon as they entered, they could sense the heat radiating from one of the walls, beyond which the fire was obviously raging, and they could hear flames crackling on the wooden roof above them.

'Left, keep left!' spluttered Miss Kojima, pushing

Jackson from behind and towards one of two concrete corridors ahead of them.

Jackson had his bearings back. He knew the corridor down which they were both now running. It led to the games hall and then, beyond that, the Masters' quarters, where hopefully they'd find Master Kojima and a way out. That was assuming, of course, that the whole place hadn't been transformed into an inferno.

The heat in the games hall was stifling. It was usually the hottest place in the complex, on account of the heat that radiated from the computers. But the superheating effect of the hot air now being funnelled in by the corridors that fed into it had turned it into an oven.

'Not far now!' shouted Jackson, running between the desks. But then a shadow passed across the exit in front of him. Jackson froze. Even in that split second, he recognized the outline.

'Thievius!' Jackson uttered in disbelief.

The good news was that Brooke and the Kojima girls had no trouble finding the building in which her robots were being held. The bad news was that the tightly packed trees and dense webs of long-stemmed woody vines surrounding the Second World War concrete bunker were on fire.

The bunker was hard enough to access. About twenty metres outside the outer wall of the complex, it was half buried in the volcanic rock of the forest floor. And its only access point, a small iron door, was secured by a modern, high-tensile steel padlock. But the wall of fire that raged all around it was so hot, the girls couldn't get within ten metres of it.

'There's no way you're breaking in there!' shouted one of the Kojima girls, over the roar of the flames.

'I have no intention of breaking in there!' said Brooke, shielding her face from the scorching heat. 'But *Fist* is breaking out!'

Brooke poked at the screen on her phone and then thrust it forwards in the air in a series of sharp movements. Even above the sound of the fire that snapped, cracked and sizzled all around them, the clang from the iron door rang out as *Fist* slammed into it.

The robot charged three times until the door had buckled sufficiently for one of his heat- and impact-resistant polybenzimidazole-coated fingers to get round it and his memory metal muscles to rip it from its hinges.

'It's too risky to try and retrieve my other robots,' yelled Brooke, turning to run after *Fist* who she directed towards the tall concrete outer wall. 'We need to get inside the main complex, pronto! Those poor kids in there are running out of time.'

The flying roundhouse kick seemed to come out of nowhere, hitting Jackson so hard in his kidneys that he almost instantly vomited.

'You're insane!' shouted Jackson. 'This place could explode into flames at any minute and you want to hang around to beat me up?'

'Don't worry, it won't take long!' Thievius's voice came from behind him.

Jackson spun round and was shocked to see the boy holding Miss Kojima in a throat lock. Her eyes were wide and it was clear she couldn't catch her breath.

'Put her down!' thundered Jackson, his hands tensing into fists.

'Only if you give me the fight you promised, *gaijin*!'

'My pleasure!' snarled Jackson, rage taking over where common sense should have prevailed.

Thievius dropped Miss Kojima, who fell to the floor clutching her throat, and then he immediately ran towards Jackson, his arms punching straight out from the side of his body like coupling rods on the wheels of a steam train.

Jackson instinctively lifted his hands to defend his face, but that meant his stomach was exposed. The impact of his attacker's fists with the muscles of his solar plexus was blunt and jarring, and again Jackson almost spewed his guts up.

As soon as Thievius was inside Jackson's guard, he grabbed his forearm and twisted his elbow joint the wrong way. Jackson screamed out in pain as he prepared for the joint to pop.

Suddenly there was the sound of splintering wood from the other side of the room. Both boys looked up, startled to see a four-legged yellow robot appear from the smoky corridor outside. *Fist* was soon followed by Brooke and the three Kojima girls.

The triplets snapped into fighting stances and were only stopped from launching a three-pronged attack by Brooke's cry.

'Wait up, ladies!' shouted Brooke, before turning her attention to Jackson.

'You got three choices, partner! *Fist*, the Karate Kids here – or something I've been working on that I just know you gonna love!'

'I'll take option three, please!' rasped Jackson, climbing to his feet before a bemused Thievius.

Brooke reached behind her and pulled the Automated Nunchucks from where they were tucked into the waist-band of her jeans. She then threw them along the ground, the sticks and chain wrapping themselves round Jack-son's foot.

Jackson quickly bent down and scooped them up. 'How do they work?' he shouted.

'They're automated! You just move them as you wish and they'll respond to your input!'

Jackson's focus shifted from the weapon in his hand to the sight of Thievius changing his stance in readiness for another attack.

Holding one of the sticks in one hand, he whirled the other stick around its central chain link at chest height and then snapped it quickly downwards. The free stick instantly rotated, shot straight down towards the centre of Jackson's body – and hit him squarely between his legs.

A sickening pain boiled up, forcing his whole body to contract. Jackson slipped down on to his knees. 'I thought you said they were automated!' he wheezed.

'Er, yeah . . . but you need to turn 'em on!' said Brooke.

Thievius didn't miss Jackson's error and, seeing the opportunity to attack, was running at him. In the split second it took Jackson to find and press the circular aluminium ARM button on the end of one of the sticks, his opponent planted a powerful snap kick into the centre of his chest.

Jackson felt as if he'd been charged by a bull. His ribcage took most of the force, but the whiplash of energy also rocked his neck and pelvis as he was thrown backwards like a discarded doll.

'Feel free to grovel at any time!' hissed Thievius.

'*You* grovel!' shouted Jackson defiantly, as he half sprang, half staggered, to his feet. For some reason he automatically adopted a kung-fu type stance, holding the nunchucks in front of him horizontally in a way he remembered the famous kung-fu film star Bruce Lee doing on a poster in the bedroom of an old school friend.

Thievius burst out laughing. 'You kidding, right? Now you think you're Bruce Lee?'

Jackson attempted the move he'd tried before, but a little more to his right than last time, and to his amazement the two sticks of the weapon rotated round the V shape of his bent elbow. Instinctively, he let go of one end and the two sections completed a full circle around his shoulder before one of the sticks landed back in his open hand.

The surprise on Thievius's face was unmistakable.

'Yeah!' said Jackson. 'I'm Bruce Lee!'

Thievius wasted no time, darting towards Jackson with an accelerated combination of aerial kicks and punches that hammered Jackson's arm and legs as he raised them to defend. With Jackson backed up against a table, Thievius looked confident he had him beaten. He was wrong. Jackson attacked.

First a wailing smack to Thievius's jaw as one of the sticks pivoted 360 degrees round the vertical stick in Jackson's hand. Then an uppercut that came from a simple flick of Jackson's wrist and would have broken the boy's nose if his super-quick reflexes hadn't enabled him to bob out of the way.

Imbued with a new sense of confidence, Jackson tried a kick. Without even thinking, his right foot struck out in a kind of mule kick aimed at Thievius's stomach. To Jackson's horror, Thievius caught the foot with both hands and twisted it ninety degrees in a fluid motion that had Jackson sprawling on the floor inside half a second.

Jackson experienced the next sequence of moves in slow motion – Thievius chambering his fist beneath his shoulder in readiness for a devastating punch, the flash of ankle exposed by the boy's wide parallel stance and Jackson's unthinking swipe of the nunchucks along the ground.

Thanks to the automatic weapon's unique combination of weight-shifting and shape-changing, the energy Jackson had put into the weapon was exponentially multiplied. By the time the oscillating polymer sticks made contact with Thievius's right anklebone, they were revolving at around 80 kilometres an hour. Jackson heard the bone crack – followed by his opponent's yelp.

'Go! I've got this one!' shouted Jackson across the hall to Brooke. 'Take Miss Kojima, she might know a way for everyone to get out of here.'

The three youngest Kojimas had rushed to their sister's aid and now hurried her out of the room.

Jackson didn't hesitate for a moment and, snatching up the nunchucks with one hand, he jumped to his feet and squatted in readiness for the boy's next assault. But the attack didn't come. Thievius just lay on the ground, whimpering like an injured animal.

'Go on then, *gaijin*, finish me off!' croaked Thievius, holding his ankle as he lay on the ground.

'I don't need to, mate,' said Jackson. 'The fire will do that for me.'

Jackson had taken one step in the direction his friends had gone, when he stopped in his tracks. Thievius was a merciless bully all right, who had beaten both his friends and was reckless in his intention to kill Jackson. But had the coldness in Jackson's heart frozen all his compassion? Had the brutality of this place and the people behind this sick nightmare, not to mention the deaths of his true parents, killed off his own sense of what was right and wrong?

As Jackson turned round and walked towards Thievius, the boy flinched.

'It's OK,' said Jackson, placing Thievius's arm over his shoulder and lifting him up. 'I ain't gonna hurt a man when he's down. But I can't speak for the pink-haired chick with the big yellow robot. Trust me, you don't want to get in her way!'

'You have to be kidding me!' shouted an exhausted Jackson as he dropped Thievius on to the cobbled floor in front of the Master guards' quarters.

He'd battled through thick, noxious smoke and hot flames to reach the part of the prison complex where Miss Kojima thought they might find her brother and a way out. But now, standing before the four wooden huts that constituted the senior guards' accommodation, Jackson stared aghast at a horrifying scene.

Two OX lifters stood beside each other. One was piloted by Yakimoto and had two huge chainsaws for hands. Jackson could see the smiling face of Miki behind the driver's cage in the centre of the second OX. He lifted the terrifying machine's two arms into the air like some deranged body builder, and Jackson saw that one was outfitted with a massive mechanical metal pincer and the other with what looked like the pilot light of a blowtorch.

Jackson grabbed Thievius by the scruff of the neck and began to back up, but then he spotted the petrified figure of Master Kojima in the corner of the yard, the KX100 keeping guard over him.

'Your friends managed to slip away, Jackson,' smirked Yakimoto from inside the armoured metal suit. 'I suspect if they'd known we had their brother, they'd have attempted some heroic last stand!' Yakimoto coughed a deep, grating cough that seemed to scrape itself up his throat from the depths of his lungs.

'You know, that nuclear poison that my father branded you with is going to eat away at you until there is nothing left!' Jackson spat the words out so they flew at Yakimoto like tiny invisible missiles.

'*Branded?*' countered Yakimoto. 'How very poetic of you, Farley. Poetic but ironic, because it's you who is *branded*. When I killed your mother I seared myself into your very heart. And your father? How did it feel to watch him slip away? Did your heart bleed? Did you feel the scar I put there, burning inside you?'

The answer on the tip of Jackson's tongue was 'Yes!' A fire did burn in his heart, a scalding heat that had never left him since the morning the police arrived in his flat in Peckham with the news about his mother. And while he'd hated Devlin Lear for most of the time he'd known him, the discovery that he was his biological father meant his death had added to the pain. But there was a way that Jackson thought he could extinguish the flames inside him.

Thievius noticed Jackson slowly reaching behind his

277

back for the weapon stuffed in his waistband. 'Don't listen to him, man!' he whispered. 'It's not worth it!' But Jackson couldn't hear anything except the howl of the swirling snowstorm that had swept his father to his death and the sombre knell at his mother's funeral.

He flew at his parents' murderer, the Automated Nunchucks a blur at the side of his head.

In the space of a couple of seconds, the weapon's polymer sticks smacked against the tubular metal of the driver's cage, but the attack didn't even cause Yakimoto to lose his smile. Then Jackson felt the cold steel of Miki's pneumatic pincer as it clamped round his waist and arms.

'It's a shame really!' sneered Yakimoto, sweating from behind the bars that separated their faces by just centimetres. 'After you, there'll be no more of your family left to kill.'

Then Jackson heard the tinny bark of the chainsaws as the chained teeth on the end of each of the OX's arms started to rotate.

This is what we do!

Even in the chaos of the entrance yard where the entire prison population had gathered in a fruitless attempt to climb the smooth concrete walls and barge open the gate, Brooke was buoyed up by an exhilarating sense of purpose. This is what she was born to do – to use her brilliant robotic creations to save lives.

The cloud of thick grey smoke that hung near the stone floor was suffocating, but Brooke considered the fire raging on the roof that bordered the open yard to be the most imminent threat. Dollops of flaming liquid plastic were dripping from its waterproof layer and had already set light to a pile of crates and pallets stacked in the corner of the yard. Even as Brooke directed *Fist* around the groupings of boys and towards the corner, the boxes burst into flames, igniting the clothes of several boys nearby.

As her robot leaped across the heads of the boys, Brooke triggered a fire-extinguishing grenade. The spinning aluminium capsule, which was about the size of a salt shaker, shot from a stunted barrel in *Fist*'s underside and penetrated the stack of boxes, exploding on impact with the hard rock floor. A wispy fog of potassium carbonate instantly expanded to fill the corner of the yard, quenching every flame it touched by starving the fire of oxygen at the molecular level – even the blazing hoodies and shirts of the terrified boys rolling on the ground.

The amazed onlookers darted out of the way as *Fist* lolloped across the yard like a bright-yellow baboon, springing up and clasping on to a long metal strut that secured a series of runners on to the gate. Brooke cut some shapes with her phone and seconds later *Fist* peeled the ten-metre-wide strut away from the gate.

Some of the older boys jumped up, ran to the edge of the gate and started pushing. Bounding vertically up the wooden and metal structure, using its hinges and electric motor box for handholds, *Fist* grabbed a higher strut and ripped that off too. Then a roar went up from the crowd as the gate slid open and the desperate young inmates streamed outside.

CHAPTER 23

As Yakimoto raised the two spinning sawblades level with Jackson's head, Master Kojima pleaded from across the yard for him to stop. But the famous gamer had only moved a nano-metre towards his friend when the KX100 directed a sharp snap kick to his knee.

Jackson felt his blood run cold. Yakimoto's scarred face leered at him, framed by the protective bars of his exoskeleton.

'Come on then! Let's get it over with!' rasped Jackson, the air he needed to shout squeezed out of his lungs by the crushing grip of Miki's mechanical hand across his chest.

As the whirling teeth closed in on his head from both sides, the noise of the two four-stroke engines pushing them around their metal guide blades tore at Jackson's eardrums as he waited for them to eat into the flesh of his neck.

But all of a sudden Jackson felt the sensation of air rushing back into his lungs as the grip from Miki's OX loosened. Then, unexpectedly, he felt himself slipping through the pincers and dropping on to the floor.

Jackson had been close to blacking out from lack of oxygen and even though he was now breathing properly again, it took a few seconds for him to come to his senses. When he did he noticed Yakimoto's confused face at the centre of an OX that was jerking and twitching uncontrollably. Then Jackson caught a flash of flying steel out of the corner of his eye and as he tracked its trajectory from the roof, straight down and into the chest plate on the front of Miki's OX, he saw it embed itself next to two other throwing stars.

Sparks flared from the buried *shuriken* which, judging by the erratic movements of the Yakuza boss's OX, had hit a vital part of the machine's electronics. Jackson jumped to his feet and dived sideways as the OX lurched towards him. Then, to his utter amazement, one of the machine's legs seemed to buckle at the knee.

In the split second it took for the OX to topple forward, Jackson worked out that it was falling directly on to its two spinning chainsaw blades. First he felt the thud through his feet as the huge machine slammed face down on to the stone floor. Then he sensed a fine spray of blood hit his cheek and heard Yakimoto's final scream.

'Father!' shouted Miki over the din of the chainsaws. 'No!' He screamed it until his voice rattled into nothing. Jackson spun round to see Miki's flared eyes burning from inside the OX as the boy leaned forward and the huge machine lurched towards him. As the lumbering metal giant closed in on Jackson, he could see the three silhouettes of the Kojima triplets dropping from the roof and running behind the OX. But their *shuriken* were spent. Jackson knew this because they weren't throwing any more and he could see that the sparkling stars already embedded in the OX's arms and shoulders were having no effect.

Something inside Jackson throbbed with an urge to survive, but backed into a corner before a vision from a nightmare, it was dulled by his own logic. *This is it! I'm finished!*

Miki said nothing as the blowtorch fixture at the end of his OX's left hand sparked into life. Without hesitation he swung the roaring spike of blue flame at Jackson's face.

Jackson ducked and avoided it but was immediately hit by the pincer, which knocked him flat to the ground.

The OX was a monstrous outline against the fiery glow of the sky. In the red light of its driver's cage Jackson could just make out Miki's face. The boy's cheeks were wet with tears but his teeth were bared in a snarl that could only belong to a killer about to strike.

Like scumbag father, like scumbag son.

But in the moment that Jackson should have felt the pulverizing grip of a pincer or the searing pain of a blowtorch, the OX seemed to hesitate. Jackson looked more closely and noticed Miki's face quivering from side to side. This wasn't an expression of rage after all – it was the face of someone receiving a high-voltage electric shock.

Jackson wasted no time and rolled to his side. As he stood up he saw the familiar spiked outline of *Punk*, stuck in the OX's back. *Punk*'s cattle-prod function had fried the OX's circuits. Miki would survive; Brooke had designed her favourite robot's main defensive measure to use a non-lethal voltage.

Several thousand volts less than he deserves, thought Jackson as he looked at the exhausted figure of the boy slumped inside the OX.

Jackson was surprised to see Miss Kojima, not Brooke, standing behind the OX, the phone she'd used to control *Punk* in her hand. He was about to thank her when he heard the guttural shouts of the three younger Kojimas. Jackson watched the final few moments of their battle with the KX100.

The machine clearly couldn't work out which of the three targets to focus on in the bombardment of kicks and punches they were directing at it. As the robot extended a section of plastic armature for a hesitant punch, the piece was ripped clean off by a jumping front kick from one of the girls. Another prong cracked as one of the sisters unleashed a blistering chain of punches.

And when a powerful downwards elbow strike caused the karate robot's program to glitch for a moment – so instead of reacting to inputs from its laser and infrared proximity sensors it just threw out random moves – the three girls set about it like hungry vultures. In a matter of seconds, the combined concussive power of the feet and hands of three expert martial artists cracked the KX100's shell wide open like a walnut.

'There!' panted one of the girls, holding up the raw LED circuit board she'd just ripped from inside the machine, a neon Japanese character flashing behind its shattered screen. 'We won! Three against one hundred!'

By the time Jackson had managed to pull a dazed Miki from the OX, burning embers blown on to the roofs of the Master guards' wooden huts had set them ablaze, blocking the escape route that Master Kojima assured him was there.

There was no choice left to the group but to battle through the superheated corridors of the complex. Some of the walls glowed with heat and one or two sections of concrete floor were so hot, they could feel the soles of their shoes sticking as they melted.

Aided by Master Kojima, Thievius shouted directions as they forged on through blinding smoke that scorched their throats as they struggled to breathe. Then Jackson saw a figure picked out by a blinding light ahead of them.

He recognized the contour of his friend immediately. It was Brooke – and the light belonged to *Fist* who was hanging from pipes in the ceiling. Brooke was wearing an oxygen mask and was flanked by several fire-fighters.

As Brooke's rescue party led the procession out of the complex to a safe position at the edge of the forest, they were greeted by Detective Yoshida and Sergeant Endo. The two men had been joined by several armed officers wearing bulletproof vests and helmets. Jackson could see many more SWAT police officers, standing guard over a ring of handcuffed Yakuza from the complex. And beyond them were large groups of the child inmates, attended by a line of ambulances and teams of paramedics.

'Get that one in handcuffs, Sergeant, and put him with the others!' demanded Detective Yoshida, stabbing his finger at Miki. 'Do we need to go in after his father?'

'No,' said Jackson, his voice hoarse from smoke inhalation. He turned to look at the twenty-metre column of flames that had engulfed the complex. 'Right about now, he's being cremated!'

'I'm so sorry about getting us mixed up with that evil lowlife, Jackson.' As Brooke spoke, Miki was led away, his eyes fixed on the two of them in an inimical stare.

Jackson looked into her face and smiled. 'It doesn't matter, Brooke. It's over.' But as he uttered the words, he was vaguely aware of a dark shadow behind her, rising from the blazing pit that encircled the complex. He tried to focus his vision through his streaming, smoke-stung eyes when he spotted a vague fiery form moving towards them at speed.

'What is it, Jackson?' enquired Brooke, noticing the change in his expression.

'*Move!*' he roared, jumping to his feet and barging Brooke to one side.

The burning Komodo dragon slammed into Jackson, its sizzling jaws clamping round his thigh and the force of its charge hurling him against the thick trunk of a tree.

Yoshida and Sergeant Endo were the first of the assembled officers to react. Six short barks from two handguns and the demonic creature was a smouldering mass of dead meat.

But it was too late for Jackson. He could hardly breathe, the shouts and cries of those around him drowned out by the thudding of his heart. With every beat, the neurotoxic liquid transmitted by the dragon's bite was pumped around his body – slowly, efficiently, poisoning him.

CHAPTER 24

Jackson's world was a blur of blue lights and shadowy faces, the trundle of trolleys and the distinctive rocking motion of a helicopter and then a jet plane.

One constant was the thudding of his heart in his ear.

That was a good sound, a sound he didn't mind hearing, a sound that told him he was alive. The fragments of conversation he caught, as he drifted in and out of consciousness, were less welcome.

'Yes, the poison can kill.'

'Komodos secrete a neurological toxin. There is a good chance he could wake up with brain damage.'

'If the Hospital for Tropical Diseases can't help him, I'm afraid the boy won't make it.'

What Jackson couldn't have guessed was that the hospital he'd heard mentioned was in Euston, in London. He was home.

He opened his eyes. He didn't want to move his head yet; something told him that a headache wasn't far away, buried by painkillers and just beyond the reach of his senses. The first thing he focused on was a bouquet of flowers on a table that stretched across his hospital bed. He felt different. It was as if he'd finally managed to put something down that he'd been forced to carry around with him for a long time. It was the hatred for Yakimoto, his son, and the pain and suffering they caused everyone they touched. It had been like another kind of venom, slowly poisoning him, deadening the pieces of him that made him different from them until he no longer knew who he was. Now they were gone and here he was, back in London. He knew it straight away, from the familiar accents of the voices moving past his room and the Radio One jingle coming from somewhere at the end of a corridor.

He felt the presence of someone in the room, but he didn't want to chance the throbbing pain he feared would come if he moved his head. It was a nurse, probably, checking charts or changing tubes. 'I'm allergic to pollen!' he said, his eyes taking in the full splendour of the fine bunch of roses.

'Don't worry, sugar, I bought you plastic!'

It was Brooke. Without thinking, Jackson snapped his head sideways and, sure enough, pain stabbed at his temples.

'Easy now, cowboy.' Brooke came forward and placed a soothing hand on his head. 'Don't move too quickly. Doc said the Komodo's toxins are still washing around somewhere in your nervous system. Everything is gonna hurt for a few days.'

'Nice T-shirt,' said Jackson, spotting the black writing on Brooke's chest, which read 'IT'S A LONDON THING'.

'Thanks! Your dad bought it me! He's really cool. He's just popped out but he'll be back in a few minutes.'

'How come you're here, Brooke? In London?'

'Never left your side, hon! Someone had to make sure you didn't go picking fights with any more dragons.'

The pain in Jackson's head had eased and he attempted to pull himself into a more upright position. The Doc was right, it hurt, an electric pain in his spine and a tingling sensation in his fingers, but he got there.

The twins. The Kojima girls. Yoshida. Their faces flashed up in his mind. He didn't even need to ask the questions; Brooke sensed what he was thinking.

'They're safe, Jackson,' she reassured him. 'Yakimoto is dead. Miki is in custody and all the kids are safe. We did good, partner!'

'What about you, Brooke? How is your dad . . . about you being here?'

'Hmmm, now that's a bit more complicated.' She let the warm smile she'd adopted for Jackson slide. 'Seems I've been given an ultimatum. Get behind my father's plans to make, I don't know what – talking vending machines for all I know – or lose my inheritance and the research grants that have made all our robot work possible.'

There was a knock at the door and Mr Farley walked in. His face lit up when he saw Jackson sitting up in bed, awake. Seeing his palpable joy and relief, Jackson knew that though Mr Farley wasn't his biological father he'd always be his dad.

'Welcome home, son!' he said, walking up to Jackson's bedside and hugging him gently.

'Your timing couldn't have been better,' he added, digging his hands into a carrier bag. 'If you'd still been asleep you'd have missed this!' He pulled out a brown paper bag, opened it up and placed it on the table in front of Jackson. Jackson didn't need to look inside; he knew what his dad had brought him just by the smell.

'Egg-and-bacon sandwiches with tomato sauce. Your favourite, son. I bought three, just in case you woke up. Seems they did the trick!' He handed Brooke one, then took a bite from his own.

'Oh, and this arrived for you this morning,' he continued with his mouth full, pulling an envelope from his inside pocket and handing it to Jackson.

Jackson read the front of the envelope. It was his name and London address in type. As Mr Farley proceeded to tell Brooke how to spot the perfect bacon-and-egg sandwich, Jackson slowly opened the envelope, his fingers still a little fuzzy, and unfolded the letter inside.

The letter was written on stiff, expensive-looking paper, with a crest embossed at the top that featured an image of the scales of justice encircled by several Latin words.

Shawcross & Partners Legal Firm
303 Strand
London
England

Dear Jackson Farley,

Since the death of Mr Devlin William Lear it has been my job and that of my colleagues at Shawcross & Partners to preside over the division of Mr Lear's estate.

As you may be aware, Mr Lear's affairs covered a wide and complex range of business interests, corporations and foundations. Since he passed away, there has also been the added complication of the need to settle several legal proceedings brought against my client.

With all judgments in these cases now satisfied, as executor of his Will I am hereby writing to inform you that you are a major beneficiary of Mr Lear's estate.

Please find enclosed a cheque made out in your name. If you have any questions or require further assistance, please do not hesitate to contact me directly on the number above.

Yours sincerely,
Thomas H. Shawcross

Jackson checked the envelope and pulled out a small slip of paper. Sure enough, it was a cheque. His name was printed in the top left. The bottom right section of the cheque was where the amount was written. Jackson had to count the zeros twice and read the figure written in words in the centre of the cheque before he could believe the value in front of his eyes.

£1,000,000,000

It was a cheque for one billion pounds.

'Anything interesting?' enquired Brooke.

Jackson looked up. Brooke had a large dollop of tomato sauce on the end of her nose. When his eyes met hers, both she and Mr Farley burst out laughing and Jackson couldn't help but join in.

'You could say it's interesting, yeah. I'll tell you about it later!' He dug his hand inside the brown paper bag beside him on the bed. 'Right now, though, I just gotta get me some of this bacon sandwich!'

ACKNOWLEDGEMENTS

I still pinch myself when I think that I'm a Puffin author and I must start by thanking the whole Puffin family, in particular our inimitable chieftain Francesca Dow and my Puffin soulmates Tania Vian-Smith, Vanessa Godden, Kirsten Grant and Lisa Hayden. I must also thank my always-awesome editor Lindsey Heaven, who, halfway through the writing of this book, had a mini Heaven! With Lindsey on maternity leave, the job of editing the final manuscript fell to Alex Antscherl, whose surname I still can't pronounce, but who I now count as a bona fide Dot.Roboteer. And I must thank editorial executive, Wendy Tse, whose mum, by the way, thinks she might have actually met Jackie Chan!

Having a maths genius as a central character means that the *sums* in the Dot.Robot books can get rather complex, so a huge 'big up' to Mark Finnemore, the coolest teacher I've ever met and the man who helped me with all the maths in *Dot.Robot*, *Atomic Swarm* and *Cyber Gold*.

During the writing of *Cyber Gold*, I began to learn

martial arts and the teachings of my two 'black belt' experts Zak Zivanovic and Terry Jacobs were instrumental in the creation of the kung-fu fighting scenes in *Cyber Gold*.

As some of you will know, my books have another dimension, the Dot.Robot Roadshow – a wild and crazy author event and the only show in town where break-dancing and robotics meet! The event has graced the stages of schools and festivals up and down the country and for this I must thank my original schools booker, Trevor Wilson, and more recently the ebullient Lizzie Blake-Thomas. My thanks also go to the many teachers, librarians and event organizers who have given up so much of their time to help introduce my books to young readers – I applaud all the hard work you do to promote reading, it is so very important!

Some authors choose to lock themselves away in order to get their creative juices flowing – whereas I prefer the hubbub of a cafe to bring my ideas to life and for the germination of my third book I chose The Tea Box in Richmond. Thank you to the hard-working staff, especially Felix, who kept me stuffed with cake and ever more exotic brews for the best part of four months! And while writing I was kept in touch with both world events and the most inane of trivia thanks to my followers on Twitter and Facebook – once again, your support and good humour were a constant source of positive energy.

There are so many other people I'd like to thank, but I'll keep it short and finish with the most important